The

Six Daughters

of

Joaquin Miguel Salvador

By
Lynn Coulibaly

The Six Daughters of Joaquin Miguel Salvador

ISBN: 0985509600
ISBN-13: 9780985509606

Printed in the United States of America

Cover artwork by Lynn Coulibaly
Cover design by Douglas Dykstra
Cover photo of artwork by Jay Pearson

For Vernon Albert Koenig,
my dear husband who left this world too soon.
My memory of you is forever filled with laughter and joy.

Acknowledgements

I began writing this book because I was intrigued with my now deceased husband Vern's family. It was his grandfather's emigration from the Azores and his subsequent raising of six daughters that I found calling me to write. While the little I knew about the real story was intriguing, my book is entirely a work of fiction.

My son, Soren Ryherd, gave me the needed push to start putting down the first words, and my daughter, Majken Ryherd, tirelessly read the early versions multiple times helping me find my footing—for that I give them my thanks as well as my love.

Wanting to keep the true spirit of the Azoreans and Portuguese woven into the story, I needed a translator to help me accomplish this. The person I serendipitously found turned out to bring so much more! John Soares, who also came from the Azores, helped me find not only the words I needed, but the heart, the humor, the hospitality, and the traditions of the Azorean people. *Muitissimo obrigado*, John.

Early editing assistance came from a learned friend, Jerry Harris, who helped me re-discover lessons long forgotten. I thank him for that.

Several people read my book and gave me constructive feedback—always encouraging me. Of particular support were my brother and sister-in-law, Leigh and Sharon Wilcox. Their heartfelt feedback reaffirmed for me, the joy in telling my story.

And a special thanks to Gloria Campbell, President of The Publishing Institute, who helped me with the final editing for publication.

Prologue

1980

Santa Cruz County, California

His eyes riveted on the thick ridge of trees descending steeply east to west, Martin Lukas Kohler leaned lightly against the cabin porch rail aware it might give way at any time. Though morning clouds shielded his view to the west completely blocking any sight of the Pacific Ocean, Luke felt comforted knowing the vast body of water was out there. As a youngster, whenever he had felt nothing was certain, he knew the ocean was one of the few things he could count on. His fifty-seven years of life had been like the familiar ocean tides—always moving—driven by ever-changing forces he never could control.

His gaze followed the top of the tree-line to the east, the highest point of the ridge where he was certain the property line lay. He was struck by the varying colors and textures of the magnificent display of trees Mother Nature had spread down the hillside before him. Luke was glad his companion didn't ask what he was thinking—at this moment there were too many emotions. The ridge was just part of a large stand of trees on a piece of land—yet spread before him, it tugged at his soul.

Glancing at the pretty, dark-haired young woman standing farther down the porch looking at the same ridge, he knew that if it had not been for a shared connection with this parcel of land, they might never have met. For Luke, their being here together signified a completion of the family circle. He wondered if she felt it as well.

With the clouds hovering above them, Luke's thoughts drifted back in time to another Santa Cruz so far away in another ocean—the north Atlantic. It was on the island of Flores in the Azores where his grandfather Joaquin Miguel Salvador had called up the courage to act on his life dream— the dream that today brought Luke and the young woman to this special parcel of land in Bonny Doon.

1889

JOAQUIN MIGUEL SALVADOR

THE ISLAND OF FLORES, THE AZORES, PORTUGAL

oday I will make my decision!

That thought in mind, pulling his thick black sweater around him, the man leaned determinedly into the cool morning breeze causing the thick mist to part as it hovered over the mossy path winding up the steep hillside. His wool fisherman's cap securely covering his ears caused his thick straight black hair to stick out and fall across his forehead. Twenty-seven-year old Joaquin Miguel Salvador's dark brows were furrowed—a sign of his determination to make the most important decision of his life today.

Another strong breeze brought the familiar odor of lavender, wildflowers, and the sea around him, but Miguel barely noticed. He stared down at the sapphire blue of the lake then sat down on the hard rock, ignoring the cold and dampness seeping through his well-worn trousers.

Miguel had discovered this rock when he was twelve. He and his best friend, Javier, had climbed up these hills to go exploring. He had claimed it as *his rock*. These days his *barco*

de pesca—his fishing boat—claimed most of his time and attention. He was either out on the water, fishing, or on the dock
working on the boat to keep it sea-worthy—leaving little time
for hiking.

Throughout the years, whenever Miguel had something
important on his mind, he escaped to his rock to sit and pon-
der. He enjoyed watching the clouds changing shapes causing
the colors of the rocks to change as he thought about the earth,
the stars, the wonders of the sea, his family, his friends, and, as
he grew older, girls.

He reflected on life on the beautiful island—and a severe
life it was. The Florean people worked very hard to exist. Yet
whatever Miguel lacked in food or clothing, he made up in
pride of being *Açoriano*—especially a Florean *Açoriano*.

Miguel sighed—his thoughts turning to his recently
deceased father, Manuel dos Santos Salvador. His *Paizinho* was
a good man though a very strict father. Never once did Miguel
question that his father cared deeply about his family. Growing
up, Miguel had often prayed that when he became an adult
and had his own son, he would live up to the same Azorean
standards his *Paizinho* had set.

Manuel dos Santos had been one of the more successful
fishermen, and one of the few in his village of Santa Cruz
to own a boat. He taught Miguel everything about fishing.
Miguel remembered as a boy of five, how, after constant begging, his father finally relented and took him out on the fishing boat. The father smiled at his son's exuberance as Miguel

hopped up and down on the way to the dock. Once they were out on the water, his father became very serious, demanding Miguel be careful and pay attention. It soon became apparent to Miguel that the ocean he loved to gaze out on from the safety of the shore was not the same one he now looked at as the water roughly slapped up against the sides of the small vessel. His awe of the mighty Atlantic Ocean grew in direct proportion to the darkness of the night that enveloped them. When it became so dark the sea became invisible, young Miguel took solace in the stars. He thought of each star as a bright, heavenly light guiding them. Suddenly the sky became filled with not just a few stars but millions of tiny lights. Though relieved to have some light, Miguel wasn't sure he liked being on the boat at night. It frightened him—a fact he would never admit to his father—and he stayed as close to his father as he could. He felt some comfort from the warmth of his father's large body and even more from his reassuring smile. As his eyelids grew heavy, Miguel wished he could be this close to his *Paizinho* more often. He fell asleep under the stars awakening to find the boat already at the dock and his father almost finished unloading the night's catch. Miguel frequently recalled this childhood adventure with his father and vowed that when he had a son, they would spend more time together.

By the time he turned thirteen, Miguel had forgotten about being afraid of the ocean and eagerly started working full time on his Papa's boat.

This morning, Miguel's thick, dark *bigode* twitched above his upper lip, his thoughts floating on the clouds of his childhood memories. Now that his father was gone, Miguel was the sole owner of his father's fishing boat. His friend, Javier, had become his partner.

The sudden quacking of several ducks taking off from the surface of the lake broke the silence bringing his attention back to the present. Miguel sighed, then rolled, and lit, a *cigarro*, inhaling deeply, knowing the sun would soon fully emerge from behind the morning clouds turning the day into the usual pleasant warm day of May.

Miguel's thoughts drifted back to his father's death. It was just over two years ago when he was laid to rest at the cemetery near the village church. Manuel dos Santos Salvador had passed away at the age of fifty-two. Many in the town of Santa Cruz said it was drink that had taken him, as it had other Azoreans they knew. Some of the old women muttered, calling it the Azorean curse. When he turned forty, Manuel had first been observed having occasional difficulty walking. His friends and acquaintances laughed and assumed he was *bêbado* from too much *vinho*, not unusual on the islands as many of the men were known to love their wine.

Manuel's stumbling had gone on for years with falls and flailing limbs becoming more frequent. Increasingly Miguel had taken over his father's fishing duties. By the time Manuel was forty-eight, he was confined to a chair, no longer able to go out on his boat.

Miguel sadly recalled the last time he had fished with his father. Manuel had fallen down a couple of times on the boat. Miguel helped him sit down and, with the water as rough as it was that night, tied a rope around his father's waist so he wouldn't fall or, worse yet, be swept overboard. Noticeably frustrated, Manuel was only able to watch as Miguel and Javier handled his work. Miguel could hardly bear to look at his father. Occasionally compelled to look, Miguel flinched at what he saw. It wasn't pain, anger, bewilderment, or confusion. It was *cheio de vergomha*—devastating embarrassment—one of the worst fears of any Azorean. The sobering memory of that night made Miguel shudder. Azoreans were a proud people regardless of their station. After that agonizing night, his father refused to leave home.

Miguel forced himself to think about his own dilemma— the need to make a decision. *What am I going to do with the rest of my life?* While his mother's grief for the loss of his father had pulled her further into her church, Miguel's grief had made him more restless. Pushing to the back of his mind his guilt about the possibility of leaving his mother, he knew he *had* to do something different. If he stayed on Flores there was no way to become more than he was right now. He was already twenty-seven years old. He knew he did not have the education that the men he had met on ships from other countries had, but he knew he was smart. He was a hard worker and, if he were given the opportunity, he knew he could learn to do other things. And, when God deemed it the right time, and

Miguel had a son of his own, he wanted him to know more than this life of hunger and hardship.

Miguel had met many people—many sailors who came from other parts of the world. He found one sailor from the neighboring island of Pico most interesting. This sailor had been working on a whaler, the *Angel of the Sea*, which sailed to the United States to a place—"*a state,*" the sailor, Durano, called it. "California." He described it as beautiful and sunny and said the Pacific Ocean sparkled like a gem on the other side of the world. "You know," he said, "many have left the Azores to discover gold in this American California." He paused so they could consider the possibility of such riches. He continued, "There is even a town in California called Santa Cruz!" He paused to give Miguel a hefty slap on the back. "Would you believe it!" he laughed. Miguel could not.

Ever since Durano had mentioned California, Miguel had not been able to get the thought of it out of his head. *Someday I'll have to go see for myself if that is true. I would love to see this California, this American Santa Cruz.*

Sitting on *his rock* this May morning with the sun peeking through the foggy mist, Miguel's thoughts once again settled on the American Santa Cruz so far away in the United States in a place called California. A strange feeling overcame him. The furrow in his brow disappeared as he recognized that this feeling was happiness. He smiled and his large black *bigode* twitched above his upper lip. At that moment he realized it was the failure to make a decision that had been tearing him apart. *Maybe in the American Santa Cruz I will find the woman of my dreams and then God will bring me a son of my own.*

Thinking about meeting *that special woman* made him acknowledge how picky he was. Over the years, he had met Florean women who he knew found him attractive and would love to be his *esposa*. He enjoyed flirting, and had even experienced many exciting and lusty nights that satisfied him for the moment but meant nothing more. "Ah yes," he said with a sigh, women seemed to be drawn to him. More than once Miguel had thanked God for that, yet none of these women was his *aquela mulher especial*.

Miguel stood up and crushed out the remaining stub of his cigarette with his boot heel. His mustache twitched, and he turned to hurry down the path towards home—eager to get on with his plan. He had made his decision!

The following Sunday, May 22, 1889, Miguel awakened feeling full of energy in anticipation of the start of the annual *Festa do Divinio Espirito Santo*—the celebration enacting the rituals of the coronation of *The Emperor.*

Stepping outside of the house, Miguel felt excitement in the air. The Island of Flores, like a big garden, abounded with beautiful flowers year round. Each year when the *Festa do Divinio Espirito Santo* was celebrated, Miguel noticed the colors of the flowers were once again at their most glorious; as though the blossoms knew the brilliant roles they were expected to play in honoring The Holy Ghost.

The people of Santa Cruz covered everything with as many flowers as they could find—every archway, every house, table, and ox or donkey-pulled cart. Intricate geometric designs made out of different colored and varieties of flowers set in rectangular sections were meticulously laid out in front of cottages in *pasadeiras*, the floral *tapetes* or carpets, weaving their way down the streets of the village leading to the church. Miguel had spent several days picking, trimming, and storing the greenery and flowers his family would display as their collective contribution to this year's tapestry carpet marking the direction of the procession honoring the Holy Spirit.

Following mass, the people stepped out of the church, their spirits lifted by the mix of fragrances from the flowers. Music could be heard from the earliest hour and continued through the day and into the night. After mass, folk dancing began in the streets and would continue to be enjoyed by people of all ages well into the night. *Crianças*—the littlest Azorean children who were barely walking—mimicked their parents with dance-like movements as they toddled about smiling and laughing. Some held one arm up in the air waving a hand overhead to the rhythm of the music while holding a *malasada*—a sweet flat doughnut—tightly in the other hand, moving it rapidly up in the air to their mouth, and back up in time to the beat of the music. Randomly throughout the village a variety of musicians played. School age boys and girls, under the strict tutelage of an adult, practiced intricate dance steps like the *chamarrita encaracolada*.

Miguel went into town looking for his best friend Javier to share some toasts of *Basalto*, his favorite wine. Perhaps, he thought, hopefully, he would meet a few new women. The thought made him stand taller. Young Portuguese women were well protected by their families making it a challenge for a young man to meet and get to know them.

Later, Miguel, enjoying the perfect day, walked along as the sun shone brightly overhead. Though *musica* was playing everywhere, he could hear the rumble of the ocean. He inhaled deeply enjoying the mixed aroma of the flowers as he walked with his arms spread out wide holding the glass of wine Javier had handed him. Moving around in time with the music, he had turned his smiling face up to capture the warmth of the sun, when the collision happened. Automatically he dropped his arms and swung them around the other person—clinging together as they stumbled on the uneven cobblestones performing a jerky dance. He put one arm down on the ground attempting to break their fall while trying to hold his glass steady so he would neither spill, nor drop, his *vinho*. Frantically, he held on to the other person to prevent both of them from falling flat.

His vision was blurred, the shape of the sun a lingering image before his eyes. He could hear the other person, obviously a female, say, "Oh *tenho muita pena, desculpe* Oh, I am so sorry."

"*Não faz mal, menina*. I wasn't watching where I was going. I'm sorry. Are you all right?"

He managed to pull himself and the woman upright. Gazing down at what must be her face blurred by the sunspot, he heard her laughing. *"Ai meu Dias como estás sujo."* The fact that she thought he was a mess seemed to make her laugh even more. It was a magnificent laugh, light, happy, and melodic.

Turning his head slightly, he could see long, shiny, silky, black hair, partly pulled up to the top of her head with white and yellow flowers circling like a crown of jewels. He shook his head trying to make the sunspot go away. It wouldn't cooperate. He turned his head and this time saw one dark twinkling eye with an arched brow looking up at him.

"Ai meu Deus," she said.

Miguel found himself stammering, a rare occurrence. "I'm sorry. I was looking for the sun. No, I mean I was looking up at the sun. I was listening to the music and smelling the flowers and . . . . " He stopped. "I'm sorry. I can't really see yet . . . . The sun was in my eyes."

"Well, let me tell you since you can't see. *Ai meu Dias como estás sujo!* My God you are a mess."

"You keep saying that. What do you mean I am a mess?" He looked down and tried to see what she was looking at. Then he saw. The wine had spilled on one side of his brown pants making a large deep red stain down his left leg and onto his boot.

He scowled and then laughed.

"My friend, Javier, told me this would be the best glass of wine I ever tried. I thought he meant the taste." His deep laugh got heartier.

"You, sir, are naturally a flirt, aren't you?"

Her statement startled him, but he could hear the laughter in her voice.

"No, No, of course I'm not," he said, feigning indignation at the thought. She laughed a little louder.

"Well," she said, "I do apologize for running into you, but other than the fact you are now wearing a most unique pair of trousers, we are all right. *Adeus! Tenha um bom dia.* I will wish you good day and leave you to enjoy the sun, the music, the flowers, and the smells. I guess you will have to find your friend Javier and let him know how spectacular the *vinho* was!" Bidding him a good morning, she walked on by him laughing lightly as she went.

"*Maldito,*" he thought, damning his luck. He really wanted to get a good look at the young woman. The sunspot still wasn't helping, although the white circle of light was getting smaller. All he could recall was the long flowered dress she was wearing. Unfortunately, many of the other women wore the same styles. *Of course there was that gorgeous long, shiny, black hair with the crown of white and yellow flowers on top!* The thought made him smile.

A group of school aged children came around a corner and down the path. They giggled, pointed at his pants, and continued happily on their way.

O sol, the sun, had circled high in the sky and was an orange orb dipping slightly toward the west. Soon *velas* would appear in the windows and the twinkling candle light would lead the way to entrances to some of the houses and shops. Tables, placed outside, would soon be filled with people celebrating for the evening. No one in Santa Cruz had much money, but on such a special occasion, the tavern owners made inexpensive seafood dishes, breads and desserts, the latter made of their special island butter and famous floral *mel*—honey. The sweet scent of flowers emanated from the honey. A variety of Portuguese wines could easily be found everywhere.

Miguel wandered around until finally admitting to himself that he was really looking for the young woman he had bumped into earlier. The background of cheerful and familiar music continued. He stopped periodically to join a folk dance giving him the opportunity to join the *chamarrita* with women friends, some new, and some he had known for years.

He had almost given up on seeing the woman he was looking for when he heard the happy, lilting laugh floating atop the other noises coming from farther down the street. Excusing himself from the people he was chatting with, he hurried down the street in the direction of the laughter. The thick crowds caused him some difficulty getting through and, because her laughter had subsided, he thought he had missed her. Then he spotted the white and yellow flower crown bobbing up and down and the melodic laughter erupted again.

He moved through the crowd following the *coroa de flores* until he saw a circle of young people talking together. Keeping his eyes firmly fixed on the crown of flowers, he approached her from behind. He had to lean forward to get her attention being careful not to touch her. "Excuse me," he said.

The human circle immediately widened allowing him room to step in beside her. There were six people—three young men and three young women. The word *casais* flitted through his mind—he didn't want to think of the young woman as part of a couple.

She glanced up and, without the sunspot blocking his view, he fully took in all that was below the shiny hair covered with the flowers. She was even lovelier than her laugh. *A olá mais uma vez*, she said looking him up and down. "I see you've managed to get yourself together." And the melodious laugh danced in the air.

To his chagrin, Miguel felt himself blush. As his pink cheeks become even redder, he realized he couldn't remember the last time he had blushed.

"These are my friends. I told them about our unfortunate meeting. No," she laughed, "I meant to say our unfortunate accident earlier today."

He glanced around the circle as the five other faces lit up in recognition, five mouths forming silent "Ohs." All eyes dropped to the side of his leg. There was a pause. He kept his eyes focused on her.

"Oh, I'm sorry," the girl said, and pointing to the right of Miguel, "This is Luiz and Marta and Adão and Antónia and Cristiano."

Miguel shook each hand as it was extended. He felt older as each person greeted him with "Nice to meet you, *Senhor*." Having completed the introduction of the man at her left, who, Miguel sadly noted, was a very handsome young man, she stopped. Miguel kept looking at her. She laughed her wondrous laugh and said "Oh yes, I am Maria Luísa Furtado," and held out her hand.

Miguel happily took it in his. "And I am Joaquin Miguel Salvador." He could hardly stop staring at her—she was so beautiful—and so very young! He was five feet nine inches tall—tall for a *Florean*. He guessed she must be about five feet four inches, the same height as his mother. Her light, olive skin glowed and her eyes shone. Her brows were not as thick as some of the women he knew and were naturally arched giving her the look he usually attributed to an educated or wealthy person. The light brown skin of her hand felt smooth and soft sending a tingle up his spine. He felt a slight tug of her hand and realized he was still holding it. He dropped it immediately. The corners of her mouth went up a little.

"I haven't seen any of you before," he said. "You aren't from Santa Cruz?"

One of the young men—Adão, he remembered—spoke up. "No, we sailed around the island from *Lajes* for the Festival. We have our own parish celebration, but we've heard the one in Santa Cruz is so much better."

Miguel didn't doubt this was true. He enjoyed listening as they took turns telling him their different observations of Santa Cruz so far.

As the group chatted, Miguel frequently glanced at Maria Luísa Furtado. She took his breath away. She was not the most beautiful woman he had ever met, but she had a special quality that shone from within. Had anyone asked, Miguel wouldn't have been able to describe any of the other women whose company he had enjoyed in recent years.

It was obvious Maria Luísa Furtado was from a family of some wealth and the way she spoke confirmed his belief she was well educated. A fleeting moment of self consciousness caught him off guard and he wondered if he smelled of fish. He hoped not. He had scrubbed with salt water the day before and again this morning. The thought of her soft, smooth skin reminded him that this was no farmer or fisherman's daughter.

There was a sudden pause in the conversation. He felt their eyes on him. He tried to think of what to say. Just as he turned to face Maria Luísa more directly, thinking what a beautiful name it was, he heard music beginning and saw many people taking off down the street to join in the popular folk dance.

The circle of young people around him started to move in the direction of the music. "May I join you?" he said. Without waiting for an answer, he moved forward staying between her and Cristiano. Miguel wasn't sure if he saw a frown on Cristiano's face though frankly he didn't care.

The dance, the popular *sapateia*, was performed in a circle. Men alternated with women. Another young woman had stepped up placing herself between Miguel and Cristiano.

Miguel, happy this moved Cristiano farther from Maria Luísa, smiled inwardly. In this dance there was little touching between men and women—leaving Miguel to look forward to the times in the dance when their palms would meet. When, at last, Maria Luísa's and his hands connected, he felt a bolt from the top of his head to his toes. The quick look that passed between them made Miguel sure she had felt it as well.

After the dance, Miguel followed Maria Luísa to the side of a nearby building where her other friends were already lined up. He noticed Cristiano had placed himself on her other side. He was happy to note that the younger man was engaged in a discussion with Adão.

Looking down at Maria Luísa Furtado, he said quietly, "Have you ever heard of a place called California in the United States?"

She laughed her special laugh. Her own dark eyes grew serious as she looked up into his dark brown ones, "No, please tell me all about this California of yours."

So he did.

1889

Maria Luísa Furtado

Lajes, Island of Flores, The Azores

Maria Luísa returned home to Lajes on the south side of the island, unable to stop thinking about the Santa Cruz man, Miguel. *Oh My!* She brought her hands to her cheeks as she felt them growing warm. Whenever she was alone with her thoughts, she remembered looking up at him. He was tall and *very* good looking with his full dark mustache and the wisps of dark hair falling down onto his forehead and curling about his ears. She admitted he was much older than she would have expected to find attractive. Pushing that thought aside, she closed her large brown eyes and relived their unexpected meeting and dance.

It wasn't long after she had returned home from Santa Cruz that her mother commented on how contented Maria Luísa looked. Maria Luísa blushed, and then told her about meeting Miguel Salvador. She disclosed that Miguel was a fisherman. Her mother expressed her concern. Maria Luísa's parents found fishermen, while necessary to provide the seafood they ate, beneath them. Unlike Maria Luísa's family who were more educated—Maria Luísa's father, Fermo Furtado, being the Government Official for the township of Lajes and an important position of which he and Maria Luísa's mother, Lígia, were very proud—fishermen were peasants.

Outside of hearing distance from their daughter, her mother and father agreed Maria Luísa would get over this infatuation. "After all," Lígia said in a knowing maternal manner, "She won't be going to Santa Cruz again for a very long time and he will be out in his boat—fishing." Her nose wrinkled as she spoke the word.

Maria Luísa was the only member of the Furtado family not surprised when a young man pulling a donkey cart of supplies from Santa Cruz delivered a letter to her. She stayed outside the family's cottage so she could read the note privately. It did not surprise her that his writing confirmed that Miguel was less educated than she. Ignoring that fact, she immediately grasped his underlying message—he shared the same feelings for her as she did for him. Maria Luísa told her mother and father she had received a nice note from Miguel saying he had enjoyed meeting her. She didn't show it to them and since it was tucked into her apron pocket, they didn't ask to see it.

By the time the second and then a third note arrived, Maria Luísa knew she was in love with Miguel. Perhaps she had known it all along. When Adriana, her older sister, had married a well-to-do man and went to live in his home, she had left Maria Luísa as the sole object of her parent's daily attention. As the youngest daughter, Maria Luísa had always been pampered. The sudden arrival of Miguel, if only through his letters, brought the first tension she had experienced in her young life between herself and her parents.

Each of her parents told her repeatedly that a smelly fisherman was not worthy of her. Some of Maria Luísa's friends agreed. Adriana could not understand her little sister. She said Maria Luísa would be much happier with Cristiano. Hearing this made Maria Luísa laugh because neither her parents nor Adriana had ever before had much good to say about Cristiano.

After several weeks of daily bickering, Maria Luísa's parents gave in. They invited Miguel and his mother to come to Lajes to meet them. The Furtados secretly hoped this would prove to be too difficult for the Salvadors and they would not accept the invitation. Maria Luísa never doubted Miguel would come. Though a little nervous, she was eager to meet his mother.

Miguel's mother was as shocked at Miguel's news as were Maria Luísa's parents. Only after her excuses fell on her son's deaf ears and he agreed that Aunt Nelia could join them, with great reluctance his mother got into the boat to sail half way around the island from Santa Cruz to Lajes.

The second trip for Miguel and his family from Santa Cruz to Lajes came the following May when the seas had calmed after the winter storms. This time it was for Miguel and Maria Luísa's wedding.

They were married one year after they collided at the Festival of the Holy Ghost. They were deliriously happy and, even Miguel's mother, Francisca Luísa, had shown a spark of light when Miguel first announced he had met the girl he wanted to marry. The spark had dimmed when she learned the girl was not from Santa Cruz and would later go out completely when Miguel confided their plan to move to the United States.

O *casamento*—the wedding—was very nice, befitting of the Government Official's daughter. The people of Lajes were proud to have the Chapel of Nossa Senhora das Angustias as well as the Church of Nossa Senhora do Rosairo available. It was the latter in which Miguel and Maria Luísa wed.

At Miguel's insistence for the wedding, Maria Luísa pulled up part of her shiny black hair and secured it with a crown of white and yellow flowers on top of her head. The rest of her thick, long, straight hair fell down the back of her beautiful white wedding gown. The gown was made by a seamstress in Lajes from exquisite material and lace Ligia Furtado secured from Lisbon. Maria Luísa's floral crown reminded him of the day they first met. As tradition dictated, Maria Luísa's parents provided a *fotografo* to take pictures. The sepia didn't show how bright the crown of white and yellow flowers shone atop her shining black hair. Nonetheless, Miguel felt certain he would always remember every detail, including the colors, whenever he looked at the picture. They were burned into his heart. He vowed to look at the picture of his radiant seventeen-year-old bride every day of his life.

Following the wedding celebration, the couple returned to Santa Cruz with Francisca Luísa and Aunt Nelia. Because Miguel's father had passed away and knowing they had plans to eventually move to America, they had decided to live with his mother in her cottage.

Manuel dos Santos and Francisca Luísa had lived their entire married life in the small, black basalt stone cottage. The largest room was a combined kitchen and eating space. Off to the side of the room were two small rooms, one for Francisca Luísa; the other, which had always been Miguel's, would now be shared with his new wife. This was not a situation any of the three would have preferred, yet it made sense with the newlywed's plans for the future—helping them save money for their journey. Each of the bedrooms was furnished with a bed and a simple dresser. In honor of his new bride, Miguel had stuffed new hay into the mattress to make it as comfortable as possible. The cottage floors were dirt which had become hard and smooth through years of frequent sweeping. When nature called, they would each trek to the outhouse located a far distance from the cottage.

They had barely settled into their new living arrangement when Miguel's thoughts turned to his work. He knew he would have to be even more diligent, if that were possible, in order to save enough money to buy them passage on any vessel sailing to the United States. Miguel was glad he had not married and had a family earlier in his life. For this reason, he had been able to save some of his money.

Maria Luísa's daily life was changed considerably after the wedding. She never wavered in her love and adoration for Miguel. She was eager to follow him across the island to Santa Cruz and, later, when the time was right, to the American Santa Cruz, but it came as a surprise to her that this time of her life was so difficult.

Immediately following their wedding and return to Santa Cruz, Miguel and Maria Luísa had only one night that could be considered their *lua de mel*, or honeymoon. Miguel was eager to finally share his bed with Maria Luísa, something he had dreamed about since meeting her at the Festival of the Holy Ghost. Maria Luísa, being very young, was timid, though not unwilling. Miguel recognized his bride was hesitant, maybe even frightened, and tried to be as gentle as a man who had been without a woman for so long could be. Maria Luísa thanked God the next morning for helping her make it through the night. The next day she thought about their first night as husband and wife. She realized she had enjoyed the moments they had spent talking about their future plans as much if not more than the intimate ones. She smiled inwardly as she realized that the intimate times weren't as bad as her sister had led her to believe they would be.

The next afternoon harsh reality set in as Miguel, unhappy to leave his bride, hurried back to his boat. He was eager to get started doing everything possible to increase his fishing business in order to make more money. They needed it if they were ever going to make their move to America.

Before Miguel had entered her life, Maria Luísa had focused on her family home. The Furtado home was large and comfortable. Once in Santa Cruz, she came face to face with an unexpected reality: her mother had been right. There really *was* a startling difference between the lifestyle of a fisherman and that of a Government Official. She was shocked to find the Salvador cottage so tiny and so bleak. Only because her new mother-in-law did a bit of baking and cooking requiring the oven to be hot, was the cottage kept from being entirely damp and miserable. With the oven's help, the place was damp and miserable only most of the time. She looked forward to being warm during the summer months unsuspecting of the fact that in summer the heat of the oven would be so overwhelming she would be eager to escape outside.

Maria Luísa soon made another surprising discovery: she no longer had much in common with the single local girls and was so much younger than many of the other married women, they usually ignored her. Maria Luísa was left to turn to Francisca Luísa and Aunt Nelia for friendship. Francisca Luísa, overwhelmed by her own loss of Manuel, was unable to pay her new daughter-in-law much attention. She did, however, expect Maria Luísa to follow her through the day's chores. She showed her where to lead the cows to graze during the day and how to find them to bring them back at the end of the day. She taught her to milk the cows. Maria Luísa, while wanting to have her time occupied, didn't find her time spent with the cows that rewarding. Aunt Nelia frequently came to the cottage. She was pleasant enough to Maria Luísa, though usually huddled with Francisca Luísa and the two of them went off to the church as soon as the chores were done. Only rarely did they think to ask Maria Luísa to accompany them.

Before leaving Lajes, Maria Luísa's mother had given her daughter some yarn to take with her. She began to spend much of her day making *xailes*. Though young, she had already learned to crochet intricate designs into these shawls and making them gave her something to do. She gave one to Francisca Luísa and one to Aunt Nelia. Later she urged her mother-in-law to trade others for food and other household items she might need. This offer made Francisca Luísa actually look at her daughter-in-law with a glimmer of affection.

The townspeople of Santa Cruz had already recognized Miguel as one of the hardest working and most successful Florean fisherman—like his father. Energized and with his goal in front of him, he worked even more diligently—he and Javier staying out on the seas all night whenever they could—the seas permitting.

The fishermen's work didn't end each morning when Miguel and Javier returned the boat to the dock. It was necessary to not only make sure the fish were cleaned and prepared for sale or drying, but to make sure their equipment was readied for the next night's venture. That meant Miguel arrived home long after Maria Luísa was up and about for the day. Miguel tried to be sensitive to his bride and wash away the fish smells with the salt water before he headed home. As the weeks passed, Maria Luísa began to look forward to being held close by her husband, yet remained somewhat disgusted with the stink lingering on her handsome husband's body.

They soon settled into a routine where she would have food ready when Miguel arrived home and then leave him to sleep for most of the day. Each afternoon, Maria Luísa felt extremely sad when he had to go back to the boat and start his fishing routine all over again. During the next two years time passed slowly for Maria Luísa. In the letters she sent back to Lajes, she never admitted to her parents how much she missed them and her family home. Her love of and loyalty to Miguel would never permit it. Almost every night, Maria Luísa crawled into their bed alone, pulled the blanket tightly around her shoulders and cried herself to sleep wondering if the dream she shared with Miguel of an American Santa Cruz would ever come true.

1892

Miguel told his best friend and fishing partner, Javier, about his decision to go to the United States and swore him to secrecy. He didn't want anyone other than their parents to know they were planning on leaving the island. He didn't want to do anything that might cause the government to not allow them to leave. Javier promised to buy the Salvador family fishing boat, previously owned by Miguel's father and now, Miguel.

After telling her parents about their plan, Maria Luísa's father immediately wrote to his Uncle Ronaldo Bras who lived in Providence, Rhode Island, in the United States and told him that within the next couple of years Maria Luísa and her new husband would be coming to the United States. He said that the couple planned to go first to Providence before traveling to California in hopes that Ronaldo could help them find a place to stay and find work so they could earn money to get them to their final destination. Fermo Furtado, although he did not want to do so because he did not like the idea of his youngest daughter leaving Flores, sent the letter.

One night, not long after their wedding as they lay together in their bed, Maria Luísa asked Miguel when he thought they would leave for America. Miguel tipped up her chin with his large, work-roughened hand, gazed into her beautiful brown eyes and said, "One day, when we least expect it, *os anjos* will smile down at us and let us know it's time. Until then we must work hard, be patient, and pray the angels will arrive soon." A religious man, Miguel never doubted God heard their prayers.

Two years later, the angels smiled on Miguel and Maria Luísa when a merchant ship, *The Queen of the Seas*, carrying a few passengers, made an emergency stop in the port at Santa Cruz. One of its passengers, an elderly and—more impor-tant—a wealthy man, had collapsed and was on the verge of dying. His wife, not all that well herself, convinced the cap-tain to take them ashore so they could seek help. Normally this type of request would be ignored, even laughed at by the captain. He would have been content to wait for the old man to die and then perform a perfunctory burial at sea. Because the wife offered the captain a large amount of gold, this did not happen and he agreed to anchor. The captain planned to deliver the ailing man and his wife to shore, remain one night, and, as quickly as possible, get the ship headed back out to sea to continue the journey to America.

Nearby, Javier stood alongside many other Floreans watching with interest as this unexpected drama took place. Hearing the news of the cause of the unscheduled stop and the captain's plan to leave the next morning, he went to find Miguel. Miguel was close to home and hurried back with Javier to find the captain who was at a bar with a couple of his crew. Confirming that the man they had brought onshore wouldn't be returning to the ship, Miguel asked if he and his wife could take the place of the ill traveler. At first the captain tried to brush him aside. Miguel hastily spoke up saying he had plenty of *reis*—money—to pay the captain. Hearing the word *reis*, the captain looked at Miguel with interest. Miguel, looked the captain straight in the eye, and convinced him to agree that if he and Maria Luísa were at the dock by six in the morning with money in hand well before the ship was ready to embark, he would allow them to board.

Miguel hurried out of the bar, stopping only long enough to give Javier a hug that almost crushed his friend's back, and then he ran all the way home to find Maria Luísa. He picked her up, swung her around, and said, "It's time, *meu amor. Os anjos estão sorrindo.*" The thought of the angels finally smiling down on them brought a look of joy to Maria Luísa's face.

Planning ahead and having very few possessions helped. It did not take long for them to pack. Following the wedding, they had identified the few items they were going to take to America. One of these items was their *Bíblia* which had belonged to Miguel's father. His mother had given it to

Miguel and his new wife at their wedding. Other than their few clothes and a hand-carved box—a *caixnha de Madeira gravada*—which was presented to them by Maria Luísa's parents as an *oferta de casamento*, they had little else to carry. Miguel opened the wedding box to retrieve the *reis*—the money—he and Maria Luísa had stashed away starting from the moment of their wedding. He prayed it would be enough to get them to America and provide them food and a roof over their heads until he could find work.

Maria Luísa wrote a hasty note to her parents in Lajes telling them about the ship's arrival and that they were finally leaving. She told them how much she loved them and how very much she and Miguel treasured their wedding gift of the hand-carved wooden box which was going with them to America.

The couple hurried to give the news to Francisca Luísa and Nelia, who were at the church. They lit candles and Miguel sought out Father Diogo to ask him to bless him and Maria Luísa for a safe journey. He asked the priest to look after his mother, Francisca, and his Aunt Nelia.

Neither Miguel nor Maria Luísa could sleep and were up well before the sun. Before leaving the cottage, Miguel left some *reis* to assure his Aunt Nelia would have some money to help care for his mother. Carpetbags in hand, Miguel and Maria Luísa ran to the dock, stopping only long enough to pick up some bread, cheese, and wine for the voyage. They were aboard the small boat well before the captain ordered it to return to the *Queen of the Seas* for the large merchant ship's return to the high seas.

Maria Luísa and Miguel excitedly boarded the large ship. It was, by far, the largest ship Maria Luísa had ever been close to, let alone, be aboard. Once on deck, the captain had one of his crew show them below to their assigned cabin—the same space the ill man and his wife had occupied.

The cabin was tiny with two very small bunk beds. Maria Luísa sniffed the air hoping not to find any lingering smell of pending death hovering about. Her next thought was that already the cabin was a better place to be with Miguel than their small room at Francisca Luísa's cottage. She wasn't going to miss the cottage. She never had felt like it was *their home*. She hugged Miguel hard as they put their luggage under the bunks. "At last, we begin our dream!" she said, happily smiling at her husband.

Together they returned to the upper deck to wave to the people on the dock who were waving back at them. Though the figures were far away, Miguel was sure he saw his mother and his aunt in the crowd. His heart ached at the sight of them, knowing he would probably never see them again. Suddenly he felt uneasy and, for a brief second, he wondered if he was doing the right thing. At the same moment, he felt Maria Luísa place her hand in his. Smiling down at her, he took a deep breath and prayed to God that he had made the right decision for the sake of this beautiful wife of his and their future family.

Maria Luísa returned his look. She wondered if he was feeling the same way she felt so long ago having to leave her own family in Lajes.

Free of its anchor, the ship didn't take long before reaching the open sea. It took even less time for Maria Luísa's stomach to start feeling queasy. She suddenly felt warm, sweaty, and very seasick. She tugged on Miguel's sleeve to get his attention indicating she wanted to go down to the cabin and lie down. Genuinely surprised by his wife's reaction, Miguel led the way to their small cabin. He admitted to himself that he hadn't thought about that part of the journey. He had lived on the sea for so many years he barely felt any motion. What motion they had encountered as the large vessel got underway was far less than he experienced on his small fishing boat. He offered to get Maria Luísa some tea, and later, some food. When Miguel said the word *food*, her already pale face drained of all remaining color.

Maria Luísa didn't like her tiny sips of tea although her husband kept urging her to try because they both knew she needed to take in some nourishment. After a few sips, her stomach began to convulse causing her to vomit forcefully. Miguel searched for a bucket and tried to help her clean up as best he could.

When she could focus, Maria Luísa saw in his eyes that Miguel was suffering with her. "You are not helping anything by staring at me," she said sharply. "Go up on deck and. . ."

the sentence was interrupted by the sounds of retching as she hung her head over the bucket.

Miguel tentatively patted his wife's shoulder, sighed, and retreated to the upper deck. Once there, while feeling sorry his wife was suffering and helpless to make her feel better, he wandered about the deck. He became intrigued with the operation of the vessel, and talked to the captain and the crew. Recognizing a true seaman, the crew members enthusiastically showed off the boat and its equipment. Miguel asked a lot of questions and soon the captain was showing him how to navigate the large ship. Miguel was amazed and excited realizing that, already in this new life, he was being given the opportunity to learn something new.

Later, going below to check on his wife, he found that not only wasn't she feeling better, she was getting worse. "What is that horrible stink?" she asked Miguel, her tone sounding accusing.

Miguel, who was used to the overwhelming smell of fish, had barely noticed. He realized from the sounds nearby that most of the other passengers weren't doing much better than Maria Luísa. He had to admit the smell of vomit wasn't good.

As the voyage continued and the days passed slowly, Maria Luísa frequently repeated her complaints about the bad smells and her need to clean up. Miguel was left to explain that the amount of fresh water was limited and the captain had said baths were not to be taken. Miguel helped the crew position barrels to catch any rainwater to add to the drinking supply. As more days passed, even the fresh food supply on board dwindled. The cook, not a very imaginative youth, did the best he could with the rations he had. Miguel, who was able to eat, thought the food was not very good but ate it without complaint. Maria Luísa didn't complain about the food. Her only desire was to not see any.

Miguel worried greatly about his tiny wife. He could only watch as she got noticeably thinner day by day. She remained sick for the entire trip and continued to lose weight until he was sure there was not any more for her to lose. For several days, Maria Luísa had been thinking about her mother-in-law's cottage. She had changed her thoughts about the cottage—at least it didn't move about. She wished she was back in their bed at Francisca Luísa's rather than in this miserable bunk on this miserable ship.

The crossing of the Atlantic took twenty days. Maria Luísa was sure she would always remember them as the most miserable twenty days of her life—provided she survived. On the twentieth day, Miguel entered the cabin wearing a big smile. Maria Luísa, who had lost all track of time, glowered at him wondering how he could have the nerve to smile when she was feeling so terrible.

He took her face tenderly in his hands and kissed her forehead. Even his deep affection for her could not entice him to touch her lips with his. "My love, soon we will be seeing the land of America! We are almost there!"

She opened her eyes and studied him carefully. "Are you sure?" she whispered weakly.

Miguel assured her he was not kidding. She forced herself to listen. She could hear others speaking excitedly. Miguel helped her clean up as best she could and because she was so weak, he had to practically carry her to the deck to join their fellow passengers. They all crowded together at the ship's rails, watching, eager to see land come into sight. With Miguel's arm firmly around her for support, Maria stood on wobbly legs and wept. Miguel, feeling deeply emotional, looked down at his wife certain that her tears were caused by the sight of Lady Liberty welcoming them to America. While it was true Maria Luísa was happy to see the statue, the tears she shed were entirely in anticipation of finally being able to leave the miserable ship.

Clustered near the rail with their fellow passengers, Miguel and Maria Luísa stood in awe, as thousands who had come before them had done, watching as the *Estátua da Liberdade* grew larger before them. As though orchestrated, an almost sacred silence fell over them. Many bowed their heads in prayer.

Miguel grinned from ear to ear, his mustache twitching happily as the ship pulled into port at Ellis Island. He thanked God and the captain for giving him the most exciting adventure of his entire life. Maria Luísa thanked God for having let her survive.

Waiting for the merchant ship to unload, Miguel looked about at his fellow passengers. He could see everyone had dressed in their best clothing hoping to make a good impression in this new land. In spite of their best intentions, they were a bedraggled looking crowd at best. They were exhausted, wrinkled, scared, and the smell clinging to them was acrid at best. Still he could see excitement in their eyes as they waited. The weary passengers disembarked onto Ellis Island and were forced into a line to file past doctors who examined each one of this new passel of immigrants for signs of disease. Miguel and Maria Luísa hugged each other and sighed in relief when they were each finally issued a landing card. These cards gave them permission to board the ferry which would carry them into New York City.

Once the crowd was onboard the ferry, it cut through the water towards the city. Her stomach forgotten for a moment, Maria Luísa gazed in amazement at the vast number of tall buildings growing bigger as the ferry approached its dock. They stepped onto land, their hearts full of gratitude. So in awe were they of the bustling din of the city surrounding them, they could hardly speak.

They carefully followed instructions given them by a kind fellow passenger from the ship; however, because of their faltering English, it took them some time to find a horse-drawn carriage to take them to the train station.

Miguel, who had heard stories of New York and America from his sailor friends, was shocked. The buildings were so high and he could not believe the sheer number of them. They had never seen such stylish carriages—all with horses, no donkeys and not a single ox. Still not feeling well and with chattering teeth, Maria Luísa looked around. She and Miguel exclaimed about each new thing they saw—each barely registering what the other was saying.

Their hands clasped together, they smiled timidly at the confusing, noisy scene. "What a place is this America," Miguel said. The slight quiver in his voice told his wife he might be finding the whole scene overwhelming. She certainly was.

Once they arrived and were inside the enormous train station, they looked for the telegraph office where they sent a message to Uncle Ronaldo telling them they would be coming to Providence the next day. They paused to say a prayer that Uncle Ronaldo would actually get the message then hurried to the ticket cage where they purchased tickets north to Providence.

Neither had seen a train before and, hardly believing their eyes, gazed at the huge iron beast in front of them. It was enormous and, with the screech of escaping steam, so loud it was frightening. With trepidation, they followed other passengers from the station to the train and climbed up the stairs into a passenger car. Miguel led the way with Maria Luísa holding firmly onto the back of his jacket. Miguel showed their tickets to several people who pointed to seats on the right side of the car. Miguel was nervous when a man in uniform came through the car checking everyone's tickets. He felt better when he heard the man say "Providence" after scanning their tickets. Not saying anything to Maria Luísa, Miguel was relieved to know they were on the right train. Until that moment, he had not been sure.

Maria Luísa sat by the window. Soon the train lurched forward and began rumbling its way north. She was happy her stomach coped better with the side to side lurches of the train than with the constant motion of the ocean. It was already evening by the time the couple had boarded the train, and soon there was nothing to look at outside the window except darkness. Exhausted, Maria Luísa soon succumbed to the rocking of the railroad car and fell asleep with her head falling to rest against Miguel's shoulder. He, too, was tired and soon was snoring lightly, his head resting on top of his wife's.

Light streamed through the windows and they awakened to hear the ticket man coming through the train car calling out loudly, "Next stop—Providence, Rhode Island." Recognizing the word *Providence*, they nervously stared out the window at the landscape of trees, bushes, occasional buildings, and water. Soon they heard the loud screech and felt the power of the brakes slow the train. They watched out the window fascinated as the train continued to slow and, with a final lurch, come to a halt in Union Station.

Miguel and Maria Luísa turned to face each other, eyebrows raised and smiling nervously, before standing up to follow several passengers who were climbing down the stairs to the platform. Once they stepped away from the train, they stopped, closed their eyes briefly, and uttered a silent prayer. Disembarking passengers streamed by them. Miguel thought each looked like they knew where they were going. He fervently wished he did.

Knowing her father's uncle, Ronaldo Bras, lived here in Providence, Maria Luísa desperately hoped he had received not only the letter her father had sent so long ago but yesterday's telegraph as well. The most important part of a Portuguese or Azorean life is family. She never doubted for a minute that if they could find Uncle Ronaldo, he would help. Staying in Rhode Island until they could earn enough money to travel west across the country of the United States to California was an important part of their plan.

Before disembarking from the train, Maria Luísa had removed a picture of her great uncle from her valise and now clasped it to her chest. The photograph was old and faded, and she wondered if she would recognize him if he was there to meet them. She had not seen him since she was a very young girl. Miguel had already decided if Maria Luísa's uncle wasn't at the station waiting for them, they would find out how to get to the post office and see if they could get directions to wherever he lived.

A wave of relief flooded through Maria Luísa when she noticed an older version of the man in the picture. She tugged on Miguel's sleeve and pointed. There Maria Luísa's great uncle, Ronaldo Bras, stood waiting on the railroad station platform. Miguel hugged Maria Luísa and told her the angels had smiled down on them once again. Ronaldo Bras held his hat in his hand and was looking anxiously at each person stepping off the train searching for his great niece. He looked their direction and Maria Luísa waved vigorously catching his attention. A huge, welcoming, and very relieved smile spread across his face as he hurried towards them. Miguel and Maria Luísa felt as relieved as he looked.

With almost as many tears flowing down his face as flowed down each of theirs, Ronaldo folded Maria Luísa into strong arms—his embrace reminding her of her own father, unseen for so long. Once free, she introduced Miguel. Ronaldo was a couple of inches shorter than Miguel. He reached out to take Miguel's extended hand and pumped it vigorously, then pulled the larger man into a welcoming embrace.

Ronaldo loaded their *malas* onto his bakery wagon, making sure the luggage was secure. Miguel and Maria Luísa were amazed at the number of conveniences the Americans had at their disposal. With Ronaldo directing them, Miguel pulled himself up onto the bakery delivery wagon with Maria Luísa following. After seating her in the middle, Ronaldo climbed up onto the wagon. Once settled, Ronaldo gave the reins a small shake and the large black horse stepped forward pulling the cart holding its three beaming passengers. Miguel put his arm around his wife and gave her a reassuring smile. They were on their way to their first, though temporary, home in America.

As they rode through the wide streets, Uncle Ronaldo, speaking the familiar dialect of their homeland, proudly told them about the city of Providence and the surrounding areas they passed. He talked endlessly, pointing out businesses, houses of people he knew, different kinds of plants, what the weather was like in Providence, and how he loved living in this city. Maria Luísa and Miguel listened politely.

Soon they heard Uncle Ronaldo say his bakery was not much farther. His bakery, he explained, was called "*Ronaldo's Bakery.*" Neither Miguel nor Maria Luísa was sure they even understood what an American bakery was. Ronaldo told them their new home, the apartment they would share with Ronaldo and his wife, was located above the bakery. Miguel and Maria Luísa heard the pride in Uncle Ronaldo's voice as he talked about his bakery and his home.

Soon Ronaldo pointed to a building on the left side of the cobblestone street. Maria Luísa and Miguel took it all in starting from the sidewalk up to the sky. To them the building appeared very large and very tall. Miguel and Maria Luísa had decided all American buildings were enormous compared to the small ones on Flores. On Flores only the churches were tall and now even the Azorean churches seemed small.

A wide expanse of glass, like nothing they had ever seen, ran across the front of the building. Ronaldo pointed to a large sign and read, "*Ronaldo's Bakery.*" They could see two sets of staircases, each having four to five stairs leading from street level up to the entrances into the building. The left stairs led directly into the bakery entrance while the right stairs led to a door with the numbers 535 on it. Ronaldo pulled the horse to a stop in front of the one on the right. "This door will take us upstairs," he said, pointing upward, "to our *apartamento*."

Once inside the apartment, Uncle Ronaldo introduced his wife, Aunt Sofia, who immediately embraced the new arrivals.

"Thank God Ronaldo got your telegram and found you at the railroad station! We have been praying to God since the day we received your papa's letter telling us that you would one day be coming, that you would find your way safely to us."

Neither newcomer had ever seen any cottage that could compare to Uncle Ronaldo and Aunt Sofia's apartment. They could not believe housing like this even existed. Maria Luísa oohed and aahed at everything as Sofia led the couple on a brief tour.

Uncle Ronaldo said, "You must consider this your home for as long as you stay in Providence. We know you will eventually leave us to move to California, but until then...," his voice trailed off as Miguel had turned about and was hugging him.

"*Muitíssimo obrigado. Deus te abênçoe.*" Thank you so much. God bless you."

Aunt Sophia showed them the room which would be theirs, explaining it was formerly occupied by their son, Bernaldo, who had moved to New York. The room held a double bed, a beautifully carved dresser, a small table on one side of the bed, and a rocking chair.

Amazed, Maria Luísa clutched the cross hanging from a slender chain around her neck.

Sofia took Maria Luísa's hand and led her back into the hallways where she opened another door. "This is the bathroom."

Miguel and Maria Luísa were speechless. They had never seen anything like it! Sofia had to pull on Maria Luísa's hand coaxing her into the room. "We will all be sharing it," Sofia explained.

For the first time in a long time Miguel heard Maria Luísa's lilting laugh. She was picturing the outhouse by the cottage in Santa Cruz. She giggled. Miguel and Ronaldo were bent over peering into the toilet as Ronaldo explained how it worked.

Waving her hand towards the large white tub sitting to one side of the room, Sofia said, "It's been such a long journey. Perhaps before supper, you would each like to have an opportunity for a bath so you can clean up a bit."

Maria Luísa started to hug her Aunt, but stopped as she realized how awful she must smell. No one objected to Sofia's suggestion that, perhaps, Maria Luísa would like to go first.

As Maria Luísa and Miguel reverently watched, Sofia filled the bathtub and gave Maria Luísa a towel. After the others departed, Maria Luísa undressed and settled into the large tub for the first real bath she had ever taken. She didn't want to get out and wouldn't have had it not been for knowing her husband was awaiting his turn and that her aunt and uncle were waiting for them.

The afternoon passed comfortably as they all became acquainted. Not long after a light supper, Miguel and Maria

Luísa said their goodnights. Crawling into the comfortable bed, they held hands and again gave thanks to God for having delivered them safely to America and guided them to Ronaldo and Sofia. Within seconds they fell soundly asleep.

The next morning, feeling refreshed, they enjoyed a marvelous and, at least for Miguel, hearty, breakfast including some large and delicious *malassadas* made by Sofia. Maria Luísa tentatively sampled a little food and tea, then waited to see how her stomach was going to react.

Ronaldo said, "I will take you downstairs to see the ovens." Sofia said she would not be joining them because she would be in the bakery helping customers. Miguel and Maria Luísa, not knowing what to expect, were more than eager to see everything.

Ronaldo led them through the doorway and around the left side of the building. He guided them down a flight of stone stairs. The fan for the ovens vented off the back side of the building into a field where the local children gathered to play. Ronaldo explained how almost every morning one of the children would yell "It smells sooo yummy!" and grab onto his or her tummy and pretend to faint. This never failed to bring gales of laughter from the other children. The story made Miguel and Maria Luísa chuckle.

After descending the stairs, they stepped into the oven area. Miguel and Maria Luísa staggered backward from the blast of heat. After they recovered, they followed Ronaldo across the solid, packed- earth floor and walked toward the flaming ovens. Ronaldo continued talking as he went although the roar of the fires made it hard to hear. He leaned close to Miguel and shouted, "I have two bakery workers—two men who help me with the ovens and baking. It's hard work and they work long hours." Taking hold of Miguel's elbow, he added to assure them, "I work long hours along with them.

He explained that his men unloaded heavy bags or barrels of flour and fired up the ovens which were heated day and night. They all helped mix the ingredients, put the loaves in the ovens, and take them out. "This," he said, with a sigh, "is in addition to keeping all the equipment, tools, and the whole place in good order."

Looking intently at Miguel, he watched for his reaction and tried to assess his new nephew's interest in what he was saying. Miguel was listening and nodding. Maria Luísa watched her husband, her eyes wide as she fanned herself with a napkin she had brought from the apartment.

Miguel and Maria Luísa saw only one man, sweeping around the oven openings. Ronaldo shouted, "My other man, Jorge, took a serious fall and broke several bones. He's not able to work and won't be for a long time." Seeing Maria Luísa's already large brown eyes widen, Ronaldo hastened to assure her the fall had not occurred at the bakery. "I'm sorry for Jorge, but I'm glad God sent you, Miguel. His timing was perfect. If you're interested and willing, I could hire you to take over for Jorge as long as Jorge can't work. "Perhaps," he said sincerely, "for as long as you want or need to stay in Providence before moving to California."

Miguel and Maria Luísa were speechless. Miguel looked at Ronaldo to see if he was serious. Seeing he was, Miguel nodded vigorously. "But of course. That would be fantastic. I know I work hard and I am sure I can learn quickly. Thank you. I shall never in my life be able to thank you enough for your generosity and kindness." Uncle Ronaldo grinned while patting Miguel on the back. He said something neither Miguel nor Maria Luísa could hear clearly because of the noise, except for one word, *"Familia."*

Ronaldo introduced them to the man sweeping the floor, Simão Azocar, his other employee. Simão was young, and closer to Maria Luísa's age, Miguel noted. The bulging arm muscles attested to his strength. His dark skin, shiny from sweat, glowed in the light of the fires from the ovens. He shook hands with Miguel and nodded toward Maria Luísa. Miguel, thinking he looked at her a little too long, forced himself to set the thought aside. Ronaldo was talking to him. "We've been short-handed since Jorge was injured a few days ago, Miguel. Would you be willing to start training this afternoon?"

Miguel was surprised. He grabbed Ronaldo's hand and shook it vigorously to assure his Uncle he was very willing. He shook hands with Simão again. Simão looked surprised, and after another glance at Maria Luísa, returned his attention to sweeping.

Leaving the ovens, the trio retraced their steps back up the outside stairs. Following Ronaldo, they entered the bakery. Maria Luísa and Miguel were intrigued by what they saw. It was a small room and stacked around it in baskets and on shelves were loaves of bread of different types, breakfast cakes, muffins, and some desserts neither Maria Luísa nor Miguel recognized. They watched as Aunt Sofia helped customers who came in empty-handed and left, their hand-carried baskets filled with breads and pastries. After a few minutes, Ronaldo said to Miguel, "Let's go see about training you in the baking business."

At dinner that evening, everyone toasted each other with wine, giving thanks for the safe arrival of Maria Luísa and Miguel, the generous hospitality of Ronaldo and Sofia, the abundant meal before them on the table, family, and especially, God, who made it all possible.

Sofia had fixed a hearty Portuguese stew which she served with a loaf of bread she had brought upstairs from the bakery. Maria Luísa didn't think life could get any better until she heard Sofia speak to her as they were completing their meal. "Maria Luísa," Miguel is going to be very busy working downstairs. It's hard work and takes the men away for many hours."

Hearing this, Maria Luísa sighed deeply. Dark thoughts carried her back to her mother-in-law's cottage where she had spent so many lonely hours waiting for Miguel to come home from the boat. Her aunt continued, "What would you think about working with me in the bakery?"

Maria Luísa could hardly believe her ears. She looked towards her husband for confirmation that she had heard her Aunt's words correctly. The stunned look on his face assured her he had. Turning back towards Sofia, she quickly responded, not wanting her aunt to change her mind. "Oh yes, Aunt Sofia, I would love to work with you. I am very strong too." All eyes turned to her in disbelief as they looked at her thin and frail frame.

"Well yes, dear, I'm sure you are." Her aunt looked dubious. "If you like, you can start with me in the morning." That led to more toasting and chatting. The last toast was made by Miguel, "To America, he said raising his glass, "where dreams can come true and family makes them happen."

Maria Luísa proved to be a capable, even if not a strong, worker. She loved being in the bakery with Aunt Sofia. At the end of the first week, she was astonished when Ronaldo handed money not only to Miguel but to her as well. "You earned it," he said as he saw how wide her eyes opened.

Miguel and Maria Luísa were shocked that Maria Luísa would actually be earning a wage. They were even more shocked when, once Ronaldo converted the money from what it would have been in Flores, they saw the amount sitting in Maria Luísa's hand. Miguel's fishing had never earned him this amount of money in a week. As for Maria Luísa, she had never earned *any* money in her young life. The women in Flores worked hard, but their only compensation came in what they could trade for what they produced. While trading her shawls had helped Francisca Luísa bring home more eggs and vegetables, neither she, nor her sister, her mother, nor Miguel's mother or aunt had ever earned actual money. She wanted to jump for joy.

That night as she and Miguel put their money in the now-empty marriage box, Maria Luísa told him how happy she was to now truly be his partner in working towards their dream of finding the American Santa Cruz. While the amount she was paid was a small percent of what he received, he was proud of his wife. He closed his eyes and as sleep carried him away, he was sure he caught a glimpse of an ocean—the Pacific Ocean.

Maria Luísa had worried that her lack of understanding of English would be a big problem for her in the bakery. She soon discovered the apartment and bakery were located in a section of Providence where many people from Portugal and the Azores had settled. When customers came into the bakery speaking English, at first, she didn't understand a word they said. An eager learner, she listened very carefully. Gradually, with Sofia's help, she picked up a word here and there. It was all new, different, and very exciting. She had no idea that she would feel so joyous in America without Miguel directly by her side. She loved her new adventure.

Miguel, an outgoing man, soon discovered that his new working partner, Simão was not much interested in conversation. Miguel noticed that the only time Simão did seem interested was on those infrequent occasions when Maria

Luísa came down to the ovens to give a message to Ronaldo or Miguel. Simão certainly wasn't interested in hearing tales about fishing or life in the Azores. The ovens were hot and the ventilation poor. The hard work didn't bother Miguel—he'd worked hard all his life.

The job demanded Miguel get up at four in order to assure that the ovens were hot and ready for the bread and other items Sofia and Ronaldo decided to bake that day. They needed to be ready for the customers who began arriving at seven a.m.. Rising early didn't bother Miguel because he was used to being out on his boat all night and into the day. What bothered Miguel was that the only other people he saw most of the work day were Simão and Ronaldo. Ronaldo, who did most of the actual baking, was in and out throughout the day. Maria Luísa's great uncle was a good and kind man, but, by necessity, he was preoccupied with the business and had little time to stop and converse.

Miguel felt isolated and alone. Though he could not exactly explain it to Maria Luísa, he felt he was not as free as he was at home in Santa Cruz. Sometimes Miguel was overcome with a longing for his home Island of Flores. Other Azoreans he met recognized his emotion, called *saudades*, a Portuguese word expressing a deep yearning within his soul for the past he had left. Whenever Ronaldo noticed this look on Miguel's face, he would pat his nephew on the back and say with true understanding, *"Muitas saudades!"* At those times Miguel was thankful for the hot heat from the ovens that dried the tears streaming down his face.

Soon Miguel began to think of the basement as a *caverna*, a cave. Keeping the ovens going was hard work and the temperature in the basement had to be kept high—over 100 degrees—even in winter. Miguel missed the sea, the sun, the moon, the stars, fresh air, Javier, his many other friends, his mother, and his aunt. Sometimes he wondered if coming to America had really been the right decision. At night he looked at his beautiful young wife and saw how happy she was. While he was happy for her, he could not help but feel sorry for himself. Deep in *the caverna* he thought about whether he would *ever* get to the American Santa Cruz and whether it was worth living in this cave.

Miguel and Maria Luísa had arrived in Providence in early November with the holiday season moving into full swing. With the starting the baking at 4 a.m., the smells of hot breads and holiday specialties filled the bakery all day long. The Fox Point area where *Ronaldo's Bakery* was located was a busy working-class area of Providence. Maria Luísa met many interesting people and, even though she missed her family greatly, she didn't suffer the heartache she had feared she might. She heard the familiar language and banter of Portuguese and her beloved Azorean dialects throughout the day as shoppers came in and out of the bakery. Several of the regular customers were employees of very wealthy homeowners who lived in the large and magnificent homes on the other side of Fox Point.

Occasionally after work, Miguel and Ronaldo went to one of the neighborhood *Tascas* for a beer. Miguel looked forward to those nights at the Pub, sharing a drink with friends and, speaking and hearing Portuguese. These times, filled with tall tales and lots of laughter, refreshed his soul enough to carry on.

Most nights he would clean up and join Maria Luísa, Ronaldo, and Sofia for savory dinners of Portuguese soups, stews, or seafood with bread and wine. *Ronaldo's Bakery*, as well as the shared apartment, was filled with laughter and good conversation. Miguel and Maria Luísa felt comfortable in their new, albeit temporary, home.

Gradually Miguel and Maria Luísa settled into their new life. Providence's large Portuguese community included many who had emigrated from the Azores, making Miguel and Maria Luísa feel welcome and safe whenever they were submerged in the familiar language of their homeland. The Portuguese, known for being kind, warmhearted, and friendly were especially so to their fellow immigrants.

Miguel was glad to have the Portuguese community's new Holy Rosary Church to turn to when, less than a year after they had arrived, he received a letter from Javier informing him of his mother's death. Miguel's grief was palpable. While not surprised, he was deeply saddened. He imagined his mother in heaven with his father. Sometimes as he was drifting off to sleep he was sure he could hear his mother's laughter. He sent money to Javier to give to Aunt Nelia and Father Diogo for his mother's casket and to the church in her memory.

Maria Luísa was surprised she felt the loss of her mother-in-law as deeply as she did. Even though they had shared the same cottage for a couple of years, Maria Luísa and Francisca Luísa were never close. *"Maybe it was because we both love Miguel,"* she decided.

On the rare days Miguel was out of *the cave*, he liked what he saw of the city. Except for the long cold winter, Maria Luísa loved Providence even though she had never been so cold in her whole life. Miguel wondered about the effect on his body as he moved between the outside with its below-freezing temperatures and the over one hundred degree temperature in *the cave*. Miraculously, his body adapted. Maria Luísa had to borrow a warmer dress from Sofia until she could make her own. She was glad she had brought a warm shawl with her.

The holidays passed. The new year arrived with the cold weather holding on. After work was finished for the day, Maria Luísa and Miguel frequently consoled each other, reminding themselves of how Durano, the sailor in Flores, had told them California would be sunny and warm. It made their resolve to work hard to travel across America greater.

The seasons changed, winter finally gave way to spring as the heavy snows slowly melted. A few flowers peeked out from the cold, damp earth, reminding Miguel of Flores and the times when he sat on his rock by his favorite lake. He missed his frequent treks up the steep hillsides above Santa Cruz. He wondered how Javier was doing. He missed his friend.

Time passed like a swift breeze for Maria Luísa and like a snail for Miguel. Spring of 1895 began to show itself. Miguel arose in the dark, but could hear birds singing. A few crocuses peeked out of the ground. Large buds promised that there would soon be flowers on the magnolia trees. Miguel and Maria Luísa were eager to see blossoms bloom in the yards and in the flower boxes around the neighborhood, sure to dispel the harshness of winter and remind them of their homeland. Each evening Maria Luísa told Miguel there had been a few more minutes of daylight. For him, the end of spring could not come fast enough. At night Miguel and Maria Luísa sat together on the small bed and took out the beautiful wedding box with its carved, delicate small flowers. It, too, reminded them of Flores and they were happy watching their money fill the box.

Ronaldo was more than a fair employer. He paid Miguel the same wage he would have paid his injured employee, Jorge—a tribute to Miguel's quick learning and hard Azorean work ethic. Ronaldo and Sofia adamantly refused to take any money for rent, insisting the couple put it towards their goal of getting to California. They were, after all, *familia. Family*, the word, once uttered, stopped all arguments to the contrary.

One chilly spring morning, a young woman named Dora, a cook's assistant for the Moffit family, came into the bakery. She was a regular and Maria Luísa had waited on her many times. Dora, too, was Azorean although not from Flores but rather from the island, *São* Jorge. Her Azorean name was Auxiliadora; she had shortened it to *Dora* to make it easier for the Americans to pronounce. Maria Luísa and Dora became friends sharing an occasional afternoon walk. This morning Dora waited until Maria Luísa was finished with another customer before she pulled her aside. With eyes twinkling she asked Maria Luísa if she would like to work some extra hours for the Moffit family, where she, Dora, worked.

She explained to Maria Luísa that George Moffitt, the head of the household, had earned his money in the jewelry business. He and his wife, Virginia, entertained a lot and almost always hired additional staff to help prepare for and serve meals at their many social events. Maria Luísa looked intently at her friend to see if she was serious. Convinced she was, she nodded vigorously. "Of course I am interested!" she said. Clutching her friend's arm she added, "I'll talk with Miguel and Aunt Sofia to be sure they won't mind."

That evening on hearing of the offer, Sofia hugged Maria Luísa. "You would be a fool not to do this. You will earn good money and you'll actually get to be inside one of the most beautiful homes in Providence. Not everyone like us gets to do that."

Miguel didn't hesitate to agree. He enfolded her in a big hug. Inwardly, he wished he was the one who would be out meeting new people.

With her husband's and Sofia's encouragement, Maria Luísa enthusiastically accepted Dora's offer. Dora responded, "Oh, it's not really *my* decision. I'll take you to the Moffit's so you can meet the head housekeeper, Beatriz Melo. It is

Senhora Melo, not me, who will actually decide if you will be hired." Maria looked unsure. Dora patted her hand assuring her there wouldn't be a problem.

As promised, that same week on Sunday afternoon Dora came to get Maria Luísa. Together they walked up the long hill to the Moffitt mansion. Maria Luísa could not believe her eyes. The grounds of the mansion were beautifully green with trimmed flowering bushes and many varieties of large trees. The young women wound their way up the path and around to the back entrance of the house. Maria Luísa saw large urns overflowing with multi-colored flowers. In the time she had been in Providence, Maria Luísa had passed many large houses with well maintained grounds though she had never been so close to one. She could not believe the size of the house. The anticipation of entering made her insides quiver. Dora led her into the house through a hallway which brought them to a large service pantry of some sort. Maria Luísa noticed a large panel with many buttons and levers on the wall. Silently she pulled on Dora's sleeve and pointed. "Oh that lets the family call for the service staff to come to whichever room they are in anywhere in the house." Maria Luísa felt her chin drop.

Dora continued moving forward with Maria Luísa staying close behind. They entered the largest room Maria Luísa had ever seen. It was a kitchen where two women were working, one older than Dora and one younger. The older woman looked up, smiled at Dora, and nodded towards Maria Luísa. "You must be Maria Luísa Furtado Salvador," she said in a strong voice. Startled, Maria Luísa was glad she was able to squeak out a simple "Yes."

Dora said, "Maria Luísa, this is Senhora Beatriz Melo. Senhora Melo is the head housekeeper."

Beatriz Melo nodded, dried her hands on a towel, and waved towards Maria Luísa and Dora indicating they were to follow her.

Leaving the kitchen through a closed door, they entered a large, sunny room filled with plants of all shapes and sizes. Senhora Melo took one chair and pointed Maria Luísa towards another across from her. She said, "Dora, why don't you go into the kitchen and get three glasses of lemonade. Bring them back and join us while I talk with Maria Luísa."

Dora soon returned with the lemonade glasses on a tray and placed the tray on a small table in front of Senhora Melo, then sat quietly as the head housekeeper talked with Maria Luísa about how she came to work in a bakery in Providence. Maria Luísa told her a very brief version of her and Miguel's story. Beatriz Melo listened politely though Maria Luísa could tell she was not interested in spending a lot of her time on this discussion.

After finishing her lemonade, Beatriz Melo stood up. The unexpected action startled Maria Luísa causing her to almost drop her own glass. She and Dora set their glasses down and stood at attention. Beatriz Melo smoothed out her stiff white apron with both hands and looked at Maria Luiza. "I am glad you will be helping us out, Maria Luísa. Our next party is a

dinner the Moffit family will hold next Saturday evening.
There will be forty people here. It will be your first time so
you will work with Dora, and she will show you what to do.
I expect you here by three thirty in the afternoon to prepare
for the event. Following that, you will help with the serving
of the meal, including the wine. You will stay until the dinner
is complete, the brandy has been served in the drawing room,
and all of the dishes have been removed from the dining room.
You and Dora will be helping with the dishes. After that you
will be free to leave."

There had been no question posed as to whether Maria
Luísa would be available or was even interested. Beatriz
Melo's tone was serious and her remarks brief and to the point.
Maria Luísa watched in awe as the older woman walked away
from them in the direction of the kitchen, her posture perfectly erect. Senhora Melo turned and Maria Luísa saw a slight
softening in her demeanor as she said, "It was nice to meet
you, Maria Luísa. It's always good to meet other Azoreans. We
are all a long way from home." She turned to look at Dora.
"Dora, the family has all gone out for the afternoon. Just this
once, if you and Maria Luísa would like to leave by the front
door, you may do so."

When the door to the kitchen had swung shut, Dora
grabbed Maria Luísa's hand and grinned. "She likes you,
Maria Luísa!" Maria Luísa wondered if, when Dora had originally mentioned the job, she had really been so sure she would

be hired. "Come on; let me show you more of this beautiful house."

They left the room which Dora said was called the solarium and began a tour of the downstairs. As they entered a large entry way, Maria Luísa could not believe her eyes. The ceilings were so tall she felt as though she were in a church. She looked down at the floor and, startled, jumped. She had been looking up and consequently missed seeing the rug she had stepped on. It was ornately woven; patterns of golden flowers interwoven with red and green vines and leaves running throughout. She quickly stepped off the rug only to discover rich dark wooden flooring shining beneath her feet. It was almost as beautiful as the rug. She had never seen anything like it. It gleamed like a dark jewel. Momentarily flustered, she was not sure where she should stand. She decided to follow Dora's lead and noted her friend was standing in the middle of the rug. Dora said, "Since the family is gone, let's look at the dining room. It's my most favorite room."

She opened a door off to the side of the entryway and stepped through with Maria Luísa following so close she was almost stepping on her heels. Maria Luísa gasped. She understood why Dora loved this exquisite room. The same glowing dark wood flooring surrounded another, even more beautiful, rug situated under the table filling the massive room. The table was the longest she had ever seen. It, too, was dark brown with carved designs circling its edges. The gleam of the table's wood was so bright it made the floor seem dull by comparison; something Maria Luísa would have thought impossible a moment ago. A long arrangement of white fresh flowers with dark greenery mixed in stood in the center of the table. Looking up, she saw an enormous light fixture descending from the ceiling—sparkling with diamond-looking crystals dripping down. Maria Luísa stood mesmerized.

"Isn't that chandelier gorgeous?" Dora was saying. Maria Luísa nodded, looking first to the chandelier and then to its reflection in the wall-sized mirror mounted on a wall behind a beautifully carved sidebar. The sidebar filled one wall, while, across from it, windows filled the other. Dora was still talking. "The first time I came in here, I was sure a prince and princess would appear," she said with a giggle. Maria Luísa glanced around, checking for herself.

Later Dora let Maria Luísa leave the Moffitt home by the front door. She walked alone down the hill to return to the bakery, stopping along the way to take a deep breath and reflect on all she had just seen. To her, the weeks, months, and years of living in a damp cottage followed by the journey aboard the horrendous ship now seemed worth it. She alternated skipping with walking the rest of the way home, eager to share her afternoon adventure with her family.

The first dinner party came and went with offers for additional work at the Moffits following frequently. One evening as Miguel and Maria Luísa sat on their bed studying the money spread before them, Miguel looked at his wife, and, in a firm tone of voice demanding her attention, said, "*Meu amor*, are you sure you still want to move to California? Things are going so well for you here in Providence. You are so happy. We could stay here and use our money to find our own place to live. Ronaldo told me Jorge is still having back problems and cannot work anymore, so I know he would allow me to continue to work the ovens."

Maria Luísa looked at her husband. The look in his eyes clearly told her he would do whatever she wanted. She felt overwhelmed by the love she saw. If it had not been for the cold winters, she would have been tempted to stay because she enjoyed working with Sofia and Dora was such a good friend. Looking into the handsome face of her husband, she clearly saw behind his loving offer the desperate hope she wouldn't agree. She had seen their roles change, with her becoming the strong one and his spirit being crushed as he labored in the cave.

She knew Miguel's dream had not wavered. He still longed to discover a new Santa Cruz, the one here in America. She knew that while he would miss Ronaldo and his new friends in Providence, to stay would leave him always wondering about his dream. It would mean working a job that was killing his spirit. She loved him even more for having asked her. Returning his gaze, she waited a minute, and then laughed her infectious laugh as she said, "Joaquin Miguel Salvador, you promised to show me the California Santa Cruz and the Pacific Ocean. It has become *our* dream, not just *your* dream.

And I am sure you must have said something when we got married about keeping me warm all year long. You know that could never happen in Providence." They laughed together. The relief that spread across his face made Miguel look ten years younger.

One evening in the last week of June, Maria Luísa, Miguel, and Sofia were waiting for Ronaldo to get home so they could start the evening meal. The door burst open. Thinking it would be Ronaldo, they were all surprised as a rather heavyset, balding man with ruddy cheeks stepped into the room. Sofia gave a sigh of relief as she saw Ronaldo following closely on the stranger's heels.

"Everybody, this is Harold!" Ronaldo stepped around the man and waved his arm in the direction of his family. "Harold Owens." He proceeded to go around the room and introduce his wife, Maria Luísa and Miguel.

"Sofia, set another place so Harold can join us for *jantar*—dinner. Miguel, how about you pour our new friend a glass of *vinho*."

Maria Luísa helped Sofia put another place setting on the table while Miguel found an additional wine glass. Within minutes everyone was seated around the table with wine glasses in hand. Sofia, Miguel, and Maria Luísa looked at Ronaldo in expectation of something—having no idea what. "I have come home with the most marvelous surprise!" Ronaldo said, looking about the table with eyes twinkling and his cheeks glowing. It was obvious to Miguel that Ronaldo and Harold must have come from one of the several neighborhood *Tascas*. Maria Luísa and Sofia looked Harold up and down thinking he was, indeed, an unexpected surprise.

Ronaldo continued to beam as he looked at his family gathered around the table. Raising his glass, he said "*Parabéns!*" and drank his wine half way down.

After the toast, Ronaldo waited another minute, looking from one to another, obviously enjoying the suspense of it all. Finally he leaned forward and said softly, "Guess where Harold is from?"

Six dark brown eyes lit on Harold, and scanned his balding head, bright blue eyes, ruddy cheeks, and his rounded belly, looking for a clue. All six eyebrows arched—six questioning eyes flashed back to Ronaldo.

"California!" Ronaldo announced proudly then drank the other half of his wine.

All eyes turned back to Harold who grinned and nodded. "Yes, it's true—Pasadena, California."

Ronaldo looked like he was about to explode. "It's a miracle! Harold came into "*Matos*" with Al Mendes and joined me for a drink. It turns out Harold here not only is from California, but he's going back to California on the fourth of July!"

At this, Miguel blew out his breath. He hadn't realized he had been holding it since Ronaldo first uttered the word "California." He shifted his look from Ronaldo to Harold.

"And . . .," Ronaldo hastily added, "Harold will be traveling by train from New York to California where he lives!" he added needlessly.

Maria Luísa's eyes widened and she stared at Harold Owens. Miguel, grinning from ear to ear, stroked his big black mustache excited to meet someone from California. It was like a reaffirmation that California actually existed. "This is true?" he asked Harold directly.

"Yes, it's true. I live in Pasadena, near Los Angeles. I came east to New York to visit my brother, Daniel, who's a physician at University Hospital Medical College. Daniel had written me that he'd finally convinced his wife, Belle, to move to California even though her family is from New York, and she's never been too keen on the West. She worries that the west is wild with Indians running about."

Indians? Maria Luísa's brows furrowed as she thought about the strange word.

"*Indios,*" Sofia said patting Maria Luísa's hand.

Just hearing the word, "*Indios*" was enough to scare Maria Luísa. She had heard stories about Indians attacking white people and cutting the hair off their heads, scalping them. She shuddered.

"Anyway," Harold was saying, "Belle finally agreed to go for a visit." He paused, "Daniel was convinced if he could get her to Pasadena she would love it there and want to stay. So our plan was that they would return to Pasadena with me. Let me tell you, Daniel is much wealthier than I am," he said with a chuckle. "He bought three tickets on the New York Central to Chicago and the Atchison, Topeka, and the Santa Fe from Chicago to California.

He raised his glass to take another sip of wine. Noticing it was empty he held it out so Ronaldo could refill it. With the glass again full, he continued. "Like Ronaldo told you, our tickets from New York are for the Fourth of July. Daniel and I decided the Fourth would be a perfect day to set out on this adventure." He paused, sighed, and continued in a lowered voice. "Sadly, Belle suddenly took ill. It's her heart, and Daniel determined it would be too dangerous for her to travel. This all happened in the last couple of weeks." He paused again as their thoughts were all on the ailing Belle. "If you want my opinion, the thought of moving west made her worry about being attacked by Indians and caused her heart to act up."

Again Maria Luísa silently whispered "*Indians.*" She looked anxiously at Sofia as she realized that getting to California meant having to travel through Indian lands. She clutched her dress in her hands and looked at her husband to see if he was worried as well. She saw he was listening intently to Harold. Maria knew he was concentrating on trying to understand all the English words. She decided he didn't understand the English word, *Indians*, vowing to tell him later.

"Today," Harold started speaking again, "I came up to Providence to visit an old friend of mine, Al Mendes. Al and I went into *Matos* to get a drink and ran into Ronaldo. Ronaldo told me your story. He told me you two," he waved his wine glass in the direction of Miguel and Maria Luísa, "unlike Belle, are *very* eager to get to California."

Without hesitation Miguel said heartily, *"Ah sim! Estamos!"* *"Oh yes! We are!"* he and Maria Luísa repeated it in unison. Everyone laughed.

"Well, when Ronaldo told me about the two of you, I had an idea." This time when he paused, Ronaldo had the wine at the ready to top off his glass. "I thought you two might use the tickets Daniel and Belle can't use and travel to California with me. It would be nice to have the company."

Miguel and Maria Luísa stared at Harold in disbelief. They looked at each other to see if they had really understood the English words. Ronaldo and Sofia watched them. Harold paused and looking directly at a questioning Miguel said seriously, "Would this be of any interest to you?"

The initial surprise had passed. Maria Luísa looked expectantly at Miguel. She was holding tight to the *crux*—the cross ever present on a chain around her neck.

Miguel hesitated a minute and then, with a worried look, said, "How much would it cost?"

Harold looking directly at Miguel recognized the pride of the man before him. He said carefully, "Ronaldo told me you've saved almost enough for the trip already." Harold had a good idea about how much it would cost for an emigrant fare. He paused and looked at an anxious Miguel. "It would be $75 for each of you; $150 in all. Would you be able to come up with that?"

Harold watched the younger man carefully, hoping he had settled on amount which would respect Miguel's pride and yet not overshoot the amount Miguel had actually saved. In a split second, Harold saw the worry in Miguel's eyes transition into joy.

Miguel glanced at Maria Luísa's wide eyes and hands covering her mouth in anticipation. Then he turned and grabbed Harold into a big bear hug. "*Obrigado. Muitissimo obrigado.* Thank you so very much. We are so very grateful to you. God must have sent you to us. We will always be in your debt."

Suddenly everyone began hugging each other and the evening meal turned into a major celebration. Sofia scurried downstairs to the bakery and brought up a tray of *Camafeus* to top off the dinner and commemorate the turn of events. The custard cream looked delicious oozing out the sides of the flaky pastry cornucopias. Ronaldo went to a cupboard and brought out a bottle of sweet *Angelica* brandy from the Azorean Island of Pico. He had been saving it for a special occasion.

Miguel and Maria Luísa could hardly contain their excitement. Just as it had been when they left Santa Cruz on Flores, they had little to take with them. As a result, it took less than a day for them to pack for California. While they had become very close to Ronaldo and Sofia and were very sad to leave them, they were extremely eager to *finally* be going to California!

The night before they were to leave, as a small token of their appreciation Maria Luísa insisted on doing all the meal preparation. Miguel had bought Ronaldo a bottle of *Terras de Lava*, the wine from the Azores said to have once been favored by the Russian Czars. Maria Luísa presented Sofia with a colorful *xaile*—a shawl—she had been secretly crocheting in the style of their beloved Flores. She placed it lovingly around her aunt's shoulders. The two women hugged and their tears flowed. Had they looked at their husbands, they would have seen traces of wetness on their cheeks as well.

1895

Having lived in Providence for three years, Miguel and Maria Luísa were used to seeing many modes of transportation. This time the train trip from Providence to New York was far less overwhelming than their first one when they arrived in America. On the morning of July fourth, Harold Owens met them at the train station in New York. He reminded them they would have to go to a different railway station to head west. Once there, they would board the New York Central to Chicago.

Miguel and Maria Luísa were extremely happy and relieved to have Harold Owens paving their way through the busy station and onto the train platform. Though far less nervous about riding on a train this time, they were a bit anxious, though eager, to begin this particular journey—the one which would end in Santa Cruz, California.

Maria Luísa held tightly onto her husband's arm as he assisted her up the steps and into the train. Entering the car to their right, they were surprised to see that this passenger car looked very different from those they had traveled on before—it was far more luxurious and less crowded. Feeling slightly out of place, they dutifully followed Harold down the aisle. Maria Luísa, noting the deep green floral fabric print covering the seats, thought it was beautiful. Halfway through the car, Harold stopped. "Here we are," he said. He pointed to two seats on the left side and said "Miguel, you and Maria Luísa will sit there." And pointing to his right, "And I will sit right here."

The men took care of the luggage as Maria Luísa eased into her seat, leaning comfortably against the back. With amusement she watched Miguel settle himself into the seat beside her. His large mustache twitched—a sign he was happy. Fascinated, they watched the other passengers board and find their seats. Maria Luísa was particularly interested in the women. Eyeing them, she became acutely aware of her own plain, blue shirtwaist dress and the modest cape she had pulled about her shoulders. The dark curls Miguel loved fell to her shoulders while a small hat sporting a simple white rose sat perkily atop her head. Maria Luísa noticed that the women who passed in the aisle were splendidly attired in dresses she assumed were newly tailored. Watching them reminded her of the guests the Moffits entertained—their coats, made of rich-looking fabrics, appeared custom-made. She thought their hats—chapeaus Dora had said they were called—were very ornate and beautiful. In spite of the warm weather some of the women wore furs. Harold predicted they would soon take them off as the temperature was sure to rise rapidly as the train crossed the country. In honor of the Fourth of July, several boarding passengers carried small American flags. The celebratory chatter of the passengers continued until a sudden hush fell as the conductor yelled "All Aboard."

Maria Luísa looked proudly at her husband. He wore his best black suit and white shirt. She could not recall his looking more handsome, except, perhaps, when he wore it last—at their wedding. Seeing his full black mustache twitching with excitement made her smile.

Glancing across the aisle, she saw Harold chatting with the gentleman seated beside him. She took the opportunity to look in wonder at this special, kind, and generous man who was responsible for moving them closer to their dream—*another angel, perhaps?*

As the train took off down the track, its gentle rocking put several passengers to sleep. For the moment Maria Luísa was far too excited to let that happen. She didn't want to miss a single minute of this adventure. She and Miguel gazed out the window, taking in as many details as they could as the train departed from the station. Though they tried valiantly to stave it off, not far outside of New York each succumbed to the rocking of the car and the redundant noise of the wheels clacking on the rails and fell asleep.

Later they were hungry, and, with guidance from Harold, they made their way to what he explained was the dining car. Maria Luísa and Miguel were extremely nervous moving through the passageway between the cars. It was very noisy and windy and the lurching of the train was frightening as they anxiously tried to maintain their balance as they moved from one car to the next. "Don't look down!" Harold yelled. "Just look straight ahead and follow me." With that advice shouted back over his shoulder, he disappeared into the next car.

Miguel followed pulling Maria Luísa behind him. Once they had stepped into the dining car, Maria Luísa and Miguel concentrated on breathing normally again. Their deep breaths turned into small gasps as before them tables with glowing silk-shaded lamps and gleaming leather chairs filled the car. Lovely, shining silverware sat proudly aside gleaming dishes. Maria Luísa whispered to Miguel that she felt like she was attending one of the Moffitt dinner parties, only this time not as a server but as a guest. His eyes widened as he nodded.

Once they were seated, a smiling black man wearing a crisp white jacket stepped forward to attend to their table. They felt like royalty. As she was eating, Maria Luísa saw one of the other woman passengers staring haughtily at her. She wondered if the woman thought she should be serving instead of being served. At one point Harold looked up, took notice, and gave the woman a withering stare. The woman's cheeks turned pink and she directed her attention back to her own companion. In spite of the excellent foods being served, Maria Luísa hardly ate anything. She told Harold she was much too excited to eat. After the meal was finished, the couple agreed with Harold's declaration that the food was delicious and the service outstanding.

Following a cup of tea for Maria Luísa and coffee for the men, Harold and Miguel escorted Maria Luísa back to her seat and then retreated to the smoking car to enjoy their cigars and cigarettes.

Eighteen hours later, the train entered Chicago's Dearborn Station. Peering out the window, the travelers thought the station, with its pink granite and red pressed brick exterior, particularly impressive. They gazed up at the clock tower and counted twelve stories rising up in the air. As impressed as they were, they were more eager for the train to leave and continue its trek westward.

At one point, the couple awakened and looked out the windows amazed to see how flat the entire area appeared to be—it was as though they could see forever. Harold explained they were in Kansas. Maria Luísa liked the flat landscape Kansas offered—giving, by far, the smoothest ride, for which she was grateful. Finally, the tedious sameness of the landscape lulled her back to sleep.

During their waking hours, Harold spent a lot of time telling Miguel about the business he was in. "Real Estate," he said proudly. "I've done very, very well in real estate. Buying land and houses was and is a smart way to invest! Once you, young man, get settled in Santa Cruz and earn some money, you, should consider investing in land. You will be glad you did." Miguel, who had heard the same thing from his Portuguese friends in Providence, felt proud that Harold showed confidence that he would become successful enough to consider doing such a thing. Maybe the American Santa Cruz would bring him and Maria Luísa more happiness than he had dared to dream.

Beneath them, miles of track slipped away and soon they were in Colorado. It took only a glance out the train windows to confirm the stories Harold had told them about the grandeur of the Colorado Mountains. They had never seen anything like them—feeling in awe as the train groaned its way up the curvy track carved out of the mountain side. Looking out the window and seeing below them, Maria Luísa tightly closed her eyes. She felt like they were suspended in air. She was afraid to look down for fear the entire train would fall. She listened to men seated around them talking about the skill and hard work it had taken to build the train track. She took more frequent and shallower breaths, and held a long, silent conversation with God. She was frightened going up the mountains and terrified coming down. She held on to Miguel's hand so tightly that periodically he had to pry her fingers off to allow the blood to circulate enough to get feeling back into his hand.

Hearing Harold announce cheerfully, "We're in New Mexico!" Maria Luísa once again thanked God for being with them. She exhaled so long and so loudly that Miguel asked her if she was all right.

Before they had left New York, Maria Luísa's worries were evident in the question she asked. "What if we run into

Indians?" After the train had rumbled down the mountainside, making her think they would career down into some steep ravine surely to die, she turned to her husband and said, "I think seeing Indians standing on flat lands beside the train would have been less frightening." It took several more mountain descents before they finally reached Santa Fe.

After the train left New Mexico and crossed into Arizona, Maria Luísa felt the rising, and stifling heat. The scenery outside looked brown, dry, and hot and she was glad the train had a bit of a cooling system. Even with it, all the women were finding fans or using their hats to fan themselves so they could feel a slight movement of air crossing their faces. She noticed that all the fur coats she had seen in New York and Chicago had completely disappeared.

Harold informed them they would be traveling through the desert of California in the late night and early morning rather than in the heat of the day. Not knowing exactly what this meant, they accepted his assurance that this was good news.

Early the next morning, Harold told Miguel with enthusiasm—and then Miguel even more enthusiastically told Maria Luísa—that they were finally in California! Looking out the passenger car window, they saw trees and some bushes, many with flowers. Gradually the track's curves seemed fewer and less jolting. Maria Luísa's color went from wan to pale. Miguel put one arm around her and squeezed. Occasionally, he blurted out, "California!" Harold Owens wore a continuous grin.

Harold chattered away, telling them about each of the small towns they passed through. The train passed large numbers of trees which, Harold explained, were citrus groves. "We grow a lot of oranges in California," he said. Finally the train rumbled into the Atchison, Topeka, and Santa Fe's western most terminal station. The conductor, in his mellifluous baritone, called out "Los Angeles" as he swept past them down the aisle. For a brief moment, there was total silence in the car, soon broken by lots of happy chattering passengers preparing to disembark. The trip had taken six and a half days.

Stepping off the train, Maria Luísa and Miguel faced a very large fountain surrounded by a blaze of red, white, yellow, and purple flowers—a clock tower standing majestically in the center. The scene reminded them of their beloved Santa Cruz on Flores. Simultaneously they declared to Harold that the Los Angeles Union Passenger Terminal was the most beautiful sight they had seen. With the sun shining down on them, and surrounded by a beautiful garden, they felt blessed.

1895

At the train station, Harold, Miguel, Maria Luísa, and several other passengers—very well attired, Maria noted—climbed aboard a horse-drawn trolley to begin their ride to Pasadena. Miguel and Maria Luísa watched scenery change as they traveled through downtown Los Angeles and then headed away from the city.

The trolley came to a stop at an enormous hotel surrounded by greenery, flowers, and tall, swaying palm trees. They unloaded their luggage and transferred it into a horse-drawn cab for the remainder of the ride to Harold's home in the Pasadena hills.

The fairly short ride took them up winding streets following the curves of the canyon rims. Some of the drop offs were extremely steep and Maria Luísa looked away rather than down into the steep canyons. They arrived in an area Harold called the Oak Knoll neighborhood where the cab finally pulled into a drive and Harold stepped out calling happily in his booming voice, "Here we are."

Having finally arrived, Miguel and Maria Luísa were momentarily speechless. They saw a beautiful house surrounded by a flourishing array of colorful growth. The Owens' house wasn't as large as the mansions they had already passed by or the Moffit home and others like it in Providence. Nevertheless, the surrounding palm trees, bamboo, and multitude of shrubs and flowers made it appear elegant. The pink *hortênsias* and red bougainvillea were very reminiscent of Flores. Miguel and Maria Luísa each took a long, deep breath—Miguel eager to savor the familiar floral scents—Maria Luísa to finally dispel the close smells of the overly warm train, trolley, and cab. She hoped to quell the almost constant feeling of nausea she had carried across the country.

Suddenly the front door of the house burst open and a round little woman came toddling out. A bright red dress covered by an even brighter pink apron brought to Maria Luísa's mind a moving, oversized flower.

"Harold! Oh, Harold, darling! You're finally home!"

The couple gave each other a big hug. Miguel and Maria Luísa couldn't resist smiling as they watched the couple embrace. With two very rounded bellies it was hard for Harold and his wife to actually get close to one another, none-the-less the love between them was obvious. The woman then turned toward the cab where Maria Luísa and Miguel stood, their valises beside them. "Aren't you a sight for sore eyes!" she chirped.

Harold paid the driver who, with a slight flip of the reins, signaled the horse to pull the cab smoothly away from the curb. Harold's wife made her way to Miguel. She shook his hand and then hurried over to Maria Luísa and swept her up in a big hug. Then she stepped back and looked at her. "Oh my, you don't look so good," she said. "Let's get you inside. You men bring in your luggage and things. I've got some lemonade and some fresh baked cookies. They're oatmeal and raisin cookies, Harold, your favorite!" She called back over her shoulder.

She hurried Maria Luísa up the stairs, into and through the house to the bathroom. "Use this blue cloth to splash your face," she directed, tapping a small counter. "There's a towel right beside it. That should help you feel better. You take your time and freshen up. Come out to the kitchen when you're done. It's going to be all right, dear. Don't worry about anything."

After a short time, Maria Luísa emerged to find Harold, Miguel, and Harold's wife, Ethel, sitting around a large table with tall cold glasses of lemonade in front of them. Each held a partially eaten oatmeal cookie. Ethel waived Maria Luísa towards an empty chair beside her where a glass of cold water awaited her. "I thought you might prefer water to lemonade," she said.

Maria Luísa sat heavily down on the chair. "Thank you. That was very kind of you."

"Yes," Ethel went on, "I know when *I* was with child, I couldn't drink lemonade at first either."

All eyes turned to Maria Luísa. Miguel's mouth dropped open and his thick black eyebrows shot up. Maria Luísa turned bright pink, a welcome change to her grey cross-country pallor.

She glanced at Ethel and Harold and then stared straight at Miguel, saying, "Don't you think it's wonderful? God's plan was always for our first child to be born in California."

Miguel, a man rarely at a loss for words, looked stunned for a moment and then leapt out of his chair and grabbed Maria Luísa out of hers. He started to swing her around and then stopped suddenly, setting her down on her chair as gently as if she were made of glass.

"Maria Luísa, oh my dear Maria Luísa! Um Bebé! We're going to have a baby? When did you know? Why didn't you tell me? Are you okay? Was it all right to go on this long trip? Oh my!" Miguel paused, looked up at the ceiling, and said softly, "It's a miracle. I was sure God had decided we were not to have any children." He paused again to catch his breath.

Maria Luísa was laughing. There was no way she could answer any of his questions or get a word in edgewise. "Oh Maria Luísa," he was blurting out in the Azorean dialect of his homeland, "*O nosso primeiro filho será Americano! Um Califoriano, Americano!*" He repeated. "Our first son will be American! A California American."

Harold and Ethel, understanding only *American* and *California*, beamed.

Miguel fell to his knees in front of Maria Luísa's chair and grasped her hand. He kept repeating that his first son would be an American. She was laughing a little harder as she watched his remarkable mustache twitch in his excitement. A tiny spot of pink graced each of her cheeks as she smiled tenderly at him. Repeatedly, she assured him she was okay and she loved him too.

They all settled back into their chairs, and toasted with another round of lemonade and water. Miguel, grasping one of his wife's tiny hands in his large one, suddenly looked very serious. "I have another announcement," he said. "Now that we are in the United States of America and finally in California, I am going to be called *Michael*! Not *Miguel* anymore. *Michael*. *Michael* is American. My son's papa will have an American name!" His speech was rapid and in a mix of English and Portuguese.

By the time Harold, Ethel, and Maria Luísa finally grasped what Miguel had said, he had moved on to say that he wanted to change his last name as well. Harold and Ethel figured out that Maria Luísa, now speaking Portuguese as rapidly as her husband, was disagreeing with what he was saying.

Harold joined in, speaking as rapidly as his guests, though in English, urging Miguel to listen to his wife.

Finally, Maria Luísa took a deep breath and said, in as calm a voice as she could muster, "Miguel, Dear. It's more of an honor for your father if you keep his family name, *Salvador*." She told him she knew many Azoreans changed their names when they came to America, but he, Miguel, didn't need to change both. Looking solemnly into his eyes, she said, "I love being a Salvador. It makes me proud."

He returned her gaze a long time; then he spoke. "We will stay *Salvadors* in honor of my father. I will be *Michael* in honor of America."

Michael, the former Miguel, accepted Harold's invitation to stay on with him and Ethel for a few more days allowing Maria Luísa time to feel better. The nausea, while not totally gone, settled down, and only bothered her a little in the very early morning hours.

Michael was eager to move on north to find his American Santa Cruz. A week later, he and Maria Luísa bid a fond fare-well to Harold and Ethel. After promising to stay in contact with their new friends, they returned to Los Angeles to board the train that would *finally* take them to Santa Cruz.

The couple was happy and felt comfortable traveling on the train by themselves. Big smiles remained on their faces and they beamed at the other passengers—all strangers—who, unable to resist, responded with smiles of their own. The train pulled out and soon they were rattling through the commu-nity of Santa Monica. They gazed out the train windows over beautiful blue waters near the Santa Monica pier, the site of the ocean making them feel at home. Michael inhaled deeply, hoping, though failing, to take in the familiar smells of the sea.

Continuing north, the train followed the steep coastal cliffs where the couple watched the ocean pounding rocks at its edge throwing white froth into the air. The size of the beaches amazed them. Flores had beaches, but all were small. These seemed to wander on forever, their golden and white sands sparkling in the sunlight. Off the east side of the train were rolling hills sporting coastal terraces—scattered herds of cattle and sheep grazing here and there. Maria Luísa squeezed Miguel's hand at the familiar sight.

The hours passed slowly. Much of the train track was inland as the land nearer to the coastline was too difficult for a train to pass. Michael and Maria Luísa marveled at the tunnels dug through the steep hillsides, but their focus remained primarily on the beach. They whispered softly to each other, re-sharing all they hoped this California Santa Cruz would have waiting for them.

A man across the aisle leaned over to tell Michael it wouldn't be long until they would be in Santa Cruz. Hearing this, Michael retrieved a small piece of paper from his jacket pocket. On the paper was the name of a woman Harold knew in Santa Cruz who had a house with rooms to rent. Michael kept the paper clutched in his large hand for a while and then stuffed it back into the pocket of his jacket, patting the pocket to be sure it was secure.

After what seemed like forever, they finally saw a sign out the window. Maria Luísa read it aloud, "*Welcome to Santa Cruz.*"

"*Bem Vindo a Santa Cruz,*" Michael repeated softly.

Michael and Maria Luísa held hands. "*Parece um sonho,*" Michael whispered to his wife as the train rumbled on. She nodded, agreeing it certainly did seem like a dream. He thought about the five years that had passed since they married in Santa Cruz on their beloved Island of Flores, sitting so far away in cluster of volcanic islands—the Azores. Finally, in August of 1895 they were actually going to be here in the other Santa Cruz—this Santa Cruz, in California, in the United States of America. The reality of the moment set in and they were overjoyed.

Many passengers were pointing excitedly towards the glistening water. The man across the aisle said, "That's Monterey Bay. Santa Cruz is on the northern part of the bay." The passenger car buzzed with excitement. Michael and Maria Luísa commented on how Monterey Bay was a beautiful blue—not as deep a blue as the ocean around Flores—but a beautiful blue. The tide splashed white frothy waves onto a golden beach which, Maria Luísa and Michael were astonished to see, absolutely overflowed with people. Huge buildings perched high on the hillside sprawled downwards, looking like they would fall into the sea at any moment.

Practically everyone on the train was pointing at the Santa Cruz Beach Boardwalk. As the train track brought them closer they could hear music coming from the calliope. They gasped when they saw the famous roller coaster for the very first time. The riders on the train who hailed from Santa Cruz were pointing and saying "Giant Dipper. Giant Dipper." As they said these strange words, they rolled their arms and hands up and down mimicking the car they could see on the roller coaster. Everyone was grinning from ear to ear. The shrieks of the riders made Michael and Maria Luísa wonder if the cries were from terror, and they watched, riveted, as the small cars reached the tops of the tracks and then plunged their riders down the other side. Fearing for the riders' safety, Maria Luísa couldn't keep her hands from flying up to cover her mouth. The train moved on. Maria Luísa and Michael couldn't stop grinning at each other. This was beyond what they had ever imagined.

Retrieving their luggage from the train, they found a cab to take them to the home of Senhora Beatrice Villego, who, as Harold has assured them she would, did have a sparsely furnished room to rent. They climbed up a short flight of stairs, took a quick look at the room, and told Senhora Villego they would take it. Michael carefully counted out the money for the first month's rent, making their new landlady very happy. Michael went back down the stairs with Senhora Villego and returned carrying their luggage which he deposited on the floor of their new, one room *home*. Maria Luísa sat in an upright chair by the window, her arms wrapped about her tummy. As soon Michael reappeared, she told him she was feeling tired and needed a nap.

Michael forced himself to lie quietly on the bed beside his beautiful wife holding her hand and allowing her to have some much-needed rest. After a brief thank you to God for his wife, his son-to-be, and his own safe arrival, he, too, drifted off to sleep.

Twenty-five minutes later, two large brown eyes popped wide open. Jiggling her husband's arm Maria Luísa wakened Michael and said, "This is silly. It's far too exciting to sleep. We're finally here in the American Santa Cruz, our new home. We'll have a lot of time to sleep later!"

Leaving the house they began their walk, following directions Senhora Villego had given them. They wandered through the town, taking the remainder of the afternoon to stroll around the beachfront area. Maria Luísa declared she was hungry. They sampled what a big red sign told them were *Famous Hot Dogs*. They had seen several people nearby eating them, suggesting they would be good. After finishing eating, they returned to their room, feeling happy but completely worn out. Michael kissed his wife good night and told her that early the next morning he would begin his search for a job. It would be difficult to say who was asleep first.

While Michael hoped he could find work in a day or two—it took him only one. Before leaving Providence, he had been encouraged by Ronald to look for work in the bakeries first. He had given Miguel a letter of reference. The thought of working in another *cave* was more than Michael could bear. With a sincere hug, he had thanked Ronaldo for the letter, taken it to the bedroom, put it in his suitcase, and promptly forgotten about it. He desperately wanted to return to the sea.

With a determined stride, he headed down the hill towards the waterfront. As he walked, he recalled having been told that the majority of emigrants from the Azores who settled in California worked in agriculture or became dairymen. *At least cows are outside and not in a cave.*

It took only a few inquires of the men working on the docks to learn who was hiring. Michael was soon talking with Mariano Silva, the owner of a small fishing fleet. Silva confirmed he was looking to hire a couple of new fishermen for his crews. Not long into their conversation, Silva recognized that Michael knew full well what life as a fisherman required. He found Michael's enthusiasm for the sea greater than what he usually saw in potential hires—it would be some months later before he understood why.

Mariano Silva felt he was a good judge of a man's character. His crew was entirely made up of Portuguese immigrants— men he knew he could count on to be the hardest workers, put in the longest hours, and never question the extremely hard labor required to bring in a good catch. He listened carefully as Michael told him about growing up in the Azores, and, starting at the age of thirteen, fishing with his father. He described what a typical fishing night had been like. Michael told him about the good times and the bad. Mariano Silva was well aware of how few of the Azorean immigrants who came to California were interested in fishing and the sea. Here he was facing an Azorean whose father had been a fisherman and who had followed in those footsteps. He, himself, had such a connection and because of that, he knew Michael was a man he wanted to have work for and with him.

Michael started to say more when Silva interrupted him saying he was going out to check on one of his boats. He asked Michael if he would like to come with him. Michael was elated.

As the boat cut across the water, Mariano explained to Michael that he owned ten boats. Five went out at night and five during the day. The crews rotated. Their biggest competition was from the Italians. A couple of Italian families had fishing companies with much larger fleets and did very well. No one questioned they were the most successful in the fishing business in the area.

He turned, his twinkling dark eyes looking straight at Michael. "However," he said with a grin, "what we lack in fleet size we make up with *Orgulho Portugues*—hard work, dedication, and commitment to each other. Yes. Portuguese pride and good team work; that's why our Silva Fleet does so well. The Italians may have *more* men—the Silva Fishing Company hires *the best* men."

Setting sail, the light wind carried them smoothly over the water until they reached the Silva boat. Michael's heart sped up. He saw a boat much larger than his boat in Flores, yet it was the same design he was used to. It had the beautiful sturdy wood siding and the variation of the lateen rigging with which he was so familiar. The larger boat he looked at held a crew of four and easily could accommodate one or two more. They tied up alongside the boat and boarded. Mariano briskly introduced Michael, telling his crew Michael was looking to join their fishing crew. The men each gave Michael a wave or a nod. He could tell by their looks that they were appraising him as a potential crewmate. Mariano turned his attention to the *Mestre* to discuss the business at hand.

As Mariano talked with the Skipper, Michael stepped closer to one of the other fishermen, John. Standing far enough away to not interfere with his work, Michael guessed John to be in his late thirties. Yelling over his shoulder, John asked Michael where he was from. After Michael told him Flores, John said he was from Pico, another island in the Azores. Michael peered closely at the man, seeing a weathered face with deep lines and squinted eyes from years of protecting them from the sun. This and gray-streaked hair sticking out from under his cap gave him a scowling look. He told Michael his father's cousin who died several years back had been from Flores. John turned his full attention back to his lines and began rapidly pulling—bringing in the catch. His thick arms were straining. Without hesitation, Michael stepped up and helped him. With Michael's help, the task went quickly. Together they swung the net full of fish over the side and lowered it to the deck.

Mariano, watched Michael help his crew member then returned to the smaller boat tied alongside. He called Michael's name, waving for him to join him. Once Michael was on board they untied the boat and headed back to Santa Cruz. By the time they were at the dock, Michael had been offered the job. He would start the next morning.

He hurried home, eager to share the incredibly good news with Maria Luísa. An almost forgotten feeling washed over him as he walked home. Then he recognized what it was—the feeling of a free man. He stroked his mustache, smiled, and tilting his head back to soak in the warmth of the sun, nodded skyward.

Michael liked working for Mariano Silva. They were a good team. The crews exhibited the traits of Azoreans so familiar to Michael— hard working, honest, fair, generous, and, down to a man, stubborn. While he would always be thankful for Uncle Ronaldo's generosity in providing him work in his bakery, he thanked God daily for bringing him back to the sea.

In their first weeks in Santa Cruz, each night before he and Maria Luísa went to bed, they lit candles, took out the beautiful hand-carved marriage box in which they were keeping their money, and gratefully added Michael's pay.

The new Michael, not unlike the old Miguel, was extremely frugal and, while he gave Maria Luísa enough to buy the food and occasional pieces of clothing they needed, he believed in saving money. After a couple of months, Michael announced he was going to follow Harold Owens' advice and take all the money they had saved and put it in a bank. He told Maria Luísa that from now on she could continue to use the marriage box for the grocery and household allowance money.

Though it had been over three years since they had left Flores, Michael continued to miss the hilly countryside of his Island. The picture of the Florean hills crept into his mind each day as he walked down the Santa Cruz hillside following the bend of the Bay until he came to the dock where the Silva Fishing Company fleet moored. He always arrived on time, eagerly climbing onto his assigned boat. He especially enjoyed the days or nights he worked alongside Mariano. Although Michael formed friendships with all of the crew, he soon considered Mariano his best friend in Santa Cruz.

Her morning sickness having completely disappeared, Maria Luísa liked to take walks each day while Michael was at work. Finding the small room they were renting confining, she was eager to be outside as much as possible. She loved exploring their new town. Drawing from her experience in the bakery and in her work for the Moffit family, she felt confident in her ability to meet and talk with people. She took advantage of meeting non-Portuguese residents of Santa Cruz as an opportunity to continue to learn more English words and phrases.

One Saturday morning as she was on her daily stroll, Maria Luísa noticed a *FOR SALE* sign posted on a run-down fence in front of a run-down house. She stopped to look. The house, fairly large with an upper story, appeared to have been built in the same Victorian style as many others she'd seen as she walked about Santa Cruz. She gazed up at the windows on the front of the house and imagined what a magnificent view there must be looking out over the hillside and Monterey Bay. High weeds and grass impeded her view of much of the house. Looking about, Maria Luísa didn't see anyone. Undaunted, she opened the gate and entered. Pushing back some of the grasses allowed her to follow the path leading her closer to the house. The once-white paint was peeling in many places and it was obvious the place needed a lot of work. With her large tummy on her tiny frame leading the way, she climbed the few stairs to the porch that surrounded the right side of the house. A thick coating of grime blocked her view when she tried peering through the windows. Noting several large windows, upstairs and down, she decided the place would be light inside if the windows were cleaned. She thought of the little room she and Michael shared at Senhora Villego's house. With her pregnancy so far along and her tummy so big, the small room felt more crowded with every passing day.

Maria Luísa continued to follow the porch around the side of the house leading to the back where she could see a shed at the end of a dirt path. She looked out towards the back through the weeds and grass, and was delighted to discover extremely large grounds which appeared to go on forever behind the house. About forty feet away from the house stood a large grapefruit tree laden with low hanging fruit. Many grapefruit had fallen and lay rotting in the overgrown grasses. A sustained loud humming told her the bees had discovered them as well.

Farther back on the property, Maria Luísa spotted another tree with heavy green fruit on it. She didn't know what kind it was so, descending the steps she saw nearby, she trudged back toward the tree. Once there, she set one of the not-quite-round green fruits aside to show Senhora Villego what it was. Maria

Luísa stood for a while gazing happily around the property. She soon realized that she was no longer seeing a patch of land covered with brush and weeds, but rather what she imagined could be there. She was picturing a huge garden of fruits and vegetables as well as bougainvillea and *hortênsia* hedges plus a multitude of flowers. "Oh my," she sighed. The sigh was accompanied by a firm kick in her mid-section which she took as an enthusiastic comment from the baby.

Returning to their apartment, Maria Luísa showed Senhora Villego the green fruit. Her landlady told her it was an avocado. She cut it open and gave Maria Luísa a taste. Maria Luísa wasn't sure she liked the soft bland flavor until Senhora Villego squeezed some lemon juice on it and added some salt. Senhora Villego said she would add the avocado to the salad she was fixing for lunch.

Maria Luísa could hardly wait for Miguel to get home. When she was excited, she still thought of him as Miguel. Michael arrived home that evening, but it was obvious to his wife that his day had been particularly hard and he was extremely tired. She decided to be patient and wait for a better time to approach him about the house. It wasn't until the following Sunday morning after church on their walk home that she talked him into taking a small detour. It led them to the house.

Michael first looked at the house and then curiously at Maria Luísa to see what she was so excited about. As he looked up at the house with its peeling paint, dirty windows, and overgrown weeds, all he could see was a lot of work. He was not impressed.

Again he looked down at his very pregnant wife whose smile never failed to take his breath away and humored her by letting her lead him around to the back of the house. He was expecting a small yard and was surprised seeing the large expanse before him. In a heartbeat, his attitude shifted from trying pleasantly to support his wife's enthusiasm, to one of genuine enthusiasm of his own. He no longer saw the house as a lot of work—instead he saw enormous potential and possibilities.

Michael strode through the grasses poking here and there with a stick. Occasionally he bent down, spreading away the weeds and grass to feel the earth. Standing under the large tree, he reached up and plucked a ripe grapefruit and tossed it playfully to Maria Luísa. Michael picked up another and tried to put it into his jacket pocket—failing to fit it in, he had to carry it instead. He looked back at the house and again shook his head as he viewed the peeling paint and sagging boards. *But the land—this land could become Salvador land.* He was grinning as he looked down and saw the hopeful and expectant look in the big brown eyes of his fully blossoming wife—in it he caught a glimpse of his future.

Leaving the property to head back to their room Michael said he would ask Senhora Villego if she would return to the house with them and read all the writing on the sign. As did all Floreans, he had learned to read in school on Flores, and

Maria Luísa could read things written in Portuguese even better than he. But, because the house sign was in English, he wanted to be sure they knew *exactly* what it said.

Senhora Villego happily accompanied them back to the house. She confirmed that the sign said the property was for sale. Of more interest to Michael, was that it said the house sat on more than an acre of land. *Anyone interested should contact Joseph Browning on Walnut Street in downtown Santa Cruz.* Senhora Villego explained that, Joseph Browning would be the real estate agent who was hired by the owner to take care of the business of selling the house. "Sometimes owners sell houses themselves, but if, for some reason, they can't or don't wish to do so, they hire someone to do it for them."

"This is what our friend, Harold Owens, does in Pasadena—real estate." Michael told her, glancing at Maria Luísa, who nodded.

Fishing was good and the hours long, causing another week to go by before Michael went looking for Mr. Browning's office. Following Senhora Villego's directions, Michael located the office in downtown Santa Cruz, where he found Joseph Browning—a short, round man with a tiny white mustache twirling upwards on each end.

Browning was a hearty fellow who clapped Michael on the back whenever he made a point about the house. He told Michael that the owner had been an old man who died a couple of years earlier leaving it to his only family member, an elderly sister who lived in Pennsylvania. She had little interest in either the house or California. She wanted to be rid of it. "As you saw, it's been sitting empty for some time. In fact, I thought I'd sold it about a year ago, but the sale fell through. The man who was interested bought something in Monterey instead." Joseph Browning shook his head and looked down at the floor like it was a sad thing. Michael didn't think so. Browning went on, "Are you looking to buy or to rent?"

Michael had told Mariano and all his fishing crewmates about the house. They all had been in Santa Cruz longer than he, and had told him many stories about their Portuguese and Azorean friends who had bought land first by renting it and later buying it. "Most of the people who are selling trust the Portuguese," they had said with pride. "They know we stand by our word." They had gone on to say, "That way you can get it at a price you can afford, and pay it off as you get the money."

With those conversations lingering in his mind as well as the lengthy lectures Harold Owens had given him, Michael spoke confidently to Joseph Browning saying, "I would like to rent the house and the property it sits on. I do this only if I can have the option to buy when I am ready." He said this in a deep strong voice intended to assure Joseph Browning that he *would* buy it—hoping that ongoing good fortune would make this true.

Joseph Browning gave him all the information about the price and the terms. Michael didn't even consider trying to negotiate the price—it seemed fair—and he could afford the rental price. He told Mr. Browning he was intending to fix up the house and work the land. He asked for assurance that if he did so, the house and property wouldn't be sold to anyone else. He left the office with Joseph Browning's promise to get the necessary paperwork in order.

Back at the house where Maria Luísa and Senhora Villego were waiting, Michael gave them the good news. He said he wanted to send a letter to Harold Owens. He asked Senhora Villego if she would help him. She agreed. Michael was eager to tell Harold that he had followed his advice and was taking his first step in his plan to invest in land whenever he could afford to do so. He felt sure Harold would be pleased.

1896

Michael and his very pregnant wife, Maria Luísa, moved into their *new* house early in January of 1896. Beatrice Villego once again assisted them by locating some used furniture that was in good condition. The furniture consisted of a bed, a mattress, a dresser, a small table, two chairs, a wood stove, and an ice box. Michael's friends, Mariano and John, from the boat helped them move in.

Each day before leaving the house, Michael looked tenderly at the swollen belly of his wife. He thought Maria Luísa had never looked more beautiful. As he worked on the boat, he envisioned his soon-to-be son standing alongside him— Michael proudly teaching him how to fish just as his own papa had taught him.

On the fifth of February, Maria Luísa went into labor and, with the help of a Portuguese midwife, delivered their first baby in their *new* home. Michael waited anxiously outside of the bedroom. On hearing the baby cry and deciding he had waited long enough, Michael burst into the room. "My son, António!" he said grinning ear to ear as he looked from his wife to the infant held by the midwife.

"Meet your daughter," Maria Luísa said weakly but bravely.

Michael was shocked. *The baby is not a boy! How could that be?* He expected to meet his son! He never considered for a single moment that the baby would be a girl. He didn't know what to say. He stood dumbly in the doorway before finally shuffling to his wife's bedside. The midwife placed the wrapped infant in Maria Louisa's arms and left the room. Michael kissed Maria Luísa on the forehead, and somewhat absently patted the blanket wrapped around the little bundle that snuggled against Maria Luísa's breast. Mumbling, Michael told Maria Luísa he was glad she was all right and that he would be outside.

Michael went outside and stood on the porch, deeply breathing in the cool air. When he returned to their room, Maria Luísa took her husband's hand and said tenderly, "We could call her Antónia."

Michael shook his head thinking to do so would be too much of a daily reminder to Michael of God's turning his back on him. He had requested a son—prayed for and expected a son—António. The name he had chosen for his son was Manuel António Salvador. Several months before the baby was born, one day at the market Michael had overheard the name *Mamie*. When his wife commented on the unusual name, he had said he liked it. Wisely, Maria Luísa gave Michael some time before she suggested they call their beautiful new daughter Mamie Antónia Salvador. Michael huffed and sputtered but finally agreed, declaring the baby would be called Mamie. Mamie she was.

Though valiantly trying to resist, Michael was gradually charmed by his dark-haired first-born child. He left her care almost entirely to Maria Luísa. When Maria Luísa handed the infant to him, he stood or sat stiffly waiting for Maria Luísa to return, eager to hand Mamie back to her mother. During the months that followed, whenever he was in church, Michael continued to question God as to why he had been sent Mamie instead of António.

Once Mamie began toddling about, her father could not help but pay more attention to her. Outside, she would often bring him a flower. She surprised him by taking hold of his hand to show him whatever new wonder she discovered. She was an interesting child with long, black, silky hair and very large soulful eyes. By the time she was four, he called her and treated her as his little princess.

As the years passed, Michael's determination to have a son never wavered even though the family expanded in size with Mamie acquiring five younger sisters. With Michael gone many days and nights each month, it fell to Maria Luísa to provide the daily oversight, guidance, and discipline required to raise a house full of six small, active girls.

She was also left to tend the expanding garden they had planted on the large parcel of land they now called home. As time passed and they could afford to do so, Michael hired first one man, and later, a second to help Maria Luísa with the heavy work of preparing the garden for spring planting.

Most every Sunday afternoon the Salvador family went on an outing to the beach. As a child, Mamie admired sand castles and enjoyed making up stories and telling the family about the princes and princesses who lived there. At home, when she created her stories, she was always *The Princess*.

Mamie and her siblings attended Holy Cross School in the heart of Santa Cruz, a school founded some thirty years earlier by the Daughters of Charity. The sisters who ran the school found Mamie to be an average student—smart enough but not interested in putting much effort into learning. Always the daydreamer, her mind wandered. Her parents gave a sigh of relief when, at the age of eighteen, she graduated.

It was an unusually cool, sunny June day when the family celebrated Mamie's high school graduation on the boardwalk. They settled in at their favorite soda fountain, *Lulu's*, to celebrate the special day with ice cream—the new graduate opting for her favorite treat, a black cow.

Though not the usual bright sunny day Santa Cruz was known for, people were not deterred from enjoying the many and varied pleasures the boardwalk offered. As usual, The

Giant Dipper roller coaster was the major attraction. The girls laughed as they heard the screams of the riders.

Not long after finishing their ice cream treats, one of Mamie's younger sisters, Alice, began complaining to her mother about not feeling well. Maria Luísa suggested the family go home. The older girls, Mamie, Flora, now sixteen, and Palmeda, twelve, turned to Papa begging him to let them stay. Papa, who was looking a bit pale and drawn himself, gave in. "Mamie," he said looking at his eldest daughter, "I'm holding you responsible." A small twinkle shone in his eye as he looked from one daughter to the next.

In unison they chorused *"Sim Papa."* Having told their papa yes, the three stood hand-in-hand watching in delight as their parents and younger sisters departed.

As soon as their parents were out of sight, they ran over to the fence to watch the roller coaster whiz by. Each held her breath as the cars climbed slowly upwards, groaning all the way to the highest point, and *then* laughed loudly when the high pitched screams filled the air as the car plunged to the bottom before starting up its next ascent.

Mamie spied a good-looking couple in the back seat of the last car. The young woman with short blonde hair and a big smile was very pretty and looked like the actress Mary Pickford. While she noticed the woman first, it was the man who held her attention. Although he was sitting down, she decided he was of medium height. He had dark, wavy hair, full eyebrows, and was laughing, displaying beautiful white teeth.

As he placed his right arm around his companion's shoulder, he gave her a roguish look. His hypnotizing smile set Mamie to romanticize about how it would be if she were with him instead of his blonde companion. The three sisters watched the roller coaster a while longer and then, tiring of that, Flora insisted they walk about.

Palmeda soon spotted a school friend walking nearby with her and begged Mamie to let her join them. Mamie agreed, telling her they would meet her in an hour at the end of the boardwalk in front of the fortune telling kiosk. Mamie and Flora, the two oldest sisters, while not sharing a lot of common interests, had fun walking about the boardwalk together.

The two girls sat on a long bench to one side of the board-walk watching the people pass by. Mamie spotted the Mary Pickford blonde and the handsome fellow she had seen on the roller coaster. She noticed the man had his arm around his companion's waist—the blonde's head thrown back in laughter. As they passed the bench where Mamie and Flora were sitting, the man looked their way, caught Mamie's eye, and winked. Then they were gone.

"Did you see him?" Mamie asked, poking Flora with her elbow.

"Who?" Flora asked

Mamie looked at her and said, "Oh, no one important."

Mamie saw the man once more that day. The sun, moving lower in the western sky, shone down on her and Flora. They decided to take off their shoes and walk along the beach.

Soon they passed the mysterious couple going the opposite direction. The man's left arm was still around the blonde and his and her shoes dangled from his right hand. His pant legs were rolled up enough to keep them from dragging in the sand. This time he didn't look their way. Mamie felt a pang of disappointment.

Two years later, Mamie, Flora, and Palmeda walked down the street on their way home after running some errands in town for their mother. Spotting her favorite bakery, Palmeda ran ahead and pressed her face to the glass to peer inside. Mamie and Flora continued walking down the sidewalk, laughing as they skipped along. Mamie spotted the man from the Giant Dipper helping a blonde into a black Ford. Mamie felt sure the blonde was not the same one she had seen him with before. The automobile was parked in front of *The Sunshine Bakery*. Mamie wondered if the car was his. She was impressed.

Seeing the man and the blonde ahead, Mamie dropped behind Flora, pretending she was waiting for Palmeda. Standing close to the back end of the man's car and trying not to be obvious, she watched him as he closed the door after the blonde had pulled herself inside. Mamie expected him to go around the front of the car. Instead he walked directly towards where she stood stopping just short of running into her.

His brown eyes twinkled. Feeling hypnotized she could not take her eyes off of him—he was so good-looking and smelled so good. Trying to remain calm, she moved to her right. He stepped to his left. She moved left. He stepped right. He laughed. "Well, Sweet Girl, I see you like to dance." His head tipped a bit to one side, "Perhaps we ought to try it some time." He glanced back over his shoulder to the car door where the blonde waited inside. "Sadly it will have to be another day." With that, he reached out with both hands, took hold of Mamie's arms and gently moved her away from the curb so he could go around. He winked, strode around the back of the car, popped the door open, got in, and revved the engine.

The man drove away with the Ford's familiar chugga-chugga sound bringing Mamie to her senses. She scooted over to the bakery window where Palmeda was watching Mamie's encounter with the good-looking stranger.

"Who was that?" Palmeda asked.

"I'm not sure," Mamie answered. She took Palmeda's hand pulling her towards Flora who was waiting for them farther on down the street.

It was another three years before Mamie saw the handsome stranger again. Visiting the boardwalk as often as she could during those years, Mamie had watched the Giant Dipper go up and down so many times she thought she'd throw up. She walked back and forth on the beach and played beach games with her younger sisters. She peered into so many shops, her sisters thought she was crazy, though her parents didn't seem to notice. If she hadn't convinced herself that the handsome stranger was her Prince, she would have given up.

One day Michael, who of late had been having more fits of coughing, asked Mamie to go to town and buy some medicine from a Chinese man that Marco, one of his friends on the boat, had recommended. Marco was sure this man, Wu, would have a special type of Chinese medicine that would help Michael's cough. Michael told Mamie to go and ask for the owner named Wu.

It took Mamie a while to find the right street which was in a part of town she had never visited before. Spotting a street sign matching the name on the sheet of paper in her hand, Mamie checked each side of the street finding it filled with bars, bookstores, and shops—none looking like the businesses she and her family usually frequented. She wondered if coming here had been a good idea. Thoughts of her father's coughing, kept her going. he was relieved to finally discover a red door with a small sign reading *"Wu Chinese Medicine"* written in English below some Chinese lettering.

Pulling the door open, Mamie was hit by a strong musty smell—conjuring up wood smoke, licorice, orange, cinnamon, peppers, and fish. Squaring her shoulders, she started up the long flight of dimly lit stairs being careful not to brush against the heavily soiled walls. At the top, she entered a shop like none she had ever seen. Shelves, overflowing with all shapes and sizes of bottles and boxes containing mysterious powders and liquids, lined the walls. The little writing she saw was in

Chinese, giving Mamie no idea what anything was, or when or how the items might be used. The smell of Mr. Wu's place, while similar to the smell in the stairway was, thankfully, a little better. She approached the counter where an ancient-looking Chinese man stood. His very long, drooping mustache fell straight down alongside the sides of his mouth and disappeared into a beard so wide it covered his blue, shiny shirt top. He remained standing behind the counter staring at her. "Mr. Wu?" She said, her voice sounding weak.

The man barely nodded.

"My father, Michael Salvador, works for the Silva Fishing Company. He's had an extremely bad cough for over a year and he's feeling more weak and tired all the time. One of his fishing crew-mates, Marco Sallo, suggested he come to you. He said you helped him when he was sick, and maybe you could give my father something to help stop his cough and get his energy back."

Mr. Wu neither moved nor said anything as he continued to stare at her. Mamie wondered if he didn't understand. She broke the silence by asking in a slightly louder voice, "Do you have anything that will help him?"

One side of Mr. Wu's mustache went up slightly. Reaching forward across the counter, he patted her hand. He held up one long, bony finger indicating she should wait. Disappearing into another room at the back, he was gone so long Mamie wondered if she had misunderstood his gesture and that he might not be coming back. Just as she was debating whether she should leave, he returned. He carried two bottles—one holding a black powder and the other a red.

Mr. Wu set them on the counter. Again holding up the same long, bony finger, he disappeared for the second time into the back room, returning almost immediately. He held a Chinese cup, a spoon, and two small bags of powder—again one black, the other red. Setting the items on the counter, he filled the cup with hot water from a kettle hanging from a hook over a small wood fireplace behind him. Taking the spoon, he put one scoop of the black powder into the cup of hot water and stirred. He looked at Mamie.

"One cup black when father wakes up morning. One cup middle day. One cup when father go bed. For cough." It was somewhat difficult to understand his words, but his animated directions made it clear. He grasped his throat and faked coughing to make the point.

"Oh, I understand," she said.

He dumped out the black tea mixture and proceeded to scoop a spoon of the red powder again adding hot water.

"One cup red first meal day. One cup meal middle day. One cup last meal day." He repeated the words twice so she would understand. "Give Father new energy. When eat red, new energy."

Mamie paid him, said her thanks, and headed down the stairs, eager to get back out into the sunlight.

Reaching the foot of the stairs, she hastily pushed the door open, hopping out onto the sidewalk eager to breathe fresh air.

Her foot barely touched the sidewalk when she abruptly collided with someone and started to lose her balance. She fell to one knee but arms circled around and pulled her upright. She heard a deep voice say, "Sorry."

Suddenly there *he* was. "It's you," he said with an easy smile. "I hoped I would run into you sometime, but I didn't intend to bowl you over."

Mamie was speechless. His smile disappeared, and he said, "Are you all right?" He held onto her arms but stepped back to look her up and down. His eyes stopped on her leg. "Oh-oh, you're bleeding."

Hearing his words, Mamie looked down, surprised to see a small trickle of blood running down her leg below her skirt. She pulled the hem of her blue skirt up enough so she could see her knee. It was scraped and a few drops of blood fell from where a bit of gravel stuck onto her torn stocking. She felt embarrassed. She looked up to find the warm, easy smile back in place. "Come with me. We'll get you fixed up."

Without waiting for her response and with a firm grip on her elbow, he steered her up the street—the opposite direction from where he had been coming. It surprised her when he opened the door to *Big Billy's Bar and Grill*, stepped in, and pulled her inside.

In the dimly lit room, Mamie could see a few customers scattered about the place at tables and at the bar. This was the first bar she had been in. She knew her father would be extremely upset if he could see her here—*Big Billy's Bar and*

Grill—certainly not a place for a young, respectable Portuguese woman. She was relieved to see a few other women sitting at some of the tables but noticed that there wasn't any food—only beer and other drinks—on any of them. The customers, who had glanced up when the door had first opened, had already returned their attention to their drinks. Mamie was standing close to the bar. Her companion put his arm around her small waist and easily lifted her onto the nearest bar stool. "Hey there, Billy," he called to the older man standing behind the bar. "Can we get a clean rag, a glass of water, and a bandage?"

Mamie watched the man behind the bar who she assumed must be Billy, grunt and then bend down below the bar putting him momentarily out of sight. Rising back up, he came towards them setting the three requested items plus scissors and tape in front of Mamie and her companion. "What you got going on here, Wally?"

Her companion laughed. "It's like this, Billy. I ran into this Sweet Girl down by Wu's place. She scraped her knee." Without asking, he pulled Mamie's blue skirt up a couple inches giving Billy a look. Mamie blushed, slapped Wally's hand away, and hastily pushed her skirt down. Billy and Wally grinned broadly at one another. Billy and the man who now had a name, Wally, chuckled. Grinning, Billy moved away to tend to a customer. Mamie looked at Wally who was holding one of the requested items. She said, "What am I supposed to do, dip this rag in the glass of water, clean off my leg, and put on the bandage?"

He smiled and with his deep brown eyes twinkling said, "Well, that would work. *I* was thinking you might like to have a drink of water. Then you could go to the ladies room and clean yourself up in more privacy." He tilted his head, raised his eyebrows in question. "Your choice."

Mamie stared into dark brown hypnotic eyes, reached out and drank several gulps of water, picked up the rag, the gauze bandage, the tape, and the scissors, and headed in the direction of the room marked "Ladies."

Returning, she didn't see him and felt disappointment and surprise, fearing he had left.

"Over here."

She looked towards the side of the room and saw him sitting alone at a table by the wall—two beers in front of him. She hesitated a moment as an image of her father floated through her mind. She could feel his displeasure clear across town. Then she saw the stranger she had been hoping to find for so long beckoning to her and couldn't resist. She crossed the room and slipped into a chair facing him across the table. He gently slid one of the two beers towards her.

"Better?" he inquired.

She was glad to be sitting, her legs felt wobbly, and she heard the tremor in her own voice as she said, "Oh yes, I'm fine. Really, thank you."

She looked directly at him, stretched her arm across the table offering him her hand determined to keep it from shaking, "We haven't actually met. I'm Mamie Salvador."

He took her cold, outstretched hand in his warm one and held it. "Mamie," he said slowly like he was thinking about how the name sounded. "I'm Wally Kohler. Henry Walter Kohler—my friends all call me Wally." He paused. "You know, you don't look Spanish. Seeing her puzzled look he continued, "Isn't the name Salvador Spanish?"

"My family is Azorean..." she said with noticeable pride in her voice. "Portuguese." My father and mother came to the United States from Flores—an island in the Azores in the Atlantic Ocean. I was born soon after they arrived here in Santa Cruz." She realized he was still holding onto her hand. She wanted him to continue holding it but knowing that was not proper, slid it slowly out of his grasp. She took hold of the beer so he would know it was not that she wanted her hand back from him, but rather it had something it had to do.

"Look," she said, "I'm sorry. I mean I'm sorry I ran into you on the sidewalk back there." She felt flustered. "I mean I didn't mean to run into you when I stepped out of the doorway back there. I should have looked before I pushed the door open and jumped out."

He didn't say anything at first and then with a charming smile said, "I think some things are meant to be."

His statement confirmed for Mamie that Wally really was her very own prince. She had been looking for him since she first saw him, and, finally, here he was With only a flicker of guilt, she didn't object later when he signaled Billy to bring them each another beer.

Wally said, "I live in San Francisco." She was surprised and rather taken aback to hear him say he ran a nightclub. *I wonder what Papa would think about that?* Ignoring that thought because she knew the answer, she leaned forward to concentrate on listening as Wally continued talking. He told her he liked coming down to Santa Cruz whenever he could get away.

"The bar and nightclub business is tough," he said, "very competitive. One of these days I'm going to own my own business. "But now there are some things I have to do first to get ready." Mamie with her soulful brown eyes, drank in every word he uttered.

Later Mamie began to feel tipsy and told Wally she better get something to eat. "Don't worry Sweet Girl. I'll take care of it." He slid out of his chair and walked briskly over to the bar in front of where Billy was standing. A short time later, Billy delivered two ham sandwiches to their table. Mamie ate hers not caring that it wasn't very good. After downing it, Mamie felt her focus return.

She listened, laughed a lot, and was mesmerized as Wally shared one entertaining story after another. It was four o'clock by the time Mamie realized she had not yet taken Papa his medicine. She held up the sack Mr. Wu had given her, showing it to Wally. "I have to go." She said. He held her hand, helping her out of her chair. He offered her a ride home. Mamie, tempted as it would be faster, didn't want to take him to her house knowing her parents wouldn't approve. She already knew she would have to be careful to avoid their smelling the beer on her breath. Finally she allowed Wally to give her ride to the top of the hill, telling him when to stop and let her out. She told him she would walk the few remaining blocks home.

Before letting her out of the car, Wally said he had to return to San Francisco the next day. He was not sure how soon he would be back, but promised to get in touch with her the next time he came to Santa Cruz. He leaned over and gave her a deep, long kiss so dizzying she wondered if she would be able to walk once she stepped out of the car. Steadying herself, she looked around to be sure no neighbor had witnessed the event, and then walked quickly home.

A month passed with Mamie worrying Wally had forgotten about her. After another three months went by without a word, Mamie was sure Wally had forgotten about her. Two more months passed—still nothing.

Late one Saturday morning, Mamie was alone in the kitchen when she heard a knock on the front door. Her mother was upstairs with her father who still wasn't feeling very well. Her sister Palmeda was at the church, and the younger girls were all working in the back garden.

Opening the door, she found herself face to face with Wally. "Hello, Sweet Girl," he said in the same sexy voice she had thought about each night for the last six months.

Mamie stepped out onto the porch and pulled the door closed behind her. She held a finger up to her lips, signaling him to speak quietly.

"My Father is sick and resting," she whispered. Taking hold of his arm, she tugged him to the side walk and down the street toward his parked car.

As they hurried down the street, Mamie tried to keep a scowl on her face. She wanted him to know she was not happy it had been so long since they had been together but could not maintain the scowl—Wally looked and smelled too good. Her prince had returned.

Standing beside the car, Wally suggested they go get a drink or go to the casino. Mamie told him she had promised her mother she would do some chores for the rest of the morning and afternoon.She suggested instead that she meet him on the boardwalk by the fortune teller's booth at five o'clock. Agreeing, Wally gave her a quick kiss on the cheek and slid back into his car.

Mamie hurried back home and went inside. It was not long before Maria Luísa came downstairs. "I thought I heard someone at the door," she said in a questioning tone.

"That was Leonor. She had to go to work today and wanted to know if I can meet her later at the boardwalk. I told her I couldn't get there until five. I hope that's okay." She leaned against the wall watching her mother pick up some carrots to cut up, hoping she wouldn't notice the lie.

"That's fine, go on. I'm going to stay with your father. He still isn't eating and I'm worried about him," she said sounding distracted. Normally she would have told Mamie to go tell her father her plans, but today because Michael was sleeping, she didn't.

Every day Maria Luísa had been carefully following Mr. Wu's exact instructions for the red and black powders Mamie had brought home. At first, the remedy had helped some, but, lately, Maria Luísa knew it was not. She had continued the routine only because it meant she was doing *something* to help her beloved husband.

Mamie gave her mother a quick hug and said, "You go back with Papa. I'll go help the girls with the garden." She escaped out the back door, grateful Maria Luísa didn't notice her eldest daughter's unusual eagerness in volunteering.

Four thirty in the afternoon finally came, and Mamie quietly left the house. Barely out the gate, she was startled when Palmeda came running out the door to catch up with her. "Where are you going?" Mamie sharply asked her eighteen-year-old sister.

"Back to the church—Rita and I are rehearsing our music for tomorrow." Palmeda, totally devoted to the church, spent as much time there as possible. Relieved her sister wouldn't be going all the way downtown, Mamie relaxed a little and, arm in arm, they started walking down the hill.

As they walked, Palmeda asked Mamie where she was going. She hesitated for a few seconds and then could not contain her excitement. She told her younger sister all about meeting Wally on the day she had gone to pick up Papa's Chinese medicine. She was speaking so rapidly and with such excitement it took her a minute to notice the shocked look on Palmeda's young face. Palmeda had stopped walking. Mamie turned to see why. Seeing the look on Palmeda's face, she grabbed her sister's arm. "Oh, Meda. He is terrific. I've never met anyone like him before. You must trust me and promise not to tell Mama or Papa. I'll bring Wally home to meet them sometime soon, just not today." For a second, Mamie was sorry she had told Palmeda anything about Wally—especially the part about his working at the bar.

As Palmeda stared at her older sister in disbelief, Mamie was envisioning a halo over her younger sister's head. A twinge of guilt ran through her as Palmeda began to speak, sounding, Mamie thought, more like her mother than her younger sister. "Mamie, you really don't know this man. You only spent one afternoon with him—and in a bar! He isn't even from Santa Cruz. You don't even know if he is telling you the truth. Mamie, use your head! Don't let him sweep you away even if he's good looking, suave, debonair, and you think he is your *Prince!*" she added with a snort.

Palmeda had moved back closer to her sister. She struck a pose pretending to be a suave, sophisticated fellow, straightening his tie, running his hand back over his head and winking while twirling an imaginary mustache. Because any show of humor was rare for Palmeda, this impromptu act made Mamie laugh. Mamie playfully shoved Meda's arm, saying, "He doesn't have a mustache!" As they continued their walk, Mamie fervently prayed her younger sister would keep this sister-to-sister confidence as strongly as she kept her commitments to the church.

When they reached the walkway leading to the entrance to the Church, Palmeda gave her oldest sister a long hug before heading up the walkway towards the entry of the church. About halfway up the walk, she turned to look back at Mamie. Mamie saw her mouth the words, "Be careful!" Mamie nodded and waved. She paused long enough to see Palmeda disappear through the church doors, and, then, with excitement again coursing through her, hurried on her way.

As promised, Wally was waiting on the bench across from the fortune teller booth. He stood up, spread his arms open to embrace her, and pulled her into him. He gave her a big hug then backed up to look at her. "Sweet Girl, I have missed you!" Mamie, feeling her cheeks turn pink, looked about nervously.

Leaving the Boardwalk, Wally—his right arm secured firmly about her waist—guided their way. They were soon several blocks away from the main street. Mamie took a deep breath, and silently asked God and her father's forgiveness as they entered a bar, *Sylvia's*. Mamie noticed it was attached to a small hotel, *The Azure*.

Mamie was happy to see that *Sylvia's* was not just a bar, but rather an attractive dining room with high backed, dark leather booths which circled the outer walls lending privacy to their occupants. The lighting was subdued but not dark. Small candles on each table sent a warm glow throughout the room. In one corner of the remaining wall sat a shiny black piano with a tuxedo-clad man playing soft jazz—the music floating gently across the room. An ornately carved bar filled the rest of that wall. A large dark mirror behind the bar reflected multiple shelves holding various sizes and shapes of liquor bottles. Mamie thought the atmosphere was extremely romantic.

Wally held Mamie's hand firmly in his and led her to a secluded back booth where he helped her slide into the booth and slid in beside her. They were sitting close together. Mamie was acutely and pleasantly aware of his thigh pressed against hers. A waiter approached immediately. Wally smiled up at him and said, "We'd like a bottle of champagne. We're celebrating."

"Very good, sir," the waiter responded. He gave Wally a reserved smile and graced Mamie with a broader one.

Mamie wished the waiter had asked Wally what exactly they were celebrating. She was curious to know. Somewhat shyly she said "Celebrating?"

"Yes," Wally said as he took her hand in his and pulled it up into the warmth of his chest, "We are celebrating running into each other exactly six months ago today." He chuckled and reached down to lightly squeeze her knee. It was the same knee she had scraped the day she had tumbled out of Mr. Wu's shop. "That has to be the luckiest day of my life."

Mamie gazed into his dark brown eyes as his head lowered close to hers. She felt warm and tingly.

The waiter returned, set two champagne coupes in front of them, and poured a bit of champagne into one, which he handed to Wally. Wally sipped and nodded his approval. The waiter filled their glasses, then pushed the bottle into a shiny, ice-filled silver bucket he had positioned on a stand at the end of their booth. This done, he discreetly disappeared.

For the first time in her life, Mamie felt sophisticated. She knew her life was never going to be the same—her world was meant to be here. *Well, not in a bar, but definitely with Wally.* She felt like he had been part of her life forever. She knew he was the man of her dreams—her Prince. When he gazed at her, she felt beautiful. When he laughed at what she said, she felt witty, clever, and smart. When he spoke, she felt loved and safe.

Mamie had never really had a boyfriend before. Her parents, typical of every Portuguese parent she had ever met, were extremely protective of their daughters. Many times throughout her twenty-four years she had seen her father, only partially joking, raise his eyes toward the heavens and say, "You see, God, *this* is why I wanted to have a son!"

As Wally talked—and he certainly seemed to enjoy talking—she felt as though she was on an emotional roller coaster. She listened to his stories and felt sad about his childhood. She felt proud as he described having entered the army and vast relief as she listened to how he had survived the battles. She even felt happy hearing him describe winning a contest in mixing drinks. She felt anxious for him when he told her about coming home from the army and having no place to go. She felt beautiful when he told her he had noticed her in the crowd at the boardwalk and on the beach. She felt safe when he slid his arm around her waist. She felt ecstatic when he told her he didn't want to be with anyone except her.

The champagne was followed by dinner including a martini for him and a glass of red wine for her. At nine o'clock, he suggested they go upstairs to his room. At first surprised when he said "upstairs," she vaguely recalled in the earlier part of the conversation he had said he was staying at *The Azure*.

Between the time they left the dining room and reached Wally's room, everything her Mama and Papa had told her about how nice Portuguese girls should conduct themselves went through Mamie's mind. The minute she stepped into the room every last one of them was forgotten.

Mamie had never been intimate with any boy before—at least not beyond a furtive kiss stolen behind the church when she was fifteen. As Wally embraced her she knew she was in for a very different experience. His deep kiss went on for what felt was a lifetime.

Mamie was afraid she was going to fall over because her knees felt so weak. Any caution she had briefly considered outside the hotel room door had long since passed. He scooped her up easily into his arms and moved a few steps and set her gently down on the edge of the bed. She could barely breathe.

Mamie's mind flashed back to all the romantic books she had ever read. Every single one of them paled by comparison to this very real—this very sensuous—moment. As all those novels she had read through the years instructed her, she surrendered herself to him.

The night passed and soon sunlight streamed through the cracks between the drapes. Mamie felt as though she had been hypnotized, though, she doubted Father Eduardo was going to accept that as an excuse at her next confession. She pushed the uncomfortable thought out of her mind so she could enjoy the time they had left before saying goodbye.

Wally escorted her out of the hotel to give her a ride back to her house. It was the very early hours of the morning and the sun was beginning to rise in the eastern sky. Mamie's thoughts bounced back and forth between what she knew for sure—her love for Wally—and the terror she felt about facing her parents.

Approaching her house, Mamie noticed all the lights were on. Thinking her parents had stayed up all night waiting for her brought sweat to her brow. She asked Wally not to drive up right in front of the Salvador house. Instead, she had him drive past her house before letting her out. A few tears fell down her flushed olive cheeks, and she held on to him as long as she could. He promised her she would hear from him and they would be together again soon.

Mamie waited until his car pulled away from the curb. She turned around and headed back down the hill pausing by the fence to catch her breath and straighten her clothing. She climbed up the front stairs and entered the house. She was not prepared for what met her.

Palmeda, Alice, Angie, and Annie were all in a huddle in the center of the room still in their nightclothes. Mamie heard gentle sobs. "What is it? What's happened?" she asked quickly crossing the room and stepping between Palmeda and Alice. "What?"

Angie looked up at Mamie. "Oh, Mamie. It's Papa. He's dead."

Mamie jumped backwards and cried out, "No! It can't be! Tell me that's not true!" she demanded of her sisters.

She and her four sisters turned simultaneously towards the stairs as an extremely pale Maria Luísa came into the living room. If anyone had said anything at that particular moment, surely the air moving from their mouths would have knocked their mother over. All the girls, except Mamie, rushed to Maria Luísa's side and, moving together as one, guided her to her favorite chair.

Falling back into the chair, Maria Luísa looked up to see Mamie standing, trembling in front of her. "Where were you, Mamie Antónia? Your Papa, he was sick and needed you to be here with him." She didn't wait for Mamie's answer instead dropped her head into her hands, the sobs shaking her small body. Mamie rushed forward, fell to the ground, and grabbed hold of Maria Luísa's knees. Her mother's arms stayed on her face, never encircling her oldest daughter.

"Oh, Mama, I'm so sorry. I didn't know. Oh, Mama." Her own guilt-ridden sobs filled the room. The priest had left just moments before Mamie had returned home. Mamie went into the bedroom where her papa's body was laid out on the bed. Candles flickered around the room. He looked peaceful and Mamie desperately wished his eyes would open and his mustache, white on one side, black on the other, would twitch in anger at her. She deserved it. She prayed to God to let her papa know how much she loved him. She remained on her knees sobbing as she clung to her father's still hand until Palmeda came and led her to her room.

As the eldest daughter, Mamie knew she must assist Mama in making all of the arrangements for Papa's mass and burial. Overwhelmed with guilt, she was glad to have something to do. She wished she were the one who had died. She could barely look at her mother. She busied herself by contacting all Papa's friends including Harold and Ethel Owens in Pasadena. Ethel explained they wouldn't be able to come for the services because Harold was still recovering from the mild heart attack he had suffered a month before, and his doctor insisted he not travel. Ethel sent her love to her dear friend, Maria Luísa, and told the girls to be strong.

Mamie continued to feel overcome by the guilt of not having been home when her family needed her so badly. Whenever she remembered her romantic tryst, and that was often, it made her feel ill. Had he known, Papa would surely have disowned her. *Oh God. What if somehow he did know? Maybe he died of heartache and shame!*"

Distraught, she was barely able to focus on the tasks at hand. Between completing each one on her list, she moved aimlessly between Palmeda who was ably handling things in the kitchen and Alice and Angie who alternated between taking care of Maria Luísa, cleaning the house, and receiving visits from the neighbors and other family friends. Mamie avoided being alone with her mother. She had never felt so terrible and so ashamed.

Michael's funeral was delayed until Flora, Michael and Maria Luísa's second born, and her husband, Mickey, could return to Santa Cruz from Anchorage, where they were living. The steamer from Anchorage had taken them as far as San Francisco where they borrowed a friend's car and drove to Santa Cruz.

When they arrived, Mama grabbed Flora in a hug and held on tight. Flora looked healthy and fit. While she felt terribly sad Papa was gone, she took her mother and each one of her sisters aside and reminded them how Papa had always talked about death. "It's just a not-so-great part of life," he would say. She reminded them Papa had felt strongly that funerals should be times of celebrating the person's life, not mourning.

She spoke with Mamie last. Having heard Mamie's story from Palmeda, Flora didn't let Mamie dwell on her guilt. "What you did is done. You can't take it back. You can't bring Papa back. You have to set it aside for now. Mama needs you. I need you. Palmeda, Alice, Angie, and Annie need you. You'll have to decide in your heart what to do about this Wally person later."

Flora sent Mickey off on some non-essential errand, then gathered Maria Luísa and all her sisters around the dining table. Seven pairs of eyes turned toward Papa's empty chair. She asked Palmeda to get out the best wine glasses and pour each a glass of *Basalto*, Papa's favorite wine.

Flora continued directing the scene by holding her wine glass and saying, "Each one of us will make a toast to Papa. I'll go first." Raising her glass, she said, "To Papa who taught me life is like a road; it has twists and turns and always brings something unexpected. Always remember that sometime you will turn a corner and find something so incredibly wonderful it takes your breath away." Then looking across the table, she said, "Palmeda, you go next."

Lifting her glass, Palmeda said, "Papa, you taught me that when you believe in God and stay close to him you will always have strength to endure anything."

Palmeda looked at Mamie and nodded, indicating it was her turn to speak next. Mamie raised her glass and said in a tremulous voice, "To Papa who called me his princess and told me lots of stories. He taught me that when in life God brings something wonderful your way, you must grab hold and follow your heart."

Mama, who had been avoiding looking at Mamie, now looked at her. It was difficult to read her expression. Flora raised an eyebrow.

Without waiting, Angie, now ten, held up her glass. Clearing her throat, she deepened her voice to sound like her father, and said, "To Papa who always said while it was a man's world out there, his girls could be anything and do anything they wanted—with his permission, of course." Everyone, including Mama laughed through the tears.

Alice followed saying "To Papa who often said, 'Oh my God, it's another girl!'" That brought more smiles and laughter around the table. "He said family was like *um bom guizado Portuguese:* a good Portuguese stew full of so many different ingredients, each rich and spicy, making each bite a unique experience to be savored."

Annie, the youngest, raised her glass. "To Papa. You taught me to see the beautiful colors of the flowers, to know how rich the dirt feels, and to always watch for the changing mood of the skies and the sea." All eyes at the table widened with surprise as sisters and mother alike wondered how seven-year-old Annie had become so poetic.

The girls then looked at Maria Luísa looking so frail—watching her push back her chair and stand up. "To you, *meu querido*, Joaquin Miguel Salvador. You gave me more *amor* than I could ever have imagined. You gave me more laughter, good times, and adventures than I could ever have dreamed or hoped for. Best of all you gave me not just one but six gifts, our beautiful daughters." She paused a moment and looked around the table at her daughters. "Before he passed, your father said to me, 'God was right. He chose the most beautiful children in the world for us. They just happened to be girls.'" Raising her glass she continued, "*Tu es o meu unico e verdadeiro amor.* You are my one true love. Wait for me. I'll be with you soon."

All six girls were smiling with tears flowing down their cheeks as their mother toasted her one true love though each looked alarmed as their mama uttered her last sentence. The older girls looked at her wondering how soon that would be while Angie and Annie just looked incredibly sad.

They continued toasting Papa remembering things he had said, things he had done, things he had caught them doing. They laughed when Mama told the story of António turning out to be Antónia. They talked about all the times they had come in unexpectedly throughout the years to find Papa embracing Mama in his big arms and giving her passionate kisses. Mama blushed and looked downward, but the smile beneath the tears told them she was remembering too.

Mickey returned to the house, surprised to see how much laughter there was amongst all the tears. He didn't know which sister to credit for making that happen, and then decided, correctly, that a good bit of the credit went to the wine.

The next day, Maria Luísa arrived at the church for mass dressed in a long, black dress covered by a black cape complete with black hood. She looked as though she were still in the Azores. Her six daughters followed her, walking two by two, dressed in black though without hoods. Mickey followed a few feet behind leaving Flora to hold on to seven-year-old Annie's hand. Each daughter carried the Bible given to her by her father, each one with his familiar handwritten signature inside.

Annie, seven, had shown creative talent at a very young age. Aware her family didn't have much money and yet wanting to be sure her Papa's funeral was beautiful, Annie had gone door to door to the neighbors and collected a huge assortment of flowers. She added them to the many they had growing in their front and backyard gardens and arranged them throughout the church. Then as a surprise to her mother and as a loving tribute to her father, she designed a *pasadeira de flores*, the floral carpet-path going up the walkway into the church. Her father had told all the girls so many times about the Festival of the Holy Ghost and the floral designs he had helped make on the street for the occasion. She used as many *hortênsias*, which Americans called hydrangeas, as she could find. She knew in her heart Papa would have loved it. Her family and all Michael's friends attending his funeral were captivated by the beauty of the floral tapestry.

Following mass, Mickey and Michael's friend, Mariano, drove them to the cemetery where the casket sat on ropes next to the freshly dug opening in the earth designated as the final resting spot for Joaquin Miguel Michael Salvador. After the priest had spoken, each of the girls stepped forward, one by one, to place a flower on the casket. Each had selected a different flower—one they knew Papa loved. The colors appeared bright and cheery against the background of the simple, dark wooden casket. Then each stepped back to stand before the chairs which had been set up for the occasion.

With three girls on each side, and Flora and Palmeda each holding an arm to steady her, Maria Luísa moved forward. She leaned over and kissed the casket. Surprising everyone, she proceeded to open the large black purse she carried over her arm. From it she withdrew a circle of white and yellow flowers. She tenderly laid it on top and in the center of the casket. Tears flowed freely from all the girls as they recognized the *"coroa"* of flowers, identical to the one in the picture of Mama from her wedding day to Papa. Her daughters were very familiar with the picture Papa always carried with him. Without fail, he had proudly shown it to each of them every year on his and Mama's anniversary. They each could recite by heart the story of his following the floral crown to meet Mama for the first time.

Flora and Mickey stayed in Santa Cruz a week following the funeral and then had to return to their home and work in Anchorage. Maria Luísa was especially sad to see them go, but accepted the fact that they had to leave sometime. After their departure, she turned her attention back to her cooking, her baking, and concentrated on the daily routine of caring for her three youngest daughters—Alice, Angie, and Annie. While the death of her beloved Michael had clearly devastated Maria Luísa, she had no choice but to try to pick up the pieces. With Michael, the primary wage earner, no longer there, she worried about money. She knew they would have to put more effort into their garden and try to sell more produce. Perhaps, she thought, she and Palmeda could also do sewing for families who might need it.

It wasn't until after Michael's funeral when Mamie finally told her mama about Wally. She had already told all of her sisters, keeping the story simple for Alice and Annie because they were so young. One afternoon a few weeks following the funeral, Mamie was home alone in the kitchen with Maria Luísa. Maria Luísa said, "Mamie, would you please bring our coffee into the living room. I feel like sitting down." Mamie was slightly startled by her mother's sudden request. These days Maria Luísa spoke to her oldest daughter infrequently and only when necessary. Mamie immediately did as her mother requested.

Once in the living room, Maria Luísa settled into her favorite chair holding her coffee cup in her hand. She waved Mamie towards the chair her papa had always claimed as "his." Surprised at this, Mamie did as her mother directed, setting her own coffee cup on the small round table beside Papa's large stuffed chair. She felt incredibly small as she settled back into the well-worn shape her father's large body left there after years of use. She imagined the feeling of her father's familiar arms around her.

"So tell me, Mamie Antónia. What is it that has given you such a struggle these past few weeks?" Maria Luísa looked so fragile, her color pallid, yet her voice was soft but commanding.

Mamie hesitated only a few seconds and then flew out of Papa's chair falling on her knees in front of her mother. Sobbing she said, "Oh, Mama, I never meant it to happen. I really didn't." Her mother neither pushed her away nor embraced her. When Mamie looked up at her, her mother gazed so deeply into her eyes, Mamie knew she was seeing deep inside her soul. Mamie began blurting out her story about going to Mr. Wu's for Papa's medicine and coming down the stairs and running into Wally. She explained how Wally was someone she and her sisters had seen before. *This wasn't exactly true because she had been with her sisters, but she had been the only one to notice him.* She confessed to her mama how she and Wally had gone to Sylvia's and had a drink—*or several,* she thought.

Her mother listened, the look on her face unreadable. Mamie didn't want to tell her about going to Wally's room so she went on and told her mother everything she knew about Wally, which, once she had said it, she realized wasn't much. Her mother listened, silently watching her daughter struggle with her story.

Mamie leaned back and looked up, her eyes pleading with her mother. Maria Luísa waited. Mamie couldn't stand it any longer and said in a voice so soft it could hardly be heard. "We made love."

It felt like an eternity and still her mother didn't speak. "Oh, Mama," she cried, "I love him. I know we are meant to be together. He is so amazing and kind. I don't think I can live without him." Her mother remained quiet. "You don't know what that feels like."

In a split second Mamie saw a lifetime of emotions flicker through her mother's eyes. Then her mother reached out and pulled Mamie towards her, put her arms around this daughter of her heart and buried her face her Mamie's silky, black hair. "*O filha da minha alma*. It's not that I don't know—I do—I know *this* man will surely break your heart. All of your life your Papa and I tried to teach you and your sisters to be true to God and what is right and what is wrong. What you did and what you are doing is wrong. It disgraces the family. If your Papa were alive, he would tell you that you have broken his heart, as you have mine. My heart is already in tiny pieces. I do not think I can bear it. *A Deus poderas mentir, mas não podes enganar.*" You may lie to God, but you cannot deceive him.

Mamie had no way of contacting Wally though she desperately wanted to tell him all about Papa's death and how guilty she felt. It was a couple of weeks following the talk with her mother when a message finally arrived from Wally. She was terribly relieved as she couldn't bear it if it had been just a one night fling and had meant nothing to him. She certainly didn't feel that way and the worst part was she strongly suspected she was pregnant. The message she received told her he would be coming to Santa Cruz on the following Friday. He asked her to meet him for dinner. He would be at Sylvia's at six.

At dinner, Mamie told her mother and sisters about the message from Wally and her plan to meet him again. Maria Luísa didn't say anything, but the look shared between them revealed to Mamie all the heartbreak and disappointment her mother was feeling.

Mamie could hardly wait for Friday. Hurrying home after working at the Grand Mercantile, she bathed and selected one of her favorite dresses—red with red shoes to match. She plucked a red flower out of the vase on the dining room table pinning it carefully in her long dark hair. She looked at herself approvingly in the mirror and then went to tell Mama she was leaving. Maria Luísa didn't look at her daughter, yet Mamie knew she had heard. It pained her to hurt her mother yet she felt as though she would die if she could not be with Wally.

Maria Luísa was not surprised when Mamie didn't return home that evening. Her heart told her she had already lost her eldest daughter. All of the girls were afraid to say anything to Mama or to each other when Mama was in the room. Mamie didn't come back all day Saturday nor Saturday night. On Sunday after church when Maria Luísa and the younger girls returned from mass, Palmeda discovered all of Mamie's belongings gone. A simple note on her bed said, "I love you all so very much. I know I have disgraced my family yet I know in my heart I am meant to be with Wally. Please forgive me. I will always love you all."

When Mamie had left on Friday to meet Wally at Sylvia's, she had not been planning to stay. When he asked her to stay with him, there was only a second of hesitation. "Yes." She would stay. He listened to her tell him all about coming home the night after they had been together and finding out her Papa had died. He was patient and sounded genuinely sorry for her and her family. He held her to him, comforting her while she cried at the loss of her father. She couldn't bring herself to tell him she thought she was pregnant.

The next morning—Sunday—she felt nervous and could barely sleep. She got up and crossed the room to sit in a chair by the window. She let him sleep in as long as he wanted. Later, when he got up and went into the bathroom, she climbed back into bed. When he came out of the bathroom, he was surprised to see her there staring intently at him. "What's the matter, Sweet Girl? Are you sick?"

He crossed the room and slid back under the covers and pulled her to him. She gently pushed him away saying, "I have something I need to tell you."

He rolled away, looked up at the ceiling, and then turned back to her. "This doesn't sound good. What is it?" His voice sounded sharp.

Mamie closed her eyes, took a deep breath, opened them, and blurted out, "I'm pregnant." Not realizing it, she had her arms crossed in front of her to protect her because she didn't know what his reaction would be. She had never seen him angry. She realized that, other than for every part of his unbelievably attractive body, she didn't know him very well. She looked at him apprehensively and repeated it in a whisper, "I'm pregnant."

Wally's jaw dropped and his eyes widened. "You're pregnant?" Again he rolled back on his back and looked up at the ceiling. He laughed. It was a big, hearty, warm laugh. He rolled back, grabbed her, and pulled her as tight to him as he could with her arms folded across her chest. "You're pregnant! I thought it was something bad, the way you were looking at me. You're pregnant!" He said it again, as though he were studying the sound of the word. "Sweet Girl! What fantastic news! He moved back and unfolded her arms so he could give her a real hug. Mamie was incredibly relieved. Silently tears rolled down her cheeks.

"Are you sure?" he asked after a moment.

She nodded.

Sunday morning, when Mamie knew her family would be at church, Wally drove her home and went inside the house with her. He paused at the large photo of Mamie's father hanging on the wall at the bottom of the stairs. He looked at the stern photo with the big, dramatic mustache—one side absolutely black—the other—stark white. It was like none he had ever seen. Her father, a handsome man, was, however, a man he was terribly glad he was not facing today. A picture of Mamie's mother hung at the top of the stairs. He understood where Mamie's overall beauty had come from. The woman in the picture had eyes that sparkled, giving her the same look he had noticed when he first saw Mamie—the look that had captured Wally's heart. He recognized the somewhat shy smile that could make a man melt. He drew in a deep breath and hurried up the stairs to Mamie and Palmeda's room to help Mamie pack her things.

Wally wasn't much help. He tried to hug and kiss her as she bent to put things into a suitcase. At every opportunity, he came up behind her, put his arms about her waist and squeezed her tightly against him. She could not concentrate and finally asked him to wait on the stairs.

When her things were all packed and in the car, Wally pulled the car away from the curb. Mamie looked back at the house where she had spent her whole life—her feelings a mixture of regret, guilt, and tremendous sadness.

One look at the man beside her reaffirmed her desires. She had to leave her family behind to start a new life with this man and for the baby she knew they were soon going to have together. It was with this resolve, Mamie and Wally drove up the coast line towards San Francisco. They had not been driving long when Wally—one hand on the steering wheel—the other holding Mamie's hand, surprised her by saying, "Sweet Girl, let's get married."

They stopped in Pacifica and checked into a roadside inn. Mamie insisted and they located a small Catholic Church. A very elderly priest agreed to marry them the next day in a smaller chapel to the side of the main church. Wally found a general mercantile store nearby where he purchased a simple thin gold band for his bride to be.

The next morning Mamie changed into a white dress she had often worn to church in Santa Cruz. On the way to the church, Wally spotted a flower stand. The flower lady helped Mamie select a couple of white flowers which the woman attached to the white shawl covering Mamie's hair. The woman told her she looked beautiful. Mamie smiled happily. Wally, always a charmer, picked up a pink flower and stuck the flower into the reddish frizzy hair of the flower lady. Her cheeks turned pink and she pushed Wally's hand away. Her grin revealed a missing tooth. She smiled at the young couple and refused Wally's money. "A wedding gift," she said.

After the simple wedding and the happy couple's brief honeymoon night, Mamie was eager to move on, eager to see San Francisco. Wally was amazed when she told him she had never been there. He had told her there would be room for her to move into his place and she was curious to see where Wally lived as well as where Wally worked. She would soon learn they were practically one and the same.

The bar where Wally worked was called *Jazzie's Gold*. Driving around to an alley alongside the building, Wally parked at a doorway, got out, and retrieved their suitcases. He handed her two small ones, and, after unlocking the door, told her to go on and up the stairs. He followed closely behind her with the larger suitcases. When she got to the top, he told her

to turn right and follow the hallway down to the fourth door
on the right at the end. She did and stood facing a red door
trimmed in black. Slightly peeling gold numbers on the door
announced it as Number 24.

Wally stepped around her, took out another key, and
unlocked the door. "Welcome home, Sweet Girl." He stepped
inside, set down the two large suitcases, turned, and after telling her to wait, took the two small ones from her hands and
set them down inside beside the others. He returned to the
hallway and, in a grand gesture, swept her up into his arms
and carried her inside. Pulling her to him in a warm embrace,
he kissed her deeply. "Welcome home, Mrs. Kohler," he said.

Coming up for air, Mamie looked around. She was not surprised to see the apartment was very small—a main room with
a kitchenette to one side. She was relieved to see it was quite
clean. The whole place looked exactly like what she imagined
a single man's apartment would look like. She smiled tenderly
at Wally. A magazine, *Photoplay*, had been tossed on the brown
sofa and a small radio and lamp sat on an end table. Two windows on one wall let some light into the apartment. She looked
out one window down over the street and saw entry ways to
several stores or shops, several surrounded by blinking lights.

To one side of the main room of the apartment were two
doors. One led to a small bedroom. The other—and Mamie
thanked God for this—a small private bathroom. Wally caught
her hand and pulled her back and into the bedroom. The bed,
looking as though it had been hastily made, practically filled

the small room. A small closet, dresser, and bedside table with a lamp completed the room. Wally again lifted her up and laid her down gently on the bed. "Sweet Girl, you light up this place. It's been waiting for you." Any unpacking had to wait.

The sound of the front door opening awakened Mamie—it was close to six p.m. She listened and soon Wally came into the bedroom carrying two cups of coffee, each with a large doughnut sitting on top. "We seem to have forgotten to have lunch. The doughnuts were as close to a wedding cake as I could find," he laughed. "They're a little dry, but the coffee's not too bad. Anyway this should hold us for another hour or so until we can have a proper dinner."

She went to the bathroom to freshen up and returned to start unpacking her suitcases. She hung up her things, pushing his clothes to one side struggling to get hers into the small closet. Later, Wally suggested they go downstairs so she could see where he worked. This took Mamie by surprise. She had thought they were in an apartment building. Apparently he lived above the place he worked. In the hallway, she could hear lots of muffled talking, laughing, and what she thought might be an argument behind the apartment doors they passed. As they started down the stairs, they had to step aside to let a couple pass. Wally knew them and his greeting was friendly. "Mamie this is Max and Heather. You'll be seeing them a lot." Squeezing Mamie's hand, he said to Max and Heather, "This is Mamie. She's with me now." And with that he kissed Mamie's cheek. Everyone laughed and Max and Heather continued up the stairs while they headed down. Mamie secretly wished Wally had introduced her as his *wife* and wondered why he had not. They continued down the stairs.

They had entered *Jazzie's Gold* by way of a backdoor located at the end of a hallway at the bottom of the stairs. *Jazzie's,* as Wally called it, was dimly lit with a long bar stretched across the room. Already eight or ten men of various ages and five women, mostly blondes with heavy make-up, low-cut blouses, and skirts above their knees, sat at or leaned against the bar. A big, burly guy stood behind the counter. Seeing them come in, he immediately called out "Hey, Wally! I need to talk to you."

Mamie watched the heads of the people sitting at the bar swivel their way. Many waved or called out jovially to Wally. "Come on, Sweet Girl," Wally said, pulling her hand and leading her to the first empty seat at the bar. "Here, Honey. You sit here. I'll fix you a drink, see what Gus wants, and be right back."

As he helped her maneuver onto the cracked leather-covered bar stool she whispered in his ear, "Just water, please." He gently squeezed her shoulder, kissed her forehead, and scooted back in the direction they had entered. He lifted the end section of the bar, ducked under it to get behind, and strode down to where the burly guy, Gus, was serving a customer. They exchanged a few words as Wally bent down, retrieved a glass, and filled it with ice and tonic. Looking down the bar at Mamie, he tossed a slice of lime into the air, caught it in the glass, gave Mamie a wink and bowed. They laughed as he brought the glass to her. Placing the drink in front of her, he leaned across the bar, and gave her another quick kiss. "Gus tells me Harry is late. The place is starting to get busy, so he needs me to give him a hand until Harry arrives. I shouldn't be very long. Will you be okay here for a bit?"

Mamie nodded and smiled. "Go ahead. Do what you need to do. I'll be fine." She felt proud of her new husband.

A little more than an hour later Harry arrived. Mamie could hear him telling Wally something about *missing the bus*. Mamie observed Wally's expression. He didn't look pleased.

In the time she was left sitting there, she nursed her tonic water and observed her surroundings. She was neither impressed nor disappointed. On the trip up the coast from Pacifica, Wally had told her he was the assistant manager and hoped to be made manager soon. This surprised her as she had gained the impression at their first meeting that he was the *Man in Charge*. There had been talk that Gus, the current manager, might have to leave as he had been having some health problems.

During the hour she watched Wally, Mamie continued to be impressed and proud. He tied a half apron around his slacks and tossed a bar towel over his shoulder. He entertained the customers as he mixed the drinks. The men appeared to enjoy his humor. The women, Mamie noted, not only laughed at his jokes but took every opportunity to brush his hand with theirs as he served them. When he served the customers at the tables, the women leaned their heads close to his and gazed seductively into his eyes as they ordered or continued to chat. A couple of them reached up to grab hold of his waist to pull him back towards them when he was backing away. One gave him a pat on the rear end. Wally laughed good-naturedly and went back to the bar to take care of their orders. Mamie frowned. This was a part of the bar business she hadn't anticipated.

Watching these interactions, she recalled the first time she had seen Wally on the boardwalk in Santa Cruz, his arm around the shoulders of the blonde on the *Big Dipper*. Mamie wondered who *that* blonde was and what had happened to her. For that matter, she wondered who the second blond woman was that she had seen getting into his car. Maybe sometime she would ask him. She sucked the last of the tonic water through her straw.

Weeks passed with Mamie meeting a lot of new people. Wally was good about introducing his "Sweet Girl" and paid a lot of attention to her when he brought her into the bar to be with him as he worked. She was increasingly impressed with his skills in running the bar. He was obviously well-liked and when it occasionally happened at the bar, that men would get into disagreements and start a fight, Wally easily stepped in, said a few words to each, and while offering to buy them each a drink, led them to separate tables or stools. The whole uproar was over practically before it began.

Mamie and Wally spent their days together and enjoyed the dinners Mamie prepared each evening before Wally left for work. Sometimes Mamie went with him. As time went on she was more content to stay in the apartment, reading, listening to the radio, or mostly sleeping.

Wally got up each morning and laughingly said he was making her breakfast by fixing her a cup of tea to drink while he enjoyed his usual brew of strong coffee. He then sat and watched her prepare their actual breakfasts. They spent their mornings talking or going for walks—Wally talking about his dreams of owning and managing his own bar. Mamie listened happily, sometimes letting her own imagination take over as he rambled on. She pictured them finding a home as her parents had done before she was born, and buying a small house for the two of them and their baby. Whenever she tried to discuss anything related to finances, Wally inevitably leaned over, kissed her nose, and said, "Don't worry, Sweet Girl."

As the months passed Wally's working hours grew longer. Mamie grew lonelier in the tiny apartment. She tried to focus on the baby, and spent time re-arranging the apartment so they could have a place to put the small crib Tez, a waitress at Jazzie's, had given her.

Mamie sewed baby clothes and carefully set aside some of her grocery money to be able to buy other things the baby would need.

Three months later, Leonard Adler Kohler was born at San Francisco County Hospital. He weighed in at seven pounds, three ounces. Mamie, though tired, was in awe. She repeatedly said how beautiful her baby boy was. Wally laughed and said,

"Remember he's *my* son. He's not beautiful—he's handsome and strong." They laughed together. Wally said they would call the baby by his full name, Leonard not Leon as some friends suggested.

Not long after Leonard was born, Gus suffered a heart attack forcing him to quit. Wally finally became manager of *Jazzie's Gold*. To his chagrin, the little additional money his new title brought in was spent providing for his wife and new baby.

For more than two years they managed to get by in their tiny apartment. Mamie's dream of having a house faded. Leonard developed into a busy toddler who loved running around. Mamie, and sometimes Wally, made it a practice to take him out in the afternoon to a local park where he could run around and work off some energy before it was time for dinner and bed. Then Wally had to go to work. When Leonard was two, Mamie discovered she was pregnant again.

This time Wally was not happy and asked Mamie, "How could you have let this happen!" He was working long hours and expressed extreme frustration the bar was not doing as well as he thought it would. Mamie noticed he was drinking more.

One evening she left Leonard in the care of a neighbor and went down to the bar unannounced thinking it would be a happy surprise for Wally, and, maybe, cheer him up. She knew it would be a well-needed evening out for her. When she first entered the bar she didn't see him and then spotted him with his arm around the waist of one of the waitresses, Valerie. He spotted Mamie, in a playful way patted Valerie's backside, and came over to find out what Mamie wanted. She told him she wanted to surprise him and be with him as she had when they were first married. His response was cool. He patted her arm absently saying, "I'll get you a tonic. When you're finished, you might as well go upstairs—it's going to be a very busy night." She didn't wait for him to bring her drink.

Although her morning sickness lingered a few weeks longer than it had in her first pregnancy, Mamie's second pregnancy went well. Tending to her active toddler, Leonard, kept her busy. Two weeks short of nine months, Martin Lukas Kohler was born. He weighed six pounds, one ounce—a good weight for the baby the doctor told her. Mamie was visibly upset when Wally didn't appear until a couple of hours after the baby arrived. His explanation about problems at the bar fell on deaf ears. Arms folded across her chest, Mamie told him she wanted to call the baby Luke, not Lukas, as he had suggested. He took one look at her, shrugged, and didn't argue. He stayed long enough to see his second baby son, then, saying he would come back the next day, left to return to work.

It was fortunate for the Kohler family that a couple who lived in the same building in a two bedroom apartment moved a few weeks after Mamie and Wally brought Luke home. This gave them an opportunity to finally have more space. Wally, Mamie, and the boys eagerly moved in. While giving

them one more bedroom, their new apartment did not have as
much light as their first one, a fact which did not help improve
Mamie's mood. While complaining about less light, Mamie
knew it wasn't actually the amount of light that was making
her irritable—it was Wally. The time he was *at work* increased
noticeably. Mamie became convinced he was spending time
with at least one of the waitresses. He hadn't stayed out over-
night, but he was going to work earlier and coming home later.
He seemed more and more distracted when it came to Mamie.
In his favor, he did appear to enjoy spending time playing with
his sons when he was at home. Mamie was grateful for that.

One evening Wally came home in a very good mood.
The boys were already sleeping. He got a beer out of the ice
box and asked her if she wanted one. She declined, wondering if he would *ever* remember that she didn't like beer and
preferred wine. Wally's smile brought her back as he fell back
into his favorite chair and said he had some good news. Mamie
returned his smile. It had been a long time since either of them
talked about any good news. Then he told her the news—he
had taken out a loan and bought a bar over on Mission Street.
It was his. He was in charge of the whole thing. His excitement
was palpable as he went on to tell her he knew it would be a
money maker—really big money.

Mamie was in shock. For several seconds, she could not
speak. Then she blurted out angrily, "How could you do that!
How could you borrow more money? How in God's name do

you think we will be able to make payments on a loan?" She
didn't recall ever raising her voice to him before but now she
was angry. She began to cry.

Wally, taken aback by her unexpected outburst, jerked
backward as though she had slapped him. Mamie caught her
breath and went on, "How do you think we will be able to eat?
How did this happen? What were you thinking for God's sake?"

Wally slowly leaned forward in his chair again. He didn't
rise. He didn't approach her. He didn't try to console her. He
didn't touch her. He waited. Finally her sobbing subsided. His
face was red as he growled, "Mamie, you need to believe me
when I say this will work. I know what I am doing. It's the
chance of a lifetime and I'm taking it. I can and will make
this work." While she could not look at him, she was acutely
aware she had become simply *Mamie*, no longer Sweet Girl.
Though crying less, Mamie's tears continued to seep down her
cheeks. Wally's voice began to rise with his anger. "Everyone
else believes I can do it. You're my wife. You should believe it
too! You should believe in me!" He stood up, banged his beer
bottle on the small table beside the chair, picked up his jacket,
and slammed out the door. He didn't return until morning.

After the slamming of the door, Mamie took several hours
to pull herself together. Without undressing, she curled up on
their bed. Normally when Wally was at work, she would pull
his pillow close to her so she could, at least, smell him. This
night she glanced at his pillow, glared, and turned away. It took
her a long time to go to sleep. When she did, she slept fitfully.

By the time the clock said it was 5 a.m., she had made a decision. For the boys' sake she would not argue with Wally. Her babies wouldn't know there were any problems. As Wally's wife, she knew she would have to accept his decision and be supportive. When he finally came home later the next morning, she didn't ask him where he had gone or what he had done. She was up and dressed and greeted him with little warmth in her voice saying, "Your breakfast will be ready after you wash up."

Mamie had to admit Wally worked hard to make the new place succeed. He named it *The Silver Moon*. She offered to help him. He turned her down. "I've got it under control," he snapped. Mamie rarely went there. She could tell when things were going well and when things were not. When it was going well, he was full of laughter and brought home inexpensive little toys for the kids. When he was quiet and didn't have anything to say or didn't want to play with the boys, she knew it was not going well. On those occasions when things were going well and he made love to his wife, Mamie hoped her prince was back and that the good times would stay forever. The rest of the time he didn't touch her. They saved their arguments for times when the boys were asleep. They held their voices down so they wouldn't waken them or arouse the neighbors.

The year Leonard turned six, Mamie began noticing she was getting clumsier and having more accidents. She would trip, bump into things, or drop them. At first it was not too bad and the boys and Wally, if he happened to be around, just laughed. By the time Luke was seven, her clumsiness had become the norm. Sometimes she felt weak and had difficulty standing for long lengths of time. She began relying on the boys, or Wally, when he was home, to do things for her.

Wally and Mamie's relationship continued to deteriorate. He was away an increased amount of time. He seemed annoyed by Mamie's new needy state. *The Silver Moon* was not doing well. The great depression made itself felt all over the country and San Francisco was no exception. With money being so tight, Wally could no longer borrow from his friends. One night after the boys were asleep, Mamie and Wally had their worst argument ever. At the end of it Wally said flatly, "I can't do this anymore, Mamie. I'm leaving." Mamie, who of late was having a difficult time speaking quickly, did not respond. He disappeared into the bedroom, returned with a bulging suitcase, and was gone.

Devastated, Mamie was not sure what she should do. Her first thoughts turned to her family. Eyes towards heaven, she prayed for her father's forgiveness. She missed him terribly. She wished she had listened to her mother. She missed each and every one of her sisters. Yet in her heart Mamie knew the real reason she could not reach out to her sisters now was the same reason she had left in the first place—she had disgraced the family. Her mother was right: Wally had broken her heart.

Two days after Wally left, Mamie knew her husband wouldn't be coming back. She knew if she was going to be able to feed the kids and pay the rent, the first thing she had to do was get a job. She was terrified. She wished she had been a better student. She wished she was smarter. She wished she was not scared of whatever was making her body do unexpected things. When she looked in the mirror, she saw an older version of herself. No princess was looking back at her. At thirty-five, she was still fairly nice looking, she thought. She stared at her eyes. *Were they always this large?*

Her boys, Leonard and Luke, were hurt and angry. They didn't understand why Pop didn't come back home. They often directed their angry outbursts towards Mamie—it was all her fault Pop had gone away. If she had only done things better and made an effort to make him happier, he would have come home. Leonard, being the oldest, at ten, acted out the most. She knew Luke was equally upset though he held it inside.

Knowing she could not afford to stay in San Francisco, Mamie, with the help of her friend Tez, moved with her two boys from San Francisco to Watsonville, a town south of Santa Cruz. In order to afford to make the move and find a cheap apartment, she sold most of their belongings.

A very determined Mamie turned on what remained of her charm, managing to persuade the owner of a nearby used car dealership to hire her to do the bookkeeping for his business. Mamie had not been a whiz at math—Angie having been the smartest sister in that regard. Having worked briefly at the

Grand Mercantile in Santa Cruz, Mamie was able to understand the simple system Wayne Talbot used to run *Wayne's World of Cars*. For Mamie the most important consideration in seeking this particular job was the fact that she could take the bus from the corner by their apartment to work. She had to walk only part of a block past the *Wayne's World of Cars* sign and enter through a side door into the office. Once there, to do her work, she could remain seated most of the day.

For the first six months when she was working, Mamie held most of her demons at bay. The next six months her difficulties in walking, and sometimes talking, became more obvious. Wayne Talbot liked her, which was fortunate because he tolerated her clumsiness and even helped her on those occasions when she needed assistance. He sometimes would walk her to the bus stop, providing her better balance by offering her his arm to lean on. Occasionally he gave her a ride home. Mamie's physical condition gradually worsened and there were many times when he could not leave the dealership. On those days he would call the school and have Leonard come to ride home on the bus with his mother. Mamie was afraid. Her frustration level was almost at the breaking point. She could not control her body; she could barely control her emotions, and she felt guilty about not being able to take better care of her boys. She worried constantly about the money. She was terrified. She knew it was only a matter of time before Wayne would have to fire her.

One Thursday afternoon as Mamie waited for Leonard to come and help her home, a tall slender man came into the office. She had never seen him before. He smiled at Mamie and said Wayne was going to meet him there in a few minutes. Mamie pointed to a coffee pot and some cups on a counter across the room and told him to help himself. They had just started to chat when Leonard burst through the door.

"Mom," he said, whining loudly. "I was going to play ball after school with Buzz. Couldn't Mr. Talbot give you a ride home?" More frequently Wayne Talbot had been driving Mamie home instead of escorting her to the bus.

Mamie, aware of the tall man standing a few feet away who had just finished pouring his coffee, felt terribly embarrassed. She sternly whispered to her son, "I'm sorry Leonard. But Mr. Talbot's very busy today. You know we can't expect him to help me all the time. He already does more than he should." The eleven-year-old boy, tall for his age, slouched and looked down at the floor. His cheeks were red and he made no effort to hide the fact that he was angry.

Wayne came in at that moment and seeing the tall man, strode over to him and greeted him warmly. As he steered the man into his office he said hello to Leonard and asked Mamie if she was going to be leaving now. Once the two men were enclosed in Wayne's office, Mamie picked up her purse, took hold of Leonard's arm, and leaned heavily into him. Together they slowly lurched the short distance to the bus stop having to stop several times for Mamie to catch her breath. Her gait was becoming more and more staggering. She felt her face redden and her breaths come faster. Perspiration formed on her forehead and upper lip. She was extremely tired. She felt extreme sadness as she looked at her embarrassed son. Somewhat roughly Leonard helped her up the stairs of the bus while avoiding looking at the driver or other passengers.

That night all Mamie wanted to do was get into bed—she was exhausted. She had supervised Luke as he scrambled eggs for their dinners. She told the boys to get to work on their home-work and left them to clean up the kitchen. As she headed to bed, she told them that once they had completed their work, they could go outside and play for an hour. She hoped they would actually do whatever assignment their teachers had given them. Once again she was tired and it was too exhausting to watch over them to see that it was done properly.

As she lay in her bed waiting to hear them come in and close up for the night, Mamie thought about her life. She prayed to God for his forgiveness for having let it go so wrong. She remembered the happy times of her childhood when her Papa had called her his little princess. She had longed to meet her prince and was so sure she had found him when she met Wally. He was as good looking a prince as she had ever hoped for. When they first met, he had made her feel happy and loved. As she picked at the shawl her mother had made for her, she realized she was a princess who had never lived in a palace—just a dark, lonely apartment.

She thanked God for blessing her with two smart, good-looking and, healthy boys, and prayed he would always watch over them.

She wondered, *What happened with Wally and me? Why did we make each other miserable instead of happy? Why did he have to buy that stupid bar? Why did he have to flirt—or God knows what—with the waitresses?* She closed her eyes. Even thinking made her tired.

What is going to happen next? I know I won't be able to work for Wayne much longer. What will happen to me? What will happen to Leonard and Luke? The tears streamed down her cheeks.

She dozed and her family filled her dreams—her sisters looking like angels, floated by in the sky, smiling down on her. Her papa sat in a big chair in the middle of the garden holding a fish in one hand and a bouquet of flowers in the other. He looked extremely sad. She noticed his big black and white mustache was not twitching. Her mother was shaking a finger at Mamie and telling her she had shamed the family. Mamie jolted awake. Gradually she realized what had really awakened her was the boys coming in for the night, letting the door slam behind them.

They came in to kiss her goodnight. Luke asked why she was all sweaty. She told him not to worry. "Tomorrow is another day and it will be better." It took her a while before she could go back to sleep.

At three-thirty the next afternoon, Mamie, seated at her desk, looked up and saw the same tall man as the day before again enter the office. "Oh, you're here to see Wayne again. I'm not sure where he is. He must be out on the lot somewhere. Do you want...."

She hadn't finished her sentence when the man moved directly in front of her and spoke, "Mamie, my name is Peter Townley. I live in Capitola." He paused then added, "You know Capitola, don't you?"

Mamie nodded, wondering why he was talking about Capitola.

"Well, I hope you won't be too upset, but after you and your son left yesterday, Wayne, who is a very good friend of mine, told me about your situation. It sounds like you are having a rough time." He paused again. Mamie felt her cheeks redden. She was angry Wayne had said anything about her to this man. As she became more angered, her arms started twitching uncontrollably.

"I can only imagine how I would feel if someone I trusted blabbed such personal things to a stranger." Mamie was startled and looked up from the desk. "Wayne and I have known each other since we were kids. No one knows better than I do what a nice, kind man he is. He told me that not only do you have a problem, so does he."

He had Mamie's attention. She had been so worried about her problems and what to do about getting by day to day that she hadn't thought about Wayne having any problems. "Wayne's problems?" she said, looking puzzled.

The tall man, Peter, pulled a chair closer to Mamie. He nodded looking serious. "Yes, you see, as much as Wayne likes you and thinks you are bright, he knows you're no longer able to do all this job demands. He told me he's going to have to let you go."

Hearing, aloud, the same words she had told herself a million times, Mamie gasped, her breath taken away. Peter Townley continued as though he hadn't noticed. Speaking in a slow gentle manner, as unrushed as though they were discussing the afternoon's weather, he said, "He tells me you're having trouble keeping up with your rent. He said your two boys—good boys—try to help you but can be a handful. That must be a big worry for you."

Mamie's large protruding eyes, riveted on Peter Townley's face, welled up with tears. It was a constant struggle for her to not let her emotions win—most days they did. She wanted to slide from her chair and hide under her desk, yet she was more scared knowing this could *actually* happen at any moment. She felt devastated hearing this stranger talking about her personal problems, not knowing how to respond. Had she known how, she wasn't sure she could have made the words come out.

Peter stood, turned away, and crossed the room returning in a minute with two cups of hot water with tea bag strings hanging over the rims. He placed one on her desk and sat down in front of her.

"I think I can help you," he said, ignoring the tears flowing freely down her cheeks. "I own a house in Capitola. It's a three bedroom house and far too big for one person. It has a small yard. It sits on top of a hill and it's not a far walk down the hill into town and to the waterfront. There's a school nearby. I work as a weatherman for a radio station and most of the time I work from home."

Mamie's eyes had not left his face, yet she had barely heard a anything since he had said the words, "I think I might be able to help you."

"You and your boys could come live with me in my house—rent free." Seeing a look of alarm in her eyes, he continued. "As I said I have known Wayne a very long time. He knew my wife before she died several years ago. He can vouch for me. I am not a womanizer or any other horrible monster you might be imagining. Wayne and I had dinner together last night. He told me about you, your sons, and your, uh, challenges. After hearing your story I tossed out the suggestion to him. He thought it was a great idea and a perfect solution for you and, frankly, for him as well."

Mamie continued to stare at Peter, and he had to repeat what he said before Mamie actually understood his offer. She could not speak and was openly weeping.

Wayne came into the office. He gave Mamie a handkerchief and, as though he had been present for the entire conversation, proceeded to tell Mamie she should seriously consider Peter's offer. "I would trust my life to Peter," he said. "In fact, during the war, I did."

The discussion continued with Mamie making only weak noises, being in no position to refuse or even argue. If she didn't accept this opportunity, she didn't know what would happen to her and Leonard and Luke. Her tears flowed and she was powerless to stop them. Finally she managed to respond, weakly and slowly, fighting to control her thickening tongue. "I have been praying to God to send me an *Anjo da guarda*," she said, speaking English and ending with the Portuguese phrase she remembered her father uttering when she was a child. "Now, Peter Townley, I see what an *Anjo da guarda* actually looks like. My Guardian Angel" she said, reverting to English, "looks like you. Only I thought an angel wore a halo not a hat."

Mamie and her two very unhappy boys moved into Peter Townley's home on the hill above Capitola. Although the boys knew their mother needed help, to eleven-year-old Leonard and nine-year-old Luke, this was just one more terrible disruption to their already bumpy lives.

1898

FLORA ESTELLE SALVADOR

SANTA CRUZ, CALIFORNIA

The second time Maria Luísa told Michael she was pregnant, he was ready. After finally adjusting to Mamie being a girl, he had prayed to God more often. At first Michael had started to tell God he forgave him for sending him a girl. Stopping in mid-prayer, he realized this wording might not be well received. Instead Michael prayed to God saying he understood why God had wanted him to have a girl first. "Meu Deus," he said, "you probably thought it would be easier for Maria Luísa to adjust to being a mother by having a girl rather than a boy. In these two years, God, you can see what a terrific mother Maria Luísa has been to our Mamie. So certainly you can see Maria Luísa and I are ready to add a boy to our family."

Eight months later when Maria Luísa awakened in the night and told Michael it was time, he happily summoned the midwife. Together Michael and the midwife waited, hovering over Maria Luísa until the baby was ready to arrive. Michael retreated outside of the bedroom waiting until he heard the baby cry. He waited for the midwife to complete his wife's care as long as he could stand it. Finally, looking up to the heavens, he took a deep breath and strode in to greet his son.

One look at Maria Luísa's face told him all he didn't want to know. After a slight stagger, a pause, and a deep breath, he advanced to his wife's side. Once again all he could manage was to kiss his wife's forehead, tell her he was glad she and the baby were all right, pat the baby's blanket, and head back out the door.

For the first few weeks, he could hardly bring himself to look at the baby. He felt strangely shy around his wife. He alternated between thinking God had let him down and wondering, rather, if he had let God down. Had he bothered to look at Maria Luísa, he would have seen his wife was full of joy and happiness.

On Sunday afternoon, Mamie was napping and Michael was sitting in his favorite chair. Carrying the baby, Maria Luísa approached him thrusting the swaddled month-old infant into his arms. "Here, Michael, take your daughter. I need to see about dinner."

Michael blustered and started to refuse, but Maria Luísa had fled. He looked down at the round faced infant sleeping soundly. Suddenly two little eyes popped open staring right at him. He was so startled he almost dropped her. His reflexes took control and his large hand clutched the blanketed infant securely to him. One of the baby's small hands popped out of the blanket and touched his hand. He started to move his hand away, but stopped as the tiny hand grabbed hold of his little finger. The baby's gray-brown eyes gazed intently into his face. A bubble appeared between the tiny, pink, bowed lips. A funny little noise followed the bubble. Michael's eyes widened. He could not help but smile. The baby sighed and closed her eyes, her tiny hand holding firmly to Michael's finger. Michael looked upwards muttering, "God, you must know what you are doing. You will send my son next time."

As the months passed, Flora Estelle Salvador began clearly looking around with a purpose. A curious child, she watched everyone and everything—each new observation seeming to make her laugh. Michael, working long hours, found himself eager to get home each night or morning, depending on his fishing cycle, to see his expanding family. He loved his little Princess Mamie. He always made it a point to see what she had to show him first and then hurried in to find Flora. Though she was a baby, he picked her up, carried her around, and showed her everything there was to see and touch in the house as well as in the garden.

Michael worked on the house and garden as much as his limited time off allowed, a pattern he'd established from the first day he and Maria Luísa moved in. The project was slow going because of a lack of time and, at first, money. Maria Luísa, loving the feeling of the sun on her skin, worked happily by her husband's side in the garden, pulling weeds, removing trash discovered in the tall grass, and clearing space to plant vegetables and fruit.

While her four-year-old sister Mamie played with her doll, Flora, now a toddler, preferred to run about the garden. She would enthusiastically try to help pull weeds, dig, carry, plant—do anything her little arms and legs would allow. Flora loved being with her mama during the day but, as soon as Papa arrived, she ignored Maria Luísa, wanting only to be with him, following him around like a puppy. As soon as she began to talk, she aimed a barrage of questions at her parents. Not stopping at the *whys* all children ask but adding the *whos, whats, wheres*, and *hows*. Flora wanted to know everything.

Flora was four years old when her mama told her that she and Mamie would have to stay with Papa because a new baby was coming to join the family. Flora just shrugged as she had already been told a million times by her papa that her little brother would be arriving soon. She looked forward to having a little brother to play with outside. Maria Luísa and Michael gave her a doll of her own. Flora would have nothing to do with the doll. She wasn't interested and the doll remained on a shelf. She preferred to work alongside Papa as he built a new little bed for her and painted it red, her favorite color. She didn't fuss at all when they moved her from the crib into the new bed, loving it when Michael called her "Papa's big girl."

Ethel and Harold Owens, having remained very good friends with Michael and Maria Luísa through the years, occasionally visited from Pasadena. On one such visit they took

Flora and Mamie out to the beach to play, staying out for most of the day. When they came home Flora saw her mama sitting up in Mama and Papa's bed holding a blanket. Flora hopped across the room with Mamie close on her heels. Coming closer to the bundle in the blanket, Flora saw a little face peeking out. Mama smiled and said to the girls, "Mamie. Flora. Come meet your new little sister, Palmeda. Papa isn't home yet. He will be surprised, don't you think?"

Flora looked at the baby and said, "Can I go back outside and wait for Papa?"

Later that night after Mamie and Flora had gone to bed and the baby had finished nursing and was sleeping soundly, Maria Luísa gave Michael a hug. "I know Miguel," she said, reverting to what she would always call him when they were alone, "you were again hoping for your son. I am sorry, but Terezinha Palmeda is a beautiful baby and will make you happy—like Mamie and Flora do. You'll see. God has blessed us with three beautiful, healthy daughters." Michael sighed and held on tight, burying his head in his wife's hair.

Years passed and the Salvador house was full of love, laughter, and high energy. Even though Mamie was the oldest daughter, she and Palmeda, called Meda, looked to Flora, now ten, as the wisest sister. Flora was the one with all the answers. They not only turned to her for general information, but knew she could be especially helpful when it came to persuading Papa to agree to something they wanted. They thought Flora was his favorite, and Flora, wise beyond her years, didn't disabuse them of that thought.

Through the coming years as the family expanded to greater numbers, Maria Luísa kept the overall household and their burgeoning garden running smoothly. A significant part of her time was spent preparing *the next meal* for the expanded number of faces sitting around the family table. On nights when Papa was home, each member of the family was expected to be seated at the table by seven p.m. exactly—not a minute later. They waited until Papa chose one of them to say the blessing and then happily devoured savory Azorean dishes such as *Caldeirada de peise* and *Pão Estenado* which Maria Luísa set before them.

Michael Salvador was fanatical about two things: education and, in spite of his disagreement with God's refusal to grant him a son, the Catholic Church. Holy Cross Church, one of the first California missions, was located down the hill from the Salvador home. There was no doubt in Michael's mind that his daughters would get a better education under the tutelage of the nuns than at the public school, therefore, the girls attended Holy Cross School located adjacent to Holy Cross Church.

Michael, always the proud Azorean, was extremely proud of the admiring glances the family never failed to receive when he and Maria Luísa arrived at church each and every Sunday morning. They were trailed by their pretty, dark-haired daughters who were always in dresses handcrafted by their mother, or, in later years, by Palmeda.

Though very smart, Flora often found school boring. She was not impressed when Sister Mary Margaret, as she frequently did, stopped her to clarify what the expected behavior was of all the young girls at the school. Flora preferred spending her time exploring the church building, school, and the grounds, learning how everything worked by plaguing each and everyone she met along the way with questions. She particularly enjoyed seeking out Father Andrew to ask him the same questions Sister Mary Margaret had already answered. Even though the answers were the same, she felt proud she had verified it from the only person at the church with more power than Sister Mary Margaret. Had God strolled in, she would have asked him. She believed getting to the true source of the information was important.

Flora Estelle Salvador enjoyed interacting more with the boys at school than the girls. The nuns speculated this was because she was surrounded by so many girls at home. She did love her sisters and was good about watching after the younger four. She was protective of them and would allow no one to cause her sisters any trouble— unless it was her. She hated being the second oldest because she was frequently reminded by the nuns that her behavior should always be at its best as her younger sisters would follow her example. *And whose example am I supposed to follow—other than Mama—*she often wondered. *Mamie daydreams too much and thinks she's a princess. Ugh! And you can bet I will never follow your example, bossy Sister Mary Margaret!*

As the girls grew older, they cherished their family get-togethers at the beach and the boardwalk. Maria Luísa packed special picnic lunches for the outing in a large red and white woven basket with a bright yellow cloth liner brought from Flores. It was guaranteed to be filled with such Azorean Portuguese delicacies as *Tortas*, *Linguiça*, *Queijo*, and *Empadas*, Flora's personal favorite. The girls liked wearing their wool jersey tank suits for swimming. They loved the water, the sand, and the people. The girls were in full agreement with their parents that life was best when the family was together.

As a small child, Palmeda demonstrated that she was the daughter who found true joy in cooking. She and her mother spent hours in the kitchen cooking, baking, singing, and laughing. Flora thanked God for Meda's passion for all of this as she certainly didn't have any interest in it. Realizing early on that the more time Meda spent in the kitchen, the less time they needed to do so, Flora and Mamie escaped whenever they could. On the other hand, Flora did love eating the food that came out of the kitchen—no matter which Portuguese dish was placed before her.

Once becoming a teenager, Flora spent much of her time daydreaming about how soon she could leave Santa Cruz to go explore the world. The first glimmer of such a possibility came to her prior to graduation from high school.

One day, reluctantly, she accompanied her best friend, Roberta, to a soda shop where they ran into some other friends.

One of these friends, Roberta's boyfriend, Timothy, introduced them to a friend of his, Joseph Isley. Hearing that Joe was a real cowboy from Montana raised Flora's curiosity, and she locked onto Joe's side, managing to slide onto the soda fountain stool next to his. Drinking their sodas, Flora could hardly keep her eyes off of Joe, thinking he was absolutely amazing.

In short order, she found out Joe was 21, worked full time on his Uncle Jack's ranch in Bozeman, Montana, and had his own horse named Tramp. Flora listened intently as Joe talked about riding bucking horses in the various rodeos throughout the west. Yes, he said, he had been riding horses since he could walk and loved horses more than anything. He gazed down at Flora's sparkling brown eyes and olive skin and said with a wink, "Well, almost more than anything."

Flora, neither coy nor flirtatious, ignored the comment. She found his descriptions of, and stories about, life in Montana fascinating: the horses, the outdoors, the rodeos, the hunting and fishing. She was captivated by Joe's tales of his adventures. Joe spent the next several hours telling her all about his life in Montana. He had never met a girl who paid so much attention to him and appeared to be *really* interested in the stories of the places he loved best and the things he loved to do. Usually girls were attracted to Joe because he was tall, tanned, good-looking, and flirtatious. He knew he only had to let his blond hair fall down over his eyes and say "Shucks" to get the girls to giggle and move a bit closer.

Somehow meeting this girl, Flora, was different. She was tiny. *Must not be over five foot two or three at the most*, he thought. She was not unattractive, yet she was certainly not beautiful, nor even very pretty. He had never seen a girl's eyes sparkle like hers and, he had to admit, he had gazed into lots of girl's eyes. He was talking about riding up into the hills to check on the fencing when Flora surprised him by interrupting, wanting to know how the fences were built, where they went, how he got the posts up the hills, and who had to dig the holes. She wanted to know how many kinds of horses his uncle raised. Did he raise anything else, maybe cattle? Had he read any *Louis L'Amour* books? He rolled his eyes thinking, *Of course I have*.

It was almost six p.m. when Flora noticed the time. Roberta and her boyfriend had long since left. "Oh gosh," she said, "I have to get home. I can't be late for dinner. Are you still going to be in town tomorrow?" she asked.

Joe said yes, explaining he and his Uncle Jack were staying with another uncle, Will, in Santa Cruz for a week and said he didn't have much he had to do. He said, "Tomorrow's Saturday. Timothy and me, we're going to a movie at the Beach Oak Theater downtown." He saw her dark eyes sparkle and added, "Do you want to go with us? Roberta is going."

She did. She said she would ask her father, and added confidently, "I'll meet you all at the theater."

Not surprising any of her sisters, Flora was able to get permission from her father to join Roberta, Timothy, and Joe. It never occurred to Flora that he might say no.

At dinner Flora was unusually quiet. She was thinking about her graduation—not too far away. The thought made her smile. She was looking forward to being out of high school. Papa was eager for her to go to work. He wanted her to go to work at the Santa Cruz Post Office where he knew there was a woman working there who was planning to quit in June to get married. So, her father concluded, he was sure they would hire a woman.

Following the movie on Saturday, Flora talked Joe into going to the library with her. *This is a very strange girl*, Joe thought. Nevertheless, since she was not unattractive, had a quick smile, her laugh was hearty, and she was fun to be with, he said okay. He assumed they were just going to pick up a book or something. He had never spent much time in libraries. Once they were actually inside the library, he was surprised to hear Flora ask the librarian where they could find books on Montana. The librarian pointed them to the stacks with geography books about the United States. Flora found a big one filled with lots of pictures and pulled it off the shelf. She led Joe to a table and sat down, indicating he should sit beside her. First she found a map of Montana and had Joe show her exactly where Bozeman was located. After he pointed to it, she started turning pages of the book asking him about practically every picture. "What's that?"

"Antelope."

"Have you been there? She asked pointing at a picture labeled Flathead Lake.

He laughed. "Yes. And guess what. There's supposedly a Monster living in Flathead Lake."

She looked at him and rolled her eyes.

"Have you seen one of those bears?"

"That's a grizzly bear," he said, a note of respect in his voice.

"What did it look like?" He looked at her, puzzled. She shrugged.

"Why do they call it Big Sky Country?"

"The sky is so blue and it goes on forever," he answered, grinning.

"What's your favorite place in Montana?"

"Kalispell."

"Why?"

"It has the best rodeo."

"I've never seen a rodeo. I'd like to go to one. How big are the mountains?"

"Huge, straight up and they touch the sky."

"Does the air really smell good? It says here the air smells good."

"Yes. Good and clean."

"Have you herded cattle?"

"Yep. I help my uncle run cattle drives in the spring and in the fall."

"Do you like to fish?"

"Yes, Ma'am!" he said with enthusiasm.

"What's it like out in the mountain streams fishing?"

"It's like being in the presence of God."

"Which do you like better, mountain streams or lakes?"

"Definitely mountain streams."

Only three times did the librarian come over and ask them to talk more quietly.

Before they entered the library, Joe had never imagined sitting and actually enjoying looking at books. He found Flora's enthusiasm contagious and soon he was as excited as Flora. After all, he had grown up in Montana and he loved it. He watched her gazing at the pictures and looking up at him expecting him to know *everything* about every bush, rock, animal, location, cloud, and building materials. He even knew what buffalo meat tasted like. As he answered each question, he decided maybe he *really did* know quite a bit. He sat a little straighter and realized he was thoroughly enjoying being with this tiny girl who asked so many questions. By the end of the afternoon, he found himself not wanting to leave. Her energy was so contagious he didn't want to let it go.

Before they parted ways, Joe asked Flora what she liked to do in Santa Cruz. She answered him with her own question. "Would you like to go on a picnic tomorrow afternoon with me and my family?" She went on to explain her family usually went to the beach on the weekend. When she saw him hesitate she hastened to assure him that they always had enough food. He could even bring his uncles if he wanted to. Joe said he would ask them if they would like to come, but he doubted they would. "My uncles have a lot of catching up with each other to do," he explained.

"But *I'll* definitely be there," he said with enthusiasm. Assuring her he knew how to get to the boardwalk, he promised to meet her there at one o'clock.

Sunday, arrived and Flora, for once, didn't need any prodding from her parents to get up and get ready to go to church. After church, the family returned home to change clothes, pick up the picnic basket Maria Luísa had prepared earlier in the morning, and headed for the beach.

Joe was waiting when Flora arrived at one o'clock. She took him to meet her family. He wore a cowboy hat but took it off when Flora introduced him first to her mother and then to her father. Joe was very polite. Michael, though considerably shorter than he, reminded Joe of a longhorn steer. His large mustache stood out on his face in the same way the longhorns did on the steers at home. *The longhorn and this man*, Joe thought, *demand a lot of respect. It would be a big mistake to under estimate either one.*

Everyone in the family liked Joe. He appeared to enjoy their company as well. Flora's sisters giggled a lot and whispered in her ear that Joe was super good looking! Flora felt sad when the picnic was over. A few days later, she was even sadder when Joe returned to Bozeman, Montana.

Almost immediately after Joe left, Flora got her father to agree that she could stop at the post office and see if she could get a part-time job after school in order to have a better chance to continue to work there after graduation. She and her father came to an agreement. She would contribute half her meager wage to the family and the other half would be hers to save. "If you go to work, remember you will still be responsible for your share of the garden chores." She agreed. Once Flora started working, Michael thought she performed like a girl on a mission—which, it turned out, she was.

Had her mission not already begun on the day of Joe's departure, it definitely would have about a month later when the first of several letters arrived for Flora from Joe. The first letter told her how much fun he had on his visit to Santa Cruz and how much he enjoyed their time together. The same day it arrived, she replied echoing his sentiments. The second letter told her how much he missed her. Her reply assured him it was mutual. The third letter told her he couldn't stop thinking about her. She responded in kind. The next letter asked her what she would think about coming to Bozeman. It was at that moment, Flora's mission became clearly defined.

In June, Flora graduated from Santa Cruz High School and moved from part-time to full-time at the post office. Her father was happy and very proud of his second daughter. As it turned out, his happiness was cut short when Flora worked just long enough to earn enough money to buy a bus ticket to Bozeman.

When she first arrived in Bozeman, Joe met her at the bus station. From that moment on they were inseparable.

Jack, Joe's Uncle, owned a ranch located slightly southwest of Bozeman. Jack looked exactly as Flora imagined a cowboy should look. He was in his mid-forties, his skin was weathered, his smile was crooked, and his clothing crumpled. Flora liked his looks—wiry yet strong. He tipped his cowboy hat in her direction and politely called her "Miss." Had it been anyone else, Flora wouldn't have been impressed. From him it seemed natural and *right*.

Jack, standing six feet one inch without boots or hat—only an inch taller than his nephew—thought Flora was about the tiniest woman he had seen and yet had the most spirit. Her spirit reminded him of the most challenging of the wild mustang ponies he had broken through the years. They were the ones he knew would turn out to be the best of his herd. He could see why Joe had not been able to stop talking about her from the moment he left Santa Cruz.

Flora, who had never ridden a horse, learned quickly. She immediately loved the feeling of adventure and freedom galloping across the hills gave her.

A postcard from Bozeman that September informed the family that she and Joe had eloped.

Joe's wedding present to his new bride was a two-year-old quarter horse. The horse, he told her, was small in size but smart— just like her. The horse was reddish brown in color, a *sorrel*, Joe explained. The mare had a white star pattern in the middle of her forehead and four white legs. Flora named her Star, saying any other name would have been disrespectful. Joe taught his young wife to care for her new companion.

Joe told Flora his quarter horse, Tramp, was a buckskin with a black mane and tail. Tramp and Star hit it off right away, as though they wanted to be like their riders—inseparable.

Uncle Jack's ranch was 2000 acres in size. He raised horses and cattle. Flora expressed her eagerness to learn all about the ranching business. Though young, Joe had been his uncle's right hand man since Joe's parents had died when he was only twelve. Jack was grooming his nephew to take over the ranch when the time came he could no longer manage it. If either man thought Flora would be hesitant to "get her hands dirty" or back away from the uglier parts of ranching, they would have been wrong. Her curiosity was undaunted, and she eagerly joined her husband in the many daily demands of working the ranch.

She worked at Joe's side as he mended fences, checked on the herd, ran the cattle, and watched for any newborn calf or cow that might be in labor. They could not afford to lose any of these newborns, Joe told her—to lose a calf was to lose money. Flora learned how to brand calves. She didn't like it, but she didn't turn away. Neither Joe nor Jack ever had the nerve or inclination to suggest Flora might be happier staying at the ranch house or helping Joe's Aunt Sal prepare meals for the ranch hands.

Along with the ranch, Flora loved the community of Bozeman. It was unlike anything she had ever known in

California. It sat surrounded by serious mountains: the Big Belt Mountains and Horseshoe Hills to the north; Gallatin Ridge to the south; the Tobacco Root Mountains, part of the Rocky Mountains with their highest peak, Hollow Top, to the west and the Bridger Mountains to the northeast.

Springtime brought the rains. Flora didn't mind. The summer was hot. She smiled and sought out the rivers. The winter was cold and the snows were deep. Never once did she complain. Quite the opposite; she appeared to thrive. She was not frightened by sightings of the wolves, grizzly bears, elk, and bison that shared the land.

While Joe was skillful at raising cattle, Flora soon learned her husband's true love was the horses. He was a natural with them. His uncle relied on Joe to select any horses they added to their growing stock. Joe was the one who broke the colts and trained the quarter horses for herding cattle. He spent time training his own horse, Tramp, already an excellent cattle pony, to become an outstanding, prize-winning rodeo pony. Joe loved the rodeos and entered as many as he could.

While Flora had a sparkle in her eye as she watched Joe at these rodeo events, he didn't offer to teach her any rodeo skills. He was amazed that she seemed content with this decision. Quickly learning and becoming conversant with the rules and demands of the sport, Flora didn't, however, hesitate to point out to anyone nearby the strengths and weaknesses of all who participated.

Flora awoke each day filled with enthusiasm and an eagerness to learn something new. Joe was extremely happy when she expressed her interest in and subsequent love of mountain stream fishing. He thought she would be bored. To her it was another discovery of the magic of Big Sky Country. Her world was small no longer! She was eighteen and she loved her life.

At home in Santa Cruz, Maria Luísa and her sisters missed Flora terribly. It wasn't until she was gone that they realized how much they turned to her for so many things. She was smart, funny, and wise beyond her years. Michael was devastated. He became quieter and a little less outgoing. He smoked more. He continued to work as hard on the house, the yard, and the garden when he was home, yet his enthusiasm was dampened. Maria Luísa watched from the window as he walked beside the bougainvillea hedge. When he reached out tenderly and touched one of the bright red blossoms he knew were Flora's favorites, Maria Luísa noticed him heave a deep sigh before he moved on.

Flora's love for her parents and siblings remained strong, yet she was so busy discovering the wonders of Montana and enjoying the company of her adventuresome cowboy husband, she barely found time to miss them. Once a month she sent her parents a postcard, hoping, in this way, they would understand why she loved Montana and the amazing sights of Big Sky Country. In Santa Cruz, the postcards she sent showing wolves, enormous snow covered mountains, grizzly bears, bucking horses, herds of cattle, fish, and snakes made the girls giggle and eyes grow wide while Maria Luísa sighed. Michael refused to look at them. Maria Luísa wrapped a ribbon around the cards and lovingly placed them in the Marriage Box.

Spring came early to Montana. Flora and Joe, deciding to enjoy the sunny but cold weather, rode up into the higher hills. As usual they were laughing and looking up at the wondrous blue sky with its few puffy white clouds when Joe's horse, Tramp, stepped into a hole. Hidden by snow the hole was near the edge of the ridge and suddenly Joe and Tramp were tumbling down the hillside through snow, rocks, and trees. Flora was appalled to see the two of them suddenly disappear. Her first inclination was to gallop down the hillside to try to get to them. She heard Tramp's terrified whinny and Joe's brief yell for Flora and then only soft thuds and breaking branches as they careened downward into a thicket of trees.

Sensing her rider's indecision, Star abruptly halted, immediately backing up away from the disappearing ridge. This motion beneath her brought Flora back to her senses. Realizing she and Star would suffer the same fate if they tried to get to Joe and Tramp, she called out several times for Joe and waited. Not getting any answer, she yelled as loudly as she could "Joe, I'm going to get help!"

Star had already turned sharply around and with a shake of the reins and touch of Flora's boot to her side, galloped swiftly, headed towards home. Flora was thankful her horse knew the way as she couldn't see anything through the tears streaming down her face. At the ranch, she spotted Uncle Jack and began yelling for his attention. Star galloped, her muscles straining, as though she knew the urgency of the ride. She stopped abruptly one step in front of Jack almost sending Flora toppling over her head.

Flora's hysterical yell sent shivers up Jack's spine. One look at her face and the absence of Joe by her side confirmed something terrible had happened. Flora was sobbing so hard Jack couldn't understand what she was saying. He pulled her out of the saddle and held her snugly against his chest telling her, "It's okay, Flora," though he knew whatever she had to say was not going to be *okay*. "Take a deep breath and tell me what happened."

Between sobs Flora spewed out the horrific tale. Jack whistled shrilly, immediately summoning the two ranch hands who were working nearby. He snapped orders at them to gather some heavy rope and blankets. He ran into the house and came out carrying his hunting rifle, Aunt Sal, having heard the ruckus, stood silently on the porch wiping her hands on her apron, alarm showing on her face. Flora climbed back up on Star's back. The small horse had, as if knowing her next assignment, already turned about face to head the way they had come down the mountain.

Like a small posse, they raced back up the Mountain, Flora and Star in the lead. With the help of the hoof prints left by Tramp and Star on the first trip, she was quick in leading them to the area where the accident occurred. They saw where the small chunk of snow-covered land had slid down the hillside. Jack, clearly in charge, ordered the small group to keep their horses a safe distance back as he dismounted and carefully edged forward to lean over the ridge looking down where the hillside had stopped its slide. The outline of Tramp and Joe was barely recognizable. Flora, having edged up beside him saw the outline of Joe and Tramp. Her heart pumped loudly against her chest.

His rope tied to his horse's saddle, Jack expertly secured it around his waist. The two ranch hands held the end of the rope a distance from the edge and began to lower him slowly. Flora held her breath as she watched Uncle Jack's descent. She prayed fervently to God for some miracle to keep Joe and Tramp alive. She prayed harder than she had ever prayed in her life. She called on any guardian angel in hearing distance of Montana to help, and even begged Sister Mary Margaret's forgiveness for past transgressions.

As she prayed, she was watching Uncle Jack's cautious descent, terrified he would fall as well. After what seemed like an eternity Jack yelled up giving them the bad news. It was too late for Joe. Flora collapsed in the snow and stayed there, sobbing, as one of the men lowered the rifle Jack requested on another rope. Flora heard one shot as Jack ended Tramp's suffering.

Joe was buried in a small cemetery in Bozeman. His aunt and uncle, his rodeo buddies, and his fellow ranch hands joined Flora at the gravesite. Joe was barely twenty-three years old; Flora was only nineteen.

Never having fully embraced Catholicism, the organized religion of her family, Flora, nevertheless, had always had a strong faith in God. Joe's death shook her and when she and Star sought solace in the vast Montana outdoors, she would sit astride her faithful companion look skyward and sob, "Why God? Why? How could you let this happen?" Anger at God raged within her.

Flora stayed on at the ranch in Bozeman only four months after Joe's death. Her heart was broken. The grandeur of her surroundings and the good intentions and kindness of Joe's aunt and uncle could not help her mend it. Even Star's soft whinnies, though comforting, could not help her overcome her grief. Packing only her clothes, a few personal belongings, and Joe's favorite buckle won for saddleback bronco riding the previous summer in the Kalispell Rodeo, she left Star to Jack's loving care and returned to her family in Santa Cruz.

Jack, suffering his own pain at the loss of his dear nephew, assured Flora she was welcome to return to Montana any time. He, Sal and Star would always be there for her. She never did.

Michael, though genuinely saddened by the news of Joe's tragic death, was happy to have Flora back home. His girls—his family—were all together again. As he always did on Sunday, he lit seven candles at the church, offering prayers, and pleading that God would keep them together and safe.

1920

MICHAEL SALVADOR

BONNY DOON

Ethel and Harold Owens' travels often took them through Santa Cruz. On these occasions, they stopped to visit with Michael, Maria Luísa, and the Salvador family. In the spring of 1920, they were once again on their way to San Francisco. Harold said he had something very important to discuss with Michael. After enjoying a delicious and sumptuous Sunday supper consisting of sea bass in garlic and wine prepared by Maria Luísa, Michael and Harold went for a walk in the cool evening air. They stood across the street from Michael and Maria Luísa's house, looking over the hillside down to the beach and out over the Bay. It was a breathtaking view. This evening they could see the deep golden-red sun positioned low on the horizon showing off its full splendor—once more on the brink of disappearing into the sea for another night.

Turning, they looked back at the house Michael had bought and begun restoring more than two decades before.

It was now a beautiful home in a magnificent setting. The house, Victorian in style, had been brought back to near original condition—an impressive demonstration of the Azorean work ethic Michael and Maria Luísa embodied. He, Maria Luísa, and their six daughters had done most all of the work themselves.

Those who had seen the house in its state of disrepair and after all the work had been done, heaped well deserved compliments on Michael and Maria Luísa. While the house with its grey-green color and white trim was lovely, it was the Salvador's garden that gained the most attention.

The small front yard, which when Maria Luísa so many years ago had first caught sight of the house, had been filled with weeds and high grasses, was now a stunning combination of flowering beauty and seasonal produce. The short fence had been repaired and painted white and was ablaze with red bougainvillea. Between it and the house were hundreds of colorful flowers lining the pathway to the stairway leading to the front door. Every inch of the rest of the space sported rows of healthy vegetables like peppers, artichokes, radicchio, basil, carrots, and squash, all bearing produce the Salvadors sold at a local farmer's market.

Not everyone saw the back of the property where Michael and Maria Luísa had added a cherry and an apple tree to go with the existing and abundantly fertile grapefruit tree. The couple grew green beans, corn, garlic, shallots, onions, blackberries, and strawberries along with a few other seasonal

edibles. Michael and Maria Luísa, like most Azorean immigrants, demonstrated an uncanny ability to use every single
spot of soil. Michael had rebuilt a shed that stood on the back
of the property to house the tools and supplies needed to care
for the produce. While he did most of the construction and
some of the heavy planting when he could, it fell on Maria
Luísa, his girls, and two hired men to maintain the garden
while he was off fishing. The produce they sold had become an
integral part of the Salvador income. Of late, Michael's health
had been failing, and he could no longer participate in the gar-
dening. As he talked to Harold, he endured a brief fit of coughing, reminding him of this fact.

"So," Harold said, placing a hand on his friend's shoulder
after the coughing had subsided, "I have found something I
think would be another good opportunity for you, Michael."

With his full dark eyebrows lifting in question and one
hand pulling on the white side of his full, drooping mustache,
Michael looked at Harold with interest.

"I recently heard from a friend in the real estate business
about a man, Bill Barkley, who owns property up in the Bonny
Doon area near the state park. It's high up in the hills, not far
from the Lockheed property, on one of the ridges. I haven't
seen it, but my friend told me that you can actually see the
ocean from that area. It's far away, but you *can* see it. The property is large—120 acres. Apparently Barkley has run into some
financial difficulties and is eager to sell. He's willing to sell it
for very little and not many people know yet that he's planning

to sell. I'm sure when the word gets out, Barkley won't have any trouble selling it. If you're interested in buying it, I'll call my friend right away. It sounds like a good opportunity for you."

Since arriving in Santa Cruz twenty-five years earlier, Joaquin Miguel/Michael Salvador had done well. The combination of what he earned fishing plus the sales of their garden produce had provided his family a good living. While his wages were not extremely high, his basic Azorean frugality and simple lifestyle had allowed him to save enough money to invest in a couple of other pieces of property. Having a highly successful California realtor, Harold Owens, as a friend had helped. Michael had discussed each property purchase opportunity with Harold prior to buying—his confidence in Harold's advice unbroken throughout the years.

Michael agreed the Bonny Doon property sounded like a good investment. Harold had convinced him that land values in California would surely go up as the years went by. As they walked back to the house, Michael told Harold he would think seriously about it and tell him his decision the next week when Harold and Ethel would be returning to Pasadena via Santa Cruz.

During the week, Michael reflected not only on the property opportunity, but more generally about his life. He had loved Maria Luísa from the very moment he bumped into her at the Festival of the Holy Ghost in Flores thirty-four years ago. God, for reasons Michael never understood nor fully accepted, had given him six beautiful daughters *and not one son*. He had tried to be the best husband and father he knew how to be. As all Azoreans did, Michael had a basic education from which he had learned how to make a good living, work hard, live frugally, and save money. Even during the hardest of times when the fish were not plentiful, Michael had managed to put some money aside. He knew he had enough to buy this Bonny Doon land. He knew Maria Luísa would support him in whatever decision he made. He also knew how poorly he had been feeling of late. He had a sense of foreboding that he was seriously ill.

When Harold and Ethel passed through Santa Cruz on their way back to Pasadena, Michael told his friend that he would purchase the Bonny Doon land as he had something special he wanted to do with it.

Before Harold left Santa Cruz, Michael confided in his close friend that he had not been feeling well and was, he admitted, somewhat concerned. A week later, following Harold's advice, Michael had a will drawn up for him and one for Maria Luísa. His will indicated his desire that his six daughters receive one sixth each, or twenty acres, of the California land in Bonny Doon. Everything else would be left to Maria Luísa.

With the will and the purchase of the land for his daughters completed, Michael felt happy, relieved, and at peace. He spent a quiet evening with Maria Luísa, the love of his life, talking about their lives together, their journey to America, the living of their dream in the American Santa Cruz. Michael sighed deeply and stroked his mustache. Maria Luísa gazed at her husband, always amazed at his mustache, which was now totally white on one side and remained dark on the other. It was magical and, she thought, he was magical. She could not imagine her life without him.

1918

FLORA AND MICKEY

ANCHORAGE, ALASKA

Following Joe's sudden death, Flora settled back into life in Santa Cruz with her parents and her sisters. She still had her laugh and quick wit, yet her enthusiasm for life was noticeably lagging. Shortly after arriving back in Santa Cruz, she took a job working for the City of Santa Cruz in the Planning Department. She found the work somewhat interesting, yet as hard as she tried to bury herself in it, her grief for Joe remained.

On weekends, Flora and her sisters went to the beach. Her father had increased his hours of work for the Silva Fishing Company. In addition to marketing the garden produce, her mother and her seventeen-year-old sister, Palmeda, were baking Portuguese delicacies to sell at *The Sunshine Bakery*.

As the months went by, Flora became increasingly restless. One rainy January morning, Flora was working the front desk of the Santa Cruz County Planning Department, answering a miscellany of questions from town's people and searching for the various deeds and documents they requested. It was a busy morning and Flora looked forward to lunch and a chance to sit down. Her stomach growled, making her frown. As the growl subsided she heard a deep, hearty laugh coming from a group of men huddled over a map—her co-worker, Don, in the center. One of the men, wearing a dark brown leather jacket, leaned back and glanced in Flora's direction. He was not a handsome man, but he had a cheerful, slightly crooked grin, white teeth, and twinkling eyes. He caught her eye, tipped his head in acknowledgment, and leaned back into the huddle.

Flora's cheeks flushed and she turned her attention back to the form she was explaining to a contractor. She handed the man the required form to take with him and again glanced down the long counter. The huddle of men was no longer there. She was surprised at the disappointment she felt. Her stomach growled again. She went to the back room, retrieved her sack lunch, and waved to Don indicating she was going to lunch.

Her friend Barbara, the Mayor's secretary, frequently joined Flora for lunch, but today Barbara was not in the room so Flora found a small table off to the side. She had just sat down when the group of men from the huddle entered the lunch room. They were in good humor, laughing at something one of them had said.

She saw the man in the leather jacket though he didn't seem to notice her as the group headed to a nearby table. He leaned over and said something to one of the other men then headed her direction. She looked around to see where he might be going and was startled when he stopped directly in front of her. He showed the same crooked grin she had noticed before. His eyes were hazel with flecks of gold. *Now why did I notice that?*

"You're Flora Salvador Isley," he announced as though giving her new information.

"Yes, I believe I still am," she answered, smiling.

Without asking her permission he slid into the chair across from her. "Don tells me: One, you're not married, and two, you like to do exciting things."

Flora's smile faded. "What?" Her voice was flat.

"Oh, please," he laughed, "that didn't come out quite the way I intended."

Flora looked directly at him. He smiled sheepishly—his face pink. His initial comment made her think his intentions weren't too honorable; yet his recovery made her wonder.

"You see, I'm afraid I don't have much time, and I don't want to miss this opportunity. I was wondering if you would consider having dinner with me this evening."

"Are you dying?" Flora inquired, lowering her voice and leaning towards him with a sympathetic look on her face.

"What! No! Whatever made you think that?"

'Well, you just said you don't have much time."

He looked at her blankly for a moment, then tipped his head back and laughed heartily. "Oh no, that's not it at all. It's just that I'll only be in Santa Cruz for a few days. When I saw you upstairs, I knew I wanted to meet you so I asked Don about you. I was going to talk with you before we came down here, but you were helping someone. I thought I'd come back upstairs after lunch to see if you were available to talk and maybe get Don to introduce us."

"Is that right?"

"Well, yes. Would you like me to have one of my friends come over to vouch for me?" he asked looking suddenly very serious.

It was Flora's turn to laugh. She looked over at his group of friends who, although they had started eating, were obviously enjoying watching their friend and trying to listen to the conversation. Seeing Flora look their way, they suddenly became very interested in their food.

"*If* Don *had* introduced us, what would he have said about you?" Flora said, turning back to the man seated across from her.

"What? Oh, of course. I'm sorry. My name is Wesley Mickens.

Everybody calls me Mickey. I was born in San Jose, but moved to Anchorage, Alaska, not long ago. This is the first time I've been back to this area since the war. I was spending some time over the holidays with my brother Art who lives here in Santa Cruz. Unfortunately, I have to head back to Anchorage this weekend so I can get back to work."

Flora noticed his smile had returned and realized she had been trying to see more of the gold flecks in his eyes—hard to do as they kept moving with the light when he moved his head. He had a boyish look about him, though she thought he was a good deal older than she. She felt an exciting energy about him.

"Well...," she started, thinking she already knew she wanted to say yes. Suddenly the image of her father's face with his penetrating dark eyes popped into her mind, instantly reminding her the man was a stranger. She shook her head slightly to make her father's image disappear. She didn't know much about this Wesley Mickens and didn't even know for sure what her colleague, Don, would actually have to say about him. She only knew she had a good feeling about him.

He locked onto her gaze and held it there, waiting for her to finish. When she didn't say anything, he said, "Well?" and then continued, "If you tell me what time you'll be through work, I could pick you up, and we could go for a stroll on the Boardwalk; maybe find a hot dog or two to eat."

Flora knew she had to make a quick decision; otherwise, this interesting man would walk away and she probably wouldn't see him again.

On impulse she said, "No, but you *can* pick me up at my home at six thirty. That way, Wesley Mickens, you will get to meet my family."

"That's terrific, Flora Isley," he said, looking genuinely pleased. He pulled a pen and a paper out of his jacket pocket and asked her to write down her address.

She did, and he took the paper from her hand. "I'll be there at six thirty tonight." He nodded, slid out of the chair, and returned to his friends.

Forgetting about meeting Barbara or being tired, Flora hurried through her lunch and dashed back to the Planning Department to find Don.

After work, Flora hurried home and told her mother she had been invited to go to the Boardwalk for hot dogs. Maria Luísa took one look at the excited expression on her daughter's face and felt instantly nervous—a feeling heightened as she pictured Michael's reaction once he got home and saw Flora's look. She didn't have to wait long to find out—the front door opened and Michael stepped in. He listened to his second oldest daughter and started to object. Noticing the way Flora stood facing him, daring him to forbid her to go, he closed his mouth, sighed deeply, and turned silently to sit down heavily in his favorite chair.

Promptly at six thirty, the doorbell rang and the Salvador family, more anxious than eager, met Mickey Mickens. Each of Flora's five sisters, all of whom had gathered eagerly in the front room, greeted Mickey with wide eyes, big smiles, and a few soft giggles. Mickey complimented Michael on the beautiful exterior of the home and Maria Luísa on the inside. "That's the most beautiful garden I've seen here in Santa Cruz."

Nothing rang false in his tone. Even Michael was somewhat charmed, though no one in the room could tell it from his scowl. His dark eyes stared into Mickey's as though searching for his soul. His brown eyes were met by equally intense hazel ones, perhaps searching for Michael's soul as well. The stare lasted a couple of seconds yet felt like forever to Flora and her sisters. All the girls were amazed when it was Michael who looked away first, his mustache twitching.

Maria Luísa broke the tension by saying, "Mr. Mickens, Flora said you planned to go out to the Boardwalk, but I'm wondering if I could convince you to try some *Pasteis De Bacalhau*, one of our family favorites. Flora's sister, Palmeda, and I prepared them. We have more than enough."

A bit anxious that she would be turned down, she added, "Unless you would prefer to eat elsewhere."

Mickey sent a brief questioning glance towards Flora, who whispered, "Cod fish cakes," then he turned to face Maria Luísa.

"That sounds perfectly delightful, Mrs. Salvador, and," he said with twinkling eyes, "it smells delicious. So if Flora agrees, I'd be delighted to accept your kind hospitality." He flashed a look towards Flora to see if she would agree. She smiled broadly, which he accepted as a yes. He then looked at Maria Luísa and said, "Mrs. Salvador, please call me Mickey; everyone does."

Michael tried to appear less than interested—the truth being, he wanted to give Maria Luísa a big hug for having invited the man. Without Flora leaving the house, he would learn more about this stranger who was clearly making his Flora look happy.

Maria Luísa asked her six-year-old daughter, Annie, to set an extra place. She directed Mickey to sit at the right of Michael, facing Flora who was on her father's left. Michael looked back at his wife, stroked the dark side of his mustache, uttered "humph," and sat down in his usual seat at the head of the table.

The Salvadors found Mickey a delightful addition to the family dinner table. He regaled them with fascinating stories of the life that had taken him to the Alaskan wilderness. In 1913 he had, he said, enlisted in the 1st Provisional Aero Squadron of the U.S. Army Signal Corps. He was with a flying training unit in San Diego. Later he served in Mexico and from there was sent to France. In France he was escorting another reconnaissance craft when his plane was hit and he was wounded. He was sent to a hospital there to recover. After the Armistice was declared, the 1st Corps Observation Group disbanded.

"I loved flying and wanted to continue to fly," Mickey said. "So instead of rejoining my squadron and going to Germany, I resigned from the Army and came back to the United States. For a few months, I worked as a pilot flying light weight construction supplies from Seattle to Anchorage, Alaska." He paused. "I have to admit that I fell head over heels in love with Alaska," he said, laughing. "I knew I wanted to live there so I recently moved to Anchorage. My Army buddy, Jeff Barlow, another pilot who's a great mechanic, and I have been working together to set up a transportation business in up there."

He went on to explain how they were able to earn some money flying supplies from Anchorage to some outlying villages. They had tried gold mining and actually had a little early luck. They saved all the money they earned to buy their own plane. "You see, when I was in the Army, I wasn't married so I could save almost all the money I earned. Jeff wasn't married either, so he did the same thing." He paused again to take a sip of wine. "Of course he got married to Norah practically as soon as he moved to Alaska. I guess he was a little lonely up there." He looked directly at Flora to see her reaction. She was grinning and her brown eyes twinkled.

Over wine and dessert, Mickey invited the entire family to come visit him in Anchorage. None of the Salvador family was fooled into thinking the invitation was actually intended for anyone except Flora, because he looked directly at her as he issued it. All the family, except Michael, politely nodded. Michael who, in spite of his best efforts not to do so, had warmed up to Mickey over the course of dinner, fell silent as he looked at Flora looking star struck at Mickey as he issued his invitation. She was, he noted, nodding very vigorously. *Too vigorously*, he thought.

By the time dinner ended, it was late. In front of Michael and Maria Luísa, Mickey asked Flora, "If it's okay with your parents, perhaps we could meet tomorrow and share a famous

Boardwalk hot dog and ice cream?" Without waiting for parental approval, Flora's answer was a resounding yes.

The following weekend brought Mickey's inevitable departure. Flora joined Mickey's brother, Art, and his wife, Vivian, at the San Jose train station to see Mickey off to San Francisco. After his family gave him their well wishes for a safe journey, Mickey pulled Flora aside. "Flora, I'm counting on you to come to Anchorage as quickly as you can. I can't explain what happened here in these last few days. I only know you and I would be—no, make that *will be* great partners for life." He paused. "Life in Alaska is the best. I mean. I know you will love living in Alaska. Let me know as soon as you can come. I'll be waiting for you." He gave her a big hug and a warm and tender kiss while his family looked discreetly away.

Sixty days later, Flora was on a train to Seattle to board a steamer to Anchorage.

1902

April 7, 1902 arrived. While Michael had planned to be home the previous night, the weather had not cooperated. A big squall blew in, trapping the boat and delaying the Silva crew's arrival back by ten hours. Fortunately they were able to handle the amount of water the boat took on. By the time the boat had returned to dock and was unloaded, Michael's newest child was already eight hours old.

When Michael had first learned Maria Luísa was pregnant again, he was joyous. He prayed faithfully and fervently each day for *this* baby to be his boy. He had decided he had not been as attentive to his prayers to God as he should have been for the first two pregnancies. He was sure God would not only hear but would answer his prayers *this time*, and he would be blessed. Michael Salvador thought, *António, my António, you will finally arrive to join your Papa.*

When he finally arrived home, Michael had no idea God would already have spoken. Four-year-old Flora sat on the porch steps waiting to greet him when he arrived. Excited as always to see him, she ran to meet him, jumping up into his widespread arms. "Guess what!" she said. "Mrs. Botolio is here."

Mrs. Botolio was a neighbor from down the street—a good friend of Maria Luísa. "And what are Mrs. Botolio and your mama doing this morning?" he asked.

"Not too much." She said as she gave him a big hug around his neck. "Mrs. Botolio is cleaning up a glass of orange juice that got spilt."

"That's nice of her," he said as he started up the stairs toward the front door. Where's Mama?"

"Oh Mama hasn't been doing anything except holding the baby and sleeping."

Michael stopped in his tracks. "The baby? The baby! He is here?" He bent over, set Flora down on the porch, vigorously reached for the door handle and raced inside.

"I don't think so," she replied in a voice so small he didn't hear her.

Michael paused at the bedroom door and looked in. Maria Luísa's eyes were closed and cuddled to her breast, he saw the familiar bundle. Maria Luísa's eyes popped open as soon as she heard Michael's boot hit the bedroom floor. She was propped up on the pillows holding the baby. One look at his wife's face told him, once again, he had no son. He walked heavily across the room and kissed Maria Luísa. Only then did he look down on the small sleeping face scrunched down in the soft little blanket. He stared at his new daughter. Maria Luísa knew what his look said, *What have you done wrong to make this happen again.* He pulled on the graying side of his large, bushy mustache several times and gave her a weak smile. Kissing her on the top of her head, and half-heartedly patting the small blanket he said, "I better check on Flora." He turned on his heel and exited the room.

Terezinha Palmeda Salvador, the third daughter of Michael and Luísa Maria Salvador, was greeted into this world by a father who, for three tries, had wanted a son. Not understanding why God had not heard his prayers or why he didn't think he deserved to have a boy he wondered, *Have I not prayed hard enough? Have I not been good enough? Have I not been kind enough? Should I have worked harder?*

As she grew up, Palmeda, not knowing of her father's disappointment and being nurtured by her loving mother and accepted by her two older sisters, thought, instead, being third had its advantages. Her oldest sister, Mamie, acted like she was a princess. Her second oldest sister, Flora, was a tomboy with a great spirit of adventure wanting to explore everything, go everywhere, and see everything. Palmeda didn't mind. When Mamie was off fantasizing and Flora was off seeking adventures, it provided her the perfect opportunity to follow more closely—sometimes exactly—in her mother's footsteps.

Very early on Palmeda discovered the church, and, by so doing, began to worm her way into her father's heart. This love started when she was only two months old, on the morning of her baptism. She had been sleeping soundly in her mother's arms, her father standing on one side and her two sisters on the other. She was jostled as Father Andrew lifted her carefully from her cozy position to hold her over the baptismal font. When the cool water touched her hair and scalp, the infant sucked in a deep breath and was about to cry out her objections. Her eyes flew fully open sending her gaze straight up into the high rafters where powerful wooden beams stretched across the ceiling. Her father thought the infant was watching the light in the upper windows, and that she was entranced by the morning sun rays streaming through stained glass windows sending out multiple colors to dance about. It was at that moment, Terezinha Palmeda Salvador's life-long love affair with the church began.

Her mother, intent on watching Father Andrew's hands and relieved that, for whatever reason, the cry never came, didn't notice her new baby's intent gaze. Her father watched in amazement as his third daughter took in the light and, seemingly, every beautiful carving on the walls and ceiling. It seemed obvious to him that she was awestruck by all she surveyed. He, in turn, was awestruck by her.

Palmeda, sometimes called "Meda," loved being with her mother as much as Flora loved being with her father. As a toddler, she was happiest when following her mother around like a small shadow, trying to do everything she was doing—especially in the kitchen. As she grew older, Meda worked side by side with her mother—cooking, baking, sewing, tending to her younger sisters, and, of course, to the ever-burgeoning garden.

Palmeda was a good student at Holy Cross School. She was studious and always courteous and attentive to the nuns. She could never figure out why her sister, Flora, continually complained about Sister Mary Margaret. She liked Sister Mary Margaret. Palmeda's interests were, first and foremost the Bible. Following that, she liked anything concerning homemaking, cooking, and sewing.

It was through their shared love of the church that Palmeda secured her place in her father's heart.

Mamie, her oldest sister, went to church because it was expected, and she liked to wear her pretty Sunday dress—her princess dress.

Flora, who usually enjoyed doing things with and learning from her father, drew a line early when it came to the church. Flora, as required by her parents, attended, "putting in her time" each Sunday, but there her interest ended. Alice, ten, who enjoyed only the social part of going to church, could not understand why Palmeda loved the church so much.

Father Andrew had served as priest of Holy Cross Church for many years. Many of the church faithful could be seen trying desperately not to nod off during his lengthy sermons. Having attended Holy Cross for years, several of these parishioners had given up trying to avoid the arms of Morpheus and caused an occasional snore to be heard by those seated nearby. Meda was embarrassed whenever this happened. Flora and Mamie giggled. From an early age while the other children fidgeted, Palmeda listened attentively to Father Andrew. She was entranced by the pageantry of the entire service—the more pomp the better. Palmeda was not sanctimonious—she truly loved God, the priests, and the nuns, finding great comfort and joy in her church.

Following a tradition started with her older sisters, Michael and Maria Luísa gave Meda a white Bible for her tenth birthday. They could not have selected anything which would have made her happier. By the time she was sixteen, her Bible was already page worn.

Palmeda, an excellent cook and baker of Azorean and other Portuguese foods, frequently baked delicious Azorean pastries like *Torta de amêndoas* to share with her fellow parishioners. She excelled with a sewing needle. The clothing she designed and created was admired by all. She made the Portuguese dresses she and her sisters wore to church festivals and other celebrations. At the young age of seventeen, Palmeda was asked to display one of her most beautiful Azorean festival costumes at the public library.

Palmeda adored her sisters although sometimes she felt a bit isolated from them. Mamie was six years older and Flora four. Her younger sisters were five, eight, and eleven years younger.

By the tender age of ten, Palmeda had earned the full trust of her mother. Her reward was to be given the responsibility of helping deliver freshly baked breads and pastries into town to *The Sunshine Bakery*. The owners of the Bakery, Adele and Thomas Gillian, welcomed these Portuguese delicacies made by Maria Luísa, and, later, by Palmeda. All the Portuguese items were well-received by the locals and tourists alike, selling out quickly. Many Santa Cruz locals arrived as soon as the Bakery opened to insure they would find the tray of *Pasteis de Nata* still full.

At the age of twelve, after making her deliveries to the Bakery on Saturdays, Palmeda began to stay and offer to help Adele Gillian sweep and clean up. It wasn't long before she was helping out in the preparation area of the bakery. By the time she was sixteen, Palmeda worked at the Bakery regularly after school and on Saturdays. While she enjoyed helping sell the baked goods, she learned all the aspects of the trade and soon had her own dreams of one day having her own bakery or maybe even a café. Flora encouraged her to pursue her dream saying, "Women can do these things as well as men, you know!"

"Maybe my bakery or café will specialize in Azorean and Portuguese items only," Palmeda mused.

Following in her two older sisters' footsteps, Meda graduated from Holy Cross High School at the age of eighteen. The very next day she began working full time at *The Sunshine Bakery*. Following the example of her Azorean parents, she

worked hard, routinely arising around four thirty in the morning to help Maria Luísa bake breads and other pastries to be
delivered to the Bakery. Then she helped her mother prepare
breakfast for her younger sisters and get them ready for school.
Promptly at 7:45, Thomas Gillian arrived in his truck to pick
up Palmeda and the baked goods and drive them down the hill
to the Bakery. Palmeda helped unload the truck and stayed to
work the rest of the day. She did this, happily, six days a week.

It was only a few weeks after she began working at the
Bakery full time that her papa, Michael, passed away. Palmeda,
like her mother and her sisters, was devastated. Flora had
recently moved to Alaska and remarried, and, soon after the
funeral, Mamie had run away. Meda, the oldest child at home,
stepped up to support Maria Luísa. While she had forgiven
Mamie for not being there at the time Papa died, she continued to harbor feelings of guilt for being an accessory to
Mamie's rendezvous with Wally that fateful evening when she
had walked her oldest sister down the hill. She went to the
church often to ask God's forgiveness for not having tried hard
enough to stop her.

Following Michael's death, the owners of *The Sunshine
Bakery* told Palmeda to take whatever time she needed to stay
at home and care for her mother. Meda was grateful to them.

Less than a week after her father's passing, her ten-year-
old sister, Angie, said to Palmeda, "Meda, we have to do something. Mama is so worried about money now that Papa is gone.
And," she paused staring straight into Palmeda's eyes, "I know

the church and praying is important to Mama and to you, but it's more important for us to figure out how we can all bring in more money."

Palmeda, who was in the kitchen cooking dinner, wiped her hands on her apron and took Angie by the hand, pulling her out to the dining room table. She knew Angie, even at ten, was smart, and right. "You're right, Angie. Right now I need to take care of dinner, but I'll go back to work tomorrow. Adele will be happy to have me come back early. I'll talk with Alice. She will have to help Mama with the cooking and the baking." A knowing looked passed between sisters at the thought of thirteen-year-old Alice in the kitchen. "You know you and Annie will have to help Mama even more with the housework and the garden."

With this, she pulled Angie close to her chest in a big hug. Angie, who didn't care for sisterly hugs, tolerated it for a minute and pulled away. Meda hurried back into the kitchen, calling back over her shoulder, "Go find Alice."

For Palmeda things gradually settled into a more normal routine. She thanked God daily for her job. She also thanked God that her father had insisted all the family be frugal with money. Other than her weekly contribution to the church, Palmeda had few things she wished to buy. Faithfully she put her earnings into the bank the way Papa had taught her. She continued to maintain a separate small savings account—not giving up entirely on her dream of one day starting her own bakery or café.

While Mamie and Flora had each left, Palmeda was content living at home with her mother and sisters. Once, at the age of fourteen, she had been enamored of an altar boy, Edward. He seemed to like her as well. Sadly, he and his family moved away, putting an end to that brief, sweet dream. Meda contented herself by imagining Edward as a successful priest, far off somewhere in a distant part of the globe helping others. She never met another young man who could meet all her godly expectations.

One busy Saturday morning, Palmeda, now twenty-seven, was carrying a tray of freshly baked bread to the front of the bakery. She was thinking about talking to Adele about moving some items in the shop around so they would be more visible through the front window. Without warning, she dropped the tray: eight loaves of freshly baked *Massa Sovada* fell clattering to the floor. The metal tray hit the counter, the case, then teetered and fell on the floor, the loaves of sweet bread bouncing before coming to their stops.

Adele appeared from the back room, saw bread all over the floor, and Palmeda sprawled amidst the loaves. Palmeda started to cry. "I, I, I don't know what happened," she said helplessly.

Hastily, Adele set the bowl she was holding down on the counter and hurried to Palmeda. "Are you hurt, Meda?" When Palmeda shook her head, she continued, "Don't worry, Meda dear. Accidents happen." Palmeda stood up and together they carried the un-sellable bread loaves to the back of the store for disposal. Softly weeping, Palmeda continued to express her apologies and offered to pay for the ruined loaves of bread. Her employer patted her arm. "Forget about it, dear. These things happen."

Palmeda knew how much the loss of the loaves of sweet bread meant to her friend and employer. Each loaf sold represented a small profit to the Bakery owners. Her accident had just reduced that week's profit. She felt terrible. That night she stayed up late at home baking a popular Azorean dessert she would give to Adele in the morning to sell.

Palmeda could not forget about dropping the bread. She remained upset at the loss of money and embarrassed at the thought of the accident itself. *How could I have been so clumsy?* she wondered. Less than a month later, she was entering the back door of the shop and stumbled. She caught herself and this time didn't fall. Feeling vastly relieved, she went on in to work. As the months went by, she found herself stumbling frequently and losing her balance when she least expected it. She became more and more clumsy at home and at work. She noticed her arms felt weaker. She no longer dared attempt to carry the heavier trays. Her legs had begun feeling weaker—she couldn't walk far without staggering and needing to sit down.

Following Michael's death, Palmeda and her sisters had insisted Maria Luísa accompany them on their usual Sunday beach outings, thinking it would be good for her. At first, their mother was reluctant and didn't want to go. Over time she gave in and went in order to get them to stop pestering her.

Palmeda's difficulty navigating at the beach worsened until she was no longer able to move through the sand without stumbling or falling. This left her sitting on the Boardwalk benches while the rest of her family walked on the beach. Usually Maria Luísa insisted on remaining with Meda. One Sunday, Palmeda announced she was going to stay home—her siblings could not convince her to change her mind. Maria Luísa, already extremely concerned about her third daughter, became even more so as frequently Palmeda was observed staggering or lurching when she walked. One day, Adele Gillian took Maria Luísa aside to ask her discreetly if she thought maybe Palmeda was having a little too much wine. The question shocked and embarrassed Maria Luísa.

Shortly thereafter, one evening at dinner her mother suggested Meda skip having wine. Palmeda, aghast, became very emotional and left the table, secluding herself in her bedroom. This reaction seemed only to confirm her mother's thinking. *She must be inebriated or taking some medicine I don't know about.* These thoughts made Maria Luísa frequently depressed, sending her into her own room to weep.

Neighbors began speculating that Palmeda was either into whiskey or, perhaps, laudanum. The parishioners at Holy Cross gossiped about her. Although the words were not intended for Maria Luísa's ears, she inevitably heard them and felt devastated. She spent almost every night with her face buried into her pillow holding conversations with God and Miguel.

Palmeda's younger sisters were extremely worried about her. They didn't believe any of the rumors—they knew their older sister too well. They were sure that while she had wine at dinner—as they all did—she never drank to excess. None had ever seen her take any medicines. Worried about her, the mean gossip made them mad and very sad.

When Palmeda confessed to her mother that the weakness in her arms and legs was increasing, Maria Luísa sent Alice to the Bakery to deliver a written message to Adele. The note stated that Palmeda was ill and could not come to work. The Gillians adored Palmeda and it was with genuine sadness that Adele sent a note back informing Palmeda and Maria Luísa that, while they were extremely sorry Meda was not feeling well, they had no choice but to hire someone else to take her place. Adele explained in the note, as nicely as she could, that with summer fast approaching and sure to bring with it more tourists and customers, the Bakery needed an employee they could rely on.

Maria Luísa did not know what to do and felt helpless. At church it became obvious her friends were keeping their distance from the Salvador family, hurting her deeply. Even Father Andrew seemed at a loss for encouraging words. Although it broke her heart, Palmeda gave up going to church all together. It took too much effort physically, and emotionally it was overwhelming.

This decision made it clear to her mother and her sisters how deeply she was suffering. Her physical challenges had been hard enough to bear—the thought of Meda separated from her church overwhelmed them all.

In August, Ethel and Harold Owens came to visit. Although Harold appeared thin and less robust than before, he had recovered from his heart attack. This was their first trip to San Francisco since his attack. Maria Luísa felt ashamed that she had not been in touch with them since before Michael's death. Over tea, she brought them up to date with details of Mamie's running off, and Flora's sad return to Santa Cruz after Joe's death, and then deciding to leave soon after for Alaska to marry Mickey. She told them everything about Michael's passing, his funeral, and how terribly she missed him.

Refilling her friends' tea cups, Maria Luísa sank heavily into her chair in the living room. As she began to tell them about Palmeda's troubles, she lowered her voice. She described everything from the stumbling and clumsiness to her inability to continue work at the Bakery and her refusal to go to the beach and to church. As she talked, she dabbed her handkerchief at her eyes which welled up with tears that spilled over and ran down her cheeks.

Holding up a finger to excuse herself, Maria Luísa left the living room and went outside of Palmeda's room, listening to see if it was quiet. She hoped Palmeda was sleeping though she knew this had become more difficult for her daughter. Hearing nothing, she tiptoed back to the living room. With great difficulty Maria Luísa confessed her concerns about Palmeda's possible use of either alcohol or laudanum. It was not lost on Maria Luísa how much wider Ethel's eyes had opened and the look of pity she saw in them. Had Miguel been alive, she never would have confessed these fears. However, he was not here, and she knew how much he valued Harold's advice.

Harold looked distressed but thoughtful. He remained silent for a time and then said, "Maria Luísa, dear, you must get Meda to a good doctor right away. I know of one in San Jose, Dr. Hiram Buckles. He was a classmate of my brother, Daniel. I'm sure he'll be able to figure out what is really going on with Meda and tell you what you should do."

Maria Luísa stared at Harold, intent on his every word. Suddenly Ethel jumped into the conversation saying, "After all, dear, lots of young people these days are listening to those Gershwins and Cole Porter. And they go see motion picture films!" She said this as though it explained everything.

Maria Luísa and Harold looked at her and then at each other in disbelief. Harold sighed deeply, shrugged, shook his head, and stood up. He crossed the room and stood before Maria Luísa extending his hand to help her stand. "You know, Maria Luísa, Michael would agree with me." He beckoned to his wife with a little wave signaling it was time for them to leave. As they gathered at the door to say goodbye, Harold pressed some money into Maria Luísa's palm. You give Meda and the other girls a big hug from me. You must promise me that you will take Meda to San Jose as soon as you can." He held onto Maria Luísa's hand until she nodded.

At her wit's end, Maria Luísa followed Harold's advice and, within days, took Palmeda to San Jose. After examining Palmeda, Doctor Buckles told them that whatever was causing these problems was definitely something neurological: he just wasn't exactly sure what it was or what was causing it. Through his years of practice he had seen a couple of other Portuguese patients who had similar symptoms. He told Maria Luísa that it was not alcohol and certainly not laudanum. "Sadly," he said, "I know of nothing that will cure whatever is causing this. My colleagues and I in the area have discussed this type of condition at length, and I can assure you that you will hear the same thing from any of them."

He prescribed medication to help Palmeda's muscles relax when they cramped up and sent Maria Luísa and Palmeda home. While Meda felt vindicated and Maria Luísa was relieved it was not alcohol, they remained depressed. They hadn't learned what the condition was and could not stop hearing the doctor's words reverberating through their heads: *he knew of no cure.*

Palmeda's condition worsened. No longer just staggering and lurching as though having spent a long night in a bar, she also began slurring her words and had difficulty in swallowing. She complained of trouble with her vision as well. Maria Luísa noticed her daughter's eyes appeared to be larger.

One day as she was fixing dinner and watching Palmeda struggle to cut up some carrots, she remembered the stories

Michael had told her about his own father's sufferings before he had died so many years ago in Flores. As she watched her daughter twitch and try desperately to control her unwanted arm movements, she remembered Miguel telling her of the time he had to tie his father, Manuel dos Santos, to the boat. She wondered if what Palmeda was experiencing was what her husband had witnessed so many years ago.

Terrified even further by these thoughts, she left the room so Meda wouldn't see her tears. Maria Luísa felt an overwhelming sadness—she had never been so afraid and so alone. No mother would wish on any loved child the future that Maria Luísa was certain her gentlest daughter, Meda, faced.

That night after Alice, Angie, and Annie were home with Palmeda, Maria Luísa went to the church alone. She lit one candle and retreated to a front-row pew where she knelt to pray for Palmeda,

"Dear God, I know you are with us all at every moment, but I do not understand why you are letting this happen to our dear, sweet Palmeda. How I wish it were not so. Please God, let Miguel be with you as you help Palmeda get through the days, months, and, maybe even the years, ahead. And God, I pray you will give *me* the strength to help my daughter. On the outside I see Meda becoming a stranger, right before our very eyes, and yet, I know she is still inside there somewhere. I pray that each day you will help her find *something* beautiful remaining in her shrinking world."

Maria Luísa sat for a long time in the church she loved. She gazed at its beautiful and solid grandeur hoping to carry its strength back to Palmeda.

By her thirtieth birthday, Palmeda was spending all her days in a wheelchair. Knowing her dream had vanished, she insisted on using the money she had saved for her own bakery or cafe to buy the wheelchair and help with the medicines Dr. Buckles recommended.

The wheelchair allowed Meda to be moved from her bedroom to the dining room and from the back door down a ramp, which Mariano Silva and a couple of Michael's fishing crew mates had built. Palmeda spent much of her time in the garden reading her Bible. Sometimes she let the book lie idle on her lap.

As she gazed at the beauty of the garden around her, Palmeda had a silent discussion with God.

Dear God. Until now I have had such a good life. So much of it has been good because your words in this Bible my parents gave me have led the way. Most of my happiness came from the family you gave me. My strength has always come from you. I have always loved being with you in our church. I never questioned why things happened. I knew you had a big plan. Now I wonder why you have allowed this demon to take over my body. I know I have to let go and trust that you will only put me through what I can bear. Forgive me, Father, for these moments when I am so scared. I'll do my best to endure the days you put before me. I just don't know how much I can take—sometimes I just want to be with you and Papa.

Her twitchy arms soon made it impossible for Palmeda to hold the Bible and her vision became too blurred to permit her to read. She had to rely on her mother and sisters to read to her. They were not only glad, but eager, to do so because they felt so helpless otherwise. Meda suffered increasing twitching and uncontrollable movements of her arms and legs. Her difficulty in speaking made her hard to understand, frustrating her immensely. She could no longer control her emotions and cried frequently. Annie, the youngest, trying to help, brought fresh flowers to place near Meda's chair, or would sing her sister's favorite hymns.

During these difficult times, Maria Luísa increased her prayers to God and Miguel asking them to help her keep up her own strength so she could help Palmeda face the daily challenges her body presented. Maria Luísa knew her daughter was fighting in ways none of them could begin to imagine. She now knew why God had bestowed such an unwavering faith in her third daughter. *He must have given her, of all my daughters, the strongest faith, to prepare her for these most difficult days.*

Maria Luísa patiently helped Meda with eating, a task which had become more difficult as the months went by. Palmeda's tongue was swollen. Even though her eyes bulged, and with increasing frequency, darted side to side, her mother could see in them her sadness, frustration, and devastation.

One winter evening while home in Santa Cruz visiting Palmeda, Angie needed a few minutes to be alone—having just left Meda and feeling overwhelmed with sadness and helplessness. She sat down heavily on the porch stairs looking across the street at the sun, an orange orb, positioned for its daily descent into the horizon. She pulled her warm navy jacket around her seeking its comfort. Suddenly she became aware of a black and white cat walking up the path leading to the stairs where she was sitting. The only white on the cat was its face. The rest of it was shiny black, the black fur surrounding the white in a perfect circle. In the early evening light, the cat's eyes looked a soft grey. It sat down directly in front of Angie and looked up at her.

"Well, hello there," Angie said. "What brings you out this evening?" The cat looked as though she expected Angie to answer her own question.

"Do you know you look like a nun wearing a black habit?"

The cat waited.

The young woman and the cat sat, eyes locked, neither blinking.

Angie's eyes widened and she asked, "Sister Mary Margaret? Is it you?"

In response the cat blinked, stood up, lightly pranced up the stairs, and hopped onto Angie's lap. Angie laughed and cuddled the cat who gave her a loud purr in return. She carried the cat into the house to where Meda was sitting in her wheelchair, her mother by her side. Maria Luísa was reading one of

Palmeda's favorite passages from the Bible. Meda's arms and legs were twitching and her eyes were darting rapidly side to side—even so, Angie felt sure she saw the cat. "Guess who came to see you, Meda." She held the cat up facing her sister so she would get the full *nun* look. "It's Sister Mary Margaret. She's come to visit." She turned the cat so her mother, too, could see the *nun-cat*.

Maria Luísa could not help but laugh and there was a loud gurgle from Meda. Angie gently placed the cat on Meda's lap. Even as Meda's legs twitched beneath her, the cat settled down and seemed happy—her purr becoming louder. Maria Luísa and Angie exchanged looks and it appeared for a moment that Meda, too, was happy. There was never a question that "Sister Kitty Mary Margaret" had become a Salvador and had a new home.

Though none of the family thought it possible, Palmeda's condition worsened even more.

With the help of Alice, Angie, and Annie, Maria Luísa continued to produce as much bread and other baked goods to sell in order to help the family to survive. Besides caring for her family, Maria Luísa needed to keep the two men who did the heavy seasonal work in the garden employed. This allowed the family to keep on selling their produce. They gave thanks to God that they had managed to maintain their thriving garden.

The Great Depression caused everyone to suffer hard times. Some days it was more difficult to find customers. Each night before getting into bed, Maria Luísa spoke with God and Miguel, thanking each of them for everything they had taught her. She constantly reassured them she was not afraid of hard work—knowing by saying these words, it helped keep up her own strength.

Regretfully, Maria Luísa had to let the other properties Miguel had worked so hard to buy and bequeath her, go for taxes.

Maria Luísa and the girls looked forward to Flora's letters from Anchorage. While times were hard in Alaska, too, Flora and Mickey were managing to do all right. Business was fairly stable because the Alaskan people, spread throughout a huge territory, always needed supplies. Whenever she could, Flora included small amounts of money for her mother. Her notes and cards were always cheery with funny stories about life in Alaska. Her letters always closed with inquiries about the well-being of feline *Sister Kitty Mary Margaret*.

With family finances severely strained, Palmeda, at the age of 35 and with a great deal of difficulty, managed to communicate to her mother her request to write a letter to Flora. She wanted her to tell Flora the truth about her illness and ask if she would buy Palmeda's 20 acres of Bonny Doon land. Palmeda instructed her mother to say that any amount Flora could pay would be enough. Although the mail to Alaska was not fast, she heard back from Flora right away. "Yes, of course I will buy it." Working for a very low fee, an attorney friend of

Michael's from Holy Cross Church helped Palmeda execute a "Quit Claim Deed" turning the land over to Flora.

By the end of the process, Palmeda had become so ill she could no longer get out of bed. Dr. Buckles came to see her and announced she had pneumonia. Being weak to start with, she was no match for the illness. Two months later, six days short of her thirty-sixth birthday, Terezinha Palmeda Salvador passed away. The family's grief was palpable. The money Flora wired helped pay for Palmeda's casket and burial in the cemetery beside her beloved Papa.

1907

ALICE FELICIDADE SALVADOR

SANTA CRUZ, CALIFORNIA

Alice Felicidade Salvador entered the world with a howl in 1907. Neither Maria Luísa nor Michael made it to the hospital in time. Maria Luísa's labor came on fast and hard in the early September morning hours. When his wife nudged him awake and told him it was time, Michael raced out of the house and down the street to get Sonia Botolio, their neighbor, to stay with the girls while he drove Maria Luísa to the hospital. He prayed the well-used car he had bought from a farmer and restored would not fail him on the trip.

In an attempt to be more comfortable lying down, Maria Luísa crawled into the back seat of the black Ford Model A. Michael drove as fast as he could through the streets of Santa Cruz, headed to the hospital. When they were half way there, Maria Luísa let out a shriek, terrifying Michael and causing him to push harder on the accelerator. Maria Luísa gasped, "The baby is coming! Stop Michael! Help me!"

Michael cranked the steering wheel sharply to the right, pulling off to the side of the deserted residential street. He threw open his door and just as he jerked open the back door, Maria Luísa let out another scream. Before he could reach for his wife, he could hear her groans and the uncontrollable sounds of her pushing. Feeling faint himself, Michael lifted her nightgown just as a little head with lots of sticky, matted-down dark hair emerged. Without any need for urging, the baby popped out with a howl. "Oh, dear God!" Michael cried, as he awkwardly caught hold of the slippery babe.

Feeling someone tugging at his arm, he glanced over his shoulder. A woman with a red scarf and dark hair hanging down over a long grey coat was vigorously nudging him aside. "Here, sir, let me help you," she said, reaching across his arms to grasp the infant. Afraid he would drop the baby, Michael let her take over. Knowing firsthand that he had yet another daughter, he glanced upwards, rolled his eyes, shrugged, and hurried to the back of the car, seeking something warm to put over his wife and baby. Finding nothing suitable, he returned to the side of the car and saw that the baby was wrapped in a red towel. The Good Samaritan told him she had grabbed a towel on her way out of the house. This smiling but nameless savior told him she would be happy to ride with him, his wife, and new baby to the hospital.

Relief swept over Michael. He helped her into the back seat with Maria Luísa and the now-quiet infant wrapped in red and being cuddled by her mother. The stranger smiled from ear to ear. Maria Luísa's smile was sweet, but she looked exhausted. His hands shaking as he tried to steady the wheel, Michael got them to their destination. He gave his wife a wan smile as he waited for the Good Samaritan, who dashed into the hospital and returned with a nurse to help Maria Luísa.

As Michael waited for a doctor to assure him that mother and baby were fine, he learned that the woman who had rescued him, Mrs. Lagio, lived in the house closest to where he had stopped the car. Hearing the car shriek to a halt, she had looked out the window and saw Michael leap out of the car. She could see the dark hair of someone reclining in the back seat. As soon as she heard the second scream she knew immediately what was happening. "I have four children of my own, you see," she said. She had grabbed her coat by the door, tossed a towel over her shoulder, and dashed out of the house.

Alice's dramatic birth gained public attention in a small article in the next day's *Santa Cruz Sentinel* with the headline "Baby Girl wins race to Hospital."

Alice easily slipped into her place as fourth in the Salvador line of daughters. She proved to be a happy and cheerful little girl. With not only her parents but three older sisters constantly directing her, she usually did as she was told. This was not difficult since most of the time her older sisters let her get her way—often a result of their having so many other interests of their own that they failed to pay attention to her. As the youngest, her parents doted on her—a luxury to be uninterrupted for

another three years. As Alice grew older, it came as not much
of a surprise that she could be somewhat selfish and demanding. She was fun-loving and cheerful. She made her demands
with such good humor, that usually everyone willingly just let
her do whatever she wanted—which was to have a good time.

While capable of being a good student, she was not. It was
clear to all around her she didn't care about school, at least not
the academics. This came as a surprise to the nuns, who had
enjoyed teaching the three older Salvador sisters. Alice excelled
in being the class clown. She made everyone laugh, loving
pranks and practical jokes. Whenever her teacher stepped out
of the room, Alice immediately came up with a *What if* idea.
"*What if*," she asked, "we all turn our chairs around and when
Sister Agnes comes back, we are all facing the back of the
room?" *What if* when Sister Agnes, or Sister Kathryn or whichever Sister the teacher was that hour, sits down, we all immediately stand up together and say the Pledge of Allegiance.
We'll say it as fast as we can!" She added the last with glee.
These pranks, along with singing all responses when called
on or all walking with a limp in their left leg, made Alice a
popular leader of her peers. She was never at a loss for mischievous, harmless ideas. With great enthusiasm, her classmates
followed. Most of the Sisters who taught her actually looked
forward to seeing what Alice would dream up next—never letting on to the children that they found any of it humorous or
clever. Alice, who cheerfully and sometimes with great pride,
admitted to having thought up the newest diversions, spent

hours after school copying words related to proper behavior on the blackboard.

Alice enjoyed playing tag, volleyball, or going swimming. Being cute, perky, flirtatious, and fun, she was well liked by almost everyone she met. She was by far the most gregarious of the Salvador family. Her father and mother failed miserably in their attempts to coerce her into being more serious. They, as the Sisters, found many of her mischievous ways so amusing it was hard to scold her.

Only once did Alice become completely serious—at the age of thirteen, when her beloved Papa died. She was as devastated as the rest of her family. Alice was tremendously relieved when Flora arrived from Alaska to help take care of Mama and the family during the funeral. She wished Flora would stay and moped for a couple of weeks after Flora left for Anchorage. Mamie, who left after Papa's death, was eleven years older than Alice who barely felt she knew her big sister. Palmeda, who was five years older than Alice, spent most of her time working, at church or in her room reading the Bible. As none of these activities appealed to Alice, she turned to her growing circle of friends for comfort.

In high school, Alice discovered her first love—beer. She found several school friends who shared her interest. By the time she was sixteen, she had learned how to dress up and make herself look older so that she easily got into the Santa Cruz Casino with her boyfriends who were always older.

Had she met him, Alice would have thanked Fred Swanton, the well known Santa Cruz businessman who, three years before she was born, had built a spectacular casino fronting the beach in Santa Cruz. Unfortunately, the casino had been destroyed by fire only twenty-two months later. Fortunately for Alice, he had the foresight to replace it.

Alice easily learned her way around the casino game tables and was unusually lucky. She credited her luck to her middle name, Felicidade, which her mother told her meant *fortune* or *good luck*. Even when money was tight at home, she begged and usually succeeded in borrowing a little money from her sisters. She almost always paid the money back the next day and even managed to make a small profit for herself. A few times she won enough to generously contribute to household expenses. On those occasions, she gave the money to Meda who wisely didn't question her younger sister about the source.

After graduating from high school, Alice went to work in the laundry and as a waitress at the famous Santa Cruz Beach Hotel. Her bubbly personality made her popular with her fellow employees, the hotel guests, and management. She had no trouble making trades with her friends at work. This allowed her to arrange her schedule to permit a lot of freedom in the evenings. Normally she would spend time at home helping her mother with the cooking and baking. She, too, like Palmeda, continued to live at home. As frequently as she could, she left home in the evening to join friends at the casino. Alice enjoyed the attention of several beaus, but she took none of them seriously. When Meda became ill and was confined to a wheelchair, without complaint, Alice added tasks previously done by Meda and helped her mother take care of Palmeda until she passed away.

One evening when Alice was thirty-three, she went to the casino alone. She was perched on a stool at her favorite blackjack table sipping beer when a noticeably tall, dark, and handsome man sat down at the other end of the table. He was alone. He ordered his martini from a waitress and handed five dollars to the dealer who gave him his chips. A couple sitting between him and Alice completed the table. The dealer dealt the first hand. At first, *tall-dark-and-handsome* didn't pay much attention to Alice. He won some and lost other hands. The couple who sat between Alice and *TD and H* was not having much luck. Alice, as usual, was doing well. She laughed and joked with the dealer and the couple beside her. She didn't leave *tall-dark-and-handsome* out of her generous smiles. Soon he was smiling back and, in a short time, they had developed a private, invisible bond. They shared knowing looks when one of the couple would make an obvious error in judgment by having the dealer *hit* them one too many times. As the evening wore on, Alice and *tall-dark-and-handsome* each had won more than they had lost.

The middle couple left. *Tall-dark-and-handsome* moved his chips and his drink over to the stool and table space beside Alice.

Alice soon learned that while he certainly was tall-dark-and- handsome, the man's real name was Nathan Overland. He sold insurance—all types of insurance, life, auto, health, homeowners— every kind. Alice assumed he would offer to sell her some insurance by the time the evening was over. He didn't.

They played at the same table another hour or so when Alice said she was going to have to get a sandwich or she would fall off the stool. He laughed and asked if she would mind if he joined her. They found an area where they could eat, drink, and continue to gamble by playing Keno from their table. They each won fifteen dollars and decided that was an omen—they brought each other good luck. Yes, they decided, they were definitely each other's good luck charm.

Feeling flush, Alice suggested they test this new theory. "What if," she said, "we play different games, side by side for one hour and at the end see which of us is the biggest winner or loser? They started at the roulette table, moved to the poker tables, tried various slot machines, and saved the craps table for last.

At one a.m., they found seats at one of the lounge areas and tallied up their wins and losses. It was a lucky night. Alice was up by $25, more than the cost of some men's suits, while Nathan had fattened his wallet by $52. They were happy— only partially because of their winnings.

They decided to meet at the casino each Friday and Saturday evening to start their play. After the first week, they decided it was such fun they should add one week night. They wrote down the name of each day of the week on a napkin, tore it up, and flipped a nickel to see who would choose. Alice won and Tuesday was added to their nights out together.

By the end of the month, they were reviewing how much fun they had together and, on-the-spot, decided to get married and be lucky all the time. Alice took Nathan home to meet the family. Maria Luísa had not regained her energy since Palmeda had passed away. Her only activity these days after the daily baking was to retire to her favorite chair in the living room, read her Bible, and gaze out the window at the family's garden. She rarely made it to church. Her decline had actually started after the death of Miguel. Once he was gone, she never again thought of him as Michael, only as her beloved Miguel. She had drawn needed strength from her faith to care for Palmeda, but once Palmeda was gone, her spirit as well as her strength sagged dramatically.

When Alice brought Nathan home to meet her mother and sisters, he immediately charmed them. Maria Luísa, who had neither the heart to argue against love at first sight, nor the strength to plan a wedding, readily agreed to the marriage and suggested they marry in the Salvador home. As Alice had never wished to be married in the church and Nathan admitted to not being very religious, this suited them just fine. Nathan had only an older brother and his brother's wife to invite to the wedding.

An elderly Father Andrew, yielding to Maria Luísa pleadings, sent Father Cisco from Holy Cross to the house to perform the ceremony.

Flora and Mickey sent their good wishes from Anchorage. Angie and her husband came and Annie came down from the northern part of the state. At the wedding Angie and Annie each stood on opposite sides of their mother. At her mother's request, Annie had filled the living room with candles and flowers. When the sisters all heard their mother wishing their father could be with them, Annie moved the picture of Michael from the stairway wall and leaned it against the mirror above the mantle, placing candles and flowers on each side. With his startling half-black and half-white mustache and his piercing eyes looking back at them, the family felt as though Michael was presiding over the marriage instead of Father Cisco.

Like Alice, the wedding was small and cheery—a happy event filled with lots of laughter and hugs. Annie stayed home with her mother while the happy couple took a few days to honeymoon in Las Vegas. When they returned to Santa Cruz, they continued to live with Maria Luísa who was getting noticeably more frail as each day passed.

Only two months after seeing her fourth daughter get married, Maria Luísa collapsed and died. She was sixty seven years old.

Nathan comforted Alice and her sisters as they mourned their mother's death. With the sadness of Papa's, Mama's, and

Palmeda's deaths never far from their thoughts, Alice and Nathan continued to live in the Salvador house, worked hard, and managed to frequent the casino. Friends considered the couple extremely lucky, envying them as they supplemented their small incomes from their regular jobs with their winnings.

As it did for all Americans, December 7, 1941, changed Alice and Nathan's lives. That morning they awakened to news that the U.S. Naval Base at Pearl Harbor, Hawaii, had been attacked by the Japanese. Alice and Nathan remained glued to the radio listening to President Franklin Delano Roosevelt proclaim it to be "a date that will live in infamy."

Along with several of his friends, Nathan enlisted in the U.S. Navy. He was sent to the Naval Training Center in San Diego then was deployed to the South Pacific. Alice, still working at the *Beach Hotel*, stayed in the family home. Throughout the duration of Nathan's absence, Alice gave up gambling and even occasionally attended Sunday Mass at Holy Cross Church. After work, she spent time helping out at the Santa Cruz USO. It was her contribution to the War Effort.

Alice, along with the rest of the country, gave a grateful sigh of relief when the end of the War was declared in September, 1945. The country was in a post-war euphoria. Alice thought God must have been listening to her prayers when Nathan came home to her relatively unscathed. He had only a few scars to show for the minor wounds he had suffered—far luckier than many of his friends.

Within two years of the War ending, Nathan and Alice Salvador Overland had resumed their pre-War activities. Not surprising any of their friends, after a particularly lucky night, when Alice won seven-hundred dollars, the couple decided, on the spur of the moment, to move to Las Vegas. They had visited the Last Frontier Resort there a month earlier and loved the excitement of Las Vegas. They agreed: it was *the* action town. With the new Flamingo Casino opening, they believed what they heard—Vegas was booming. Over their winnings and beer, they decided a move there made good sense. They decided that if they "played their cards right"—this statement bringing forth gales of laughter from each of them—they would do very well in Vegas, be able to buy a house, and maybe later start a family.

Neither Nathan's brother nor Alice's sisters were happy with this idea. None could understand why the two of them didn't see the great risk in this plan, but the couple's jubilation over their decision could not be squelched. Alice contacted Harold Owens for advice on selling the Santa Cruz home. The proceeds from the sale would, as Maria Luísa had indicated in her will, be divided equally among Flora, Alice, Angie, and Annie, her only daughters who she knew were still living.

Alice and Nathan decided to use Alice's share as a down payment on the purchase of a home in Las Vegas. Nathan arranged a job transfer from Santa Cruz to Las Vegas with his employer, the American Insurance Company. It wasn't long before the couple was happily settled in Las Vegas, soon to be known as "Sin City."

The first year everything went as planned. Their home was small and, more important to them, located not far from the famous *Las Vegas Strip*. Nathan continued to be a highly successful insurance salesman. Lady Luck had followed them from the casino in Santa Cruz to the Vegas tables. During the first year, they tucked a little of their earnings away in the bank. With Alice's share of the money from the Salvador house sale and their bank savings, their future looked bright.

Shortly into their second year in Vegas, Lady Luck began turning her back on them. At first it was gradual with one of them losing more heavily than the other. One lost, the other won, and then it switched. After these nights, they bolstered each other's spirits. They managed to keep on the winning side of things for another six months, and then the winning stopped. Lady Luck completely spurned them.

They dipped into their savings and soon the savings were gone.

Living only on their small wages was hard. Not much new business was to be found and Nathan was no longer selling many insurance policies. Alice called her sister, Angie, begging her to buy Alice's portion of the Bonny Doon property. "It's the only asset we have," she pleaded. "We need the money, Ange!" she added, using her sister's nickname.

At first, Angie adamantly refused Alice's pleas. Angie and her husband George had managed to save Angie's portion of the money from the sale of her parent's home. Alice then told Angie if she didn't get that money, she and Nathan would lose their house. "If you don't buy it, I'll have to look outside the family for a buyer for my part of the Bonny Doon property."

When Alice said the words, *look outside the fa*mily, Angie felt as though Papa was in the room listening. She could feel his disappointment. Alice continued her sales pitch, emphasizing the unspoken bond between the sisters that mandated they help each other in hard times. Plus, she added, "I really want *you* to have the property, not some outsider. *Papa* would want the property to stay in the family." With this, Angie gave in and wired Alice the money. A Quit Claim Deed turning her twenty acres of Bonny Doon property over to Angie made it final.

When she received the Bonny Doon money, Alice and Nathan immediately left Las Vegas for Atlantic City. They were positive their luck would return there. Nine months later, Angie received a letter from Alice saying she had been diagnosed with pancreatic cancer. Her doctors told her and Nathan that she had only a short time to live. Three months later, the call came from Nathan telling Angie that Alice had passed away in the night. Nathan asked Angie to tell her sisters that in spite of what the family may have thought about how he and Alice had lived, they had loved each other very much. "From the night I met her in the casino in Santa Cruz to the last night when we said goodbye, she was the most beautiful, loving, happy, and funny person I have ever known. We talked about it and agreed if we had it to do over again, we would have done it all again, exactly the same way." Nathan decided to make his permanent home in New Jersey.

1910

Three years after Alice had joined the family, Michael greeted his fifth daughter, Angelina Gabriela Salvador. The year was 1910. He made it to the hospital this time and waited in the lobby near the delivery room. Three other fathers-to-be were waiting as well. Each had cigars sticking out of his pocket signaling plans to celebrate his respective newborns' arrival. When the doctor came out to find him, Michael was saying a silent prayer to God for the thousandth time. *Please God, I have waited patiently—well, maybe not as patiently as I should have, but patiently for my son. Please God, let it be today.*

The unusually cheerful doctor slapped Michael on the back. "Your beautiful wife and daughter are waiting to see you." With sagging shoulders and shuffling feet, Michael obediently followed the doctor. He couldn't bring himself to look at the waiting husbands as he passed. Michael was glad he hadn't brought any cigars.

As a child, Angie, neither beautiful nor even pretty, had an interesting look about her. Sometimes she reminded Michael of a spring robin with its head tilted listening for a worm to make its move. As a toddler, Angie would seek out Flora, twelve years her elder, if her older sisters were around, because Flora was not only good natured and kind, but always showed her something interesting. It was not lost upon Flora that even at an early age, Angie actually listened. She was very bright, especially with numbers, and very early on, she displayed a dry sense of humor.

Angie quickly learned that Palmeda, seven years older than she, enjoyed working in the kitchen with Mama. Angie, following the lead of her other older sisters, Mamie, Flora, and Alice, didn't volunteer to do any more than her assigned chores when it came to the kitchen.

Because of the age differences with her sisters, Angie became accustomed and content to being alone. She often chose to spend time outdoors with her adopted stray cats, Hobo and Peepers—her closest friends.

Angie went through elementary and high school without any problems. Her grades were very good, her teachers reporting to her proud parents that she was an excellent student. She enjoyed reading and excelled at math. While she got along well with the other students, none of them were close friends. She preferred to spend time at home with her sisters and her cats—often choosing the cats first.

Angie was the daughter most like Michael—hard working, even-tempered and fair. She valued education, didn't mind following all the rules, and she was the most frugal of the sisters. She used, as her father occasionally pointed out to his other daughters, *common sense*. Through these behaviors, Michael and Maria Luísa saw Angie as demonstrating the most valued, and in some instances, the most honored characteristics of her Azorean heritage. They were very proud of their fifth daughter, but because they worked such long hours, they rarely, if ever, told her that.

When Angie was three, her sister Flora left for the first time to go to Montana. Angie hardly knew her. Flora returned a year later only to leave again when Angie was five. In those two brief years when Flora was home, Angie treasured her time with Flora. In spite of the difference in ages, the sisters developed a bond.

Angie, only ten years old when her father died, was mature beyond her age. When her papa died, Angie instantly set aside any remaining childish inclinations, with the exception of the devotion to her cats, to assist her sisters Meda and Alice in helping their mother through the ordeal and caring for her seven-year-old sister, Annie. She also helped keep the garden's produce production going and, even though she was so young, always listened carefully to any discussion of family finances. She was the sister who kept one eye firmly on the dwindling family income.

Eight years following her father's death, at the age of eighteen in June of 1928, Angie graduated from high school. She found a job at the Mercantile where her sister Mamie had briefly worked. She earned enough money to enroll in Santa Cruz Community College, but soon after Angie enrolled, her sister, Meda, began having problems with her coordination. Along with her mother and sisters, Angie watched with a heavy heart as Meda's problems worsened and was upset even more when her sister became the increasing target of ugly rumors.

It saddened Angie to see Palmeda struggle with such a strange, horrible, and crippling disease. She hated and didn't understand it. With Flora in Alaska and Mamie having run away with the mysterious Wally, Angie didn't have anyone to talk to about Palmeda's situation. She chose not to talk to her mother who was already too upset, and Alice, while caring about Meda, didn't seem serious enough, and Annie was too young.

It didn't surprise Maria Luísa that Angie, being so much like Michael, proved to be a very responsible young woman. Attending college in order to get a better job was just one way in which Angie showed her commitment to her family. She not only helped her mother with the daily chores, but soon took over management of the family finances.

Angie frequently wrote to Flora, keeping her informed about the family situation. For her part, Flora sent money from Alaska whenever she could. In spite of the geographical distance between them, the bond between Angie and Flora grew tighter.

It was when Angie turned twenty and had completed her two year program at Santa Cruz Community College that, quite by accident Harold Owens proved to be, not only a guardian angel, but cupid as well.

In 1930, Harold and Ethel visited Santa Cruz and advised Maria Luísa to take Palmeda to a doctor. Before taking their leave, Harold had a brief chat with Angie about her schooling. Already well aware of Angie's abilities in math and impressed with her accomplishment at the college, he invited her to visit them in Pasadena. He told Angie he knew of a bank that would be a great place for her to work, in a small town called Arcadia, not far from Pasadena.

Angie, very pleased at the prospect of finding a good job which would enable her to earn more money to help her family. She convinced Maria Luísa to let her travel to Pasadena and, that, if she was offered the job, to take it.

Though Angie was not an adventurer like Flora, she was not afraid of traveling by train on her own to Los Angeles where, as promised, Harold met her and escorted her to his and Ethel's home in Pasadena. The following day he drove her to Arcadia for an interview with his friend, Thomas Hansen, manager of the Arcadia National Bank. Following the interview, Thomas Hansen would see that Angie boarded the Red

Car, a trolley, which would carry her safely back into downtown Los Angeles where she would take the train for home.

The interview went well and Angie left delighted with the
promise of a job. When the Red Car stopped to pick up Angie
and two other people, Hansen waved at the motorman. "Hey,
George. This is my friend, Angie Salvador. She's catching the
train in L.A. to go home to Santa Cruz. Will you be sure she
gets off at the right stop?"

Receiving a nod, a smile, and a friendly wave in return,
Hansen turned to Angie. "This is George Brazil, the best
motorman on the Red Line! You're in good hands." With that
he helped Angie on board watching as she positioned herself
behind the motorman.

Angie waved goodbye to Thomas Hansen and settled
back in her seat. Although confident she knew what she was
doing, she was secretly relieved that someone would be looking out for her. She occasionally glanced at the scenery going
by, but most of her attention was spent studying and chatting
with George Brazil.

Angie guessed George to be ten or more years older than
she. She would later find out the difference was actually fifteen. Though soft spoken, he was friendly and helpful to his
passengers who, Angie noted, all seemed to know and like him.

By the end of the ride, Angie felt comfortable with George.
At one point near the end of the line, she found herself wondering if George liked cats. *Now why did I think of that?*

When they came to Angie's stop, she got off. She was pleased to see George get off as a new motorman arrived and stepped up to take his place. Angie accepted George's offer to escort her to the train station and wait with her until the train to Santa Cruz arrived.

By the time she was on the train headed back to Santa Cruz, Angie knew she was not only eager to start the job at the bank but to spend more time with George Brazil, the Red Line Motorman. With those two thoughts in her head and the rumble of the train rails, she dozed and dreamt of moving from Santa Cruz to Arcadia.

Angie was always so quiet and stayed home so much that Maria Luísa, when she took time to think about it, worried about her daughter's future. When Angie returned home and began chattering about George, Maria Luísa was elated hoping Angie might have found someone with whom to share her life. Listening to level-headed Angie describe George, there was nothing to dislike about him—except, perhaps that he lived so far away.

Angie made the move to Arcadia and went to work at the bank. She rode the Red Car as often as she could, and it was not long until she and George were married. The wedding took place in Holy Cross Church in Santa Cruz. Angie, the new bride, moved into George's house in Arcadia. Because Peepers and Hobo had passed away, Angie arrived in Arcadia with no cats in tow, but the no-cat situation would soon change.

Arcadia, located in the foothills of the San Gabriel
Mountains, was neither a wealthy nor a poor community.
Angie and George's home was small with two bedrooms, a dining room, a living room, a bathroom, and a kitchen. A large
screened porch, a solarium of sorts, led off the back into a
good-sized backyard. A small driveway with a one-car garage
at the end, sat on the right side of their typical stucco-style
California house. They had one car, which, except for getting
them to and from work, the market, and the veterinarian, usually remained on the driveway, allowing them to use the garage
for storage.

Before agreeing to marry him, Angie had verified that
George did, indeed, like cats, though not as well as Angie did.
Could anyone? he wondered. His new wife, almost immediately, began showing up with homeless felines of various sizes,
shapes, and colors. Soon the solarium porch became the cats'
home. During their married life the fewest number the couple
had at any one time was five. Angie loved them all. They were
looked after, pampered, and cherished. Friends speculated
they were the children Angie and George never had.

On a cool Saturday in 1935, Angie received a phone call
from Flora in Anchorage. Throughout the years Flora had
lived in Alaska, she and Angie had exchanged many letters—
the phone call was unexpected. Flora, the sister Angie considered the strongest of the family, sounded shaken as she told
Angie that Mamie had died in Capitola.

"What?" Angie said, flabbergasted.

"Yes, I got a letter from a Maxwell Haggerty, an attorney in Capitola. He sent me a newspaper article about Mamie's death as well as a copy of Mamie's will."

Stunned, Angie asked. "What did they say?"

"The newspaper article says, quote, 'Mamie A. Kohler suffered a painful back injury two years ago.'" She paused before continuing, "'Mrs. Kohler,' it reads, 'has been ill since that time.' It goes on to say, 'she was 39 years, 8 months and 17 days old.'" Flora continued reading from the article, "'A Mass was held at St. Joseph's Church in Capitola. Internment was at Holy Cross Cemetery in Santa Cruz.' She is survived by two sons."

"My God," Angie whispered, "she was buried near the family. How did we not know?"

Flora continued, "The will is very simple, as you might expect. It says Mamie had $282.80 in the bank. She must have been trying to save some money for her boys. She left her share of the Bonny Doon property equally to her sons Leonard and Luke." Flora paused. "My God—two sons! Teenagers!"

She continued, "Listen to this. 'In the event of my death before either of my above named children reach the age of majority, then and in that event I respectfully request the Honorable Court to appoint as my children's guardian, Flora Isley.'"

"That makes good sense," Angie interjected.

"And listen to this last thing she wrote: To my former husband, Walter Kohler, I purposely omit to leave him anything for reasons best known to ourselves.'"

"I can only imagine what all those reasons were!" Angie said sharply.

Flora plowed on, reading the boys' ages. "There is no way Mickey and I can bring those two boys to Anchorage. Ange, *you* have to take them." This wasn't a question. Flora stated it as the obvious solution.

Angie gasped—the thought was so overwhelming she fell silent. She knew in her heart that Flora was probably right—about it not being realistic to move the boys to Alaska. As much as she had enjoyed having a younger sister, she had never pictured herself in a mothering role. At the time she married George, they had discussed children. Angie was adamant she didn't want to have any. In truth, she was afraid that the condition that had affected her grandfather and her sister Palmeda might be passed on. George, who was thirty-six when they married, said he was perfectly fine with not having children. He wanted their life together to be uncomplicated and simple.

"Flora! According to what you just read, I am only ten years older than Luke and seven years older than Leonard!" she said in a weak attempt to convince her sister that this was not a good plan.

"You'll do a good job, Ange," Flora hurried to reassure her. "I'm sure you must be smarter than they are. They are children!"

"For heaven's sake, Flora," Angie said louder, "Leonard must be in high school. At least, I hope Mamie kept them in school!"

Hanging up the phone, Angie, in the same way that Flora had announced to her that the boys must live with them, announced the same thing, practically verbatim, to George. Seeing the look on his wife's face and being the kind and wise man he was, he didn't voice any objections and knew he didn't have another solution to offer.

Flora had informed Angie that the newspaper obituary article said Mamie had worked for a car dealer named Wayne in Watsonville. Going to the telephone book, it didn't take Angie long to find Wayne at Wayne's World of Cars. Wayne, who hadn't known anything about Mamie's family because she never discussed it, wasn't aware she had a sister. He already knew about Mamie's death. "I always liked Mamie," he told Angie. He started to ask her why, if Mamie had a sister, she wasn't around to help Mamie, but he didn't. Once he knew she was looking for the boys, without any hesitation, he gave her the telephone number for Peter Townley in Capitola. "I was the one who introduced her to Peter Townley. He's a life-long friend of mine—an exceptionally nice and kind man. I told him all about Mamie and her problems, and that she and her boys desperately needed a place to go."

Angie hung up the phone realizing she hadn't asked Wayne what he meant when he said *all of her problems*. The statement had frightened her. She felt extremely sad that if her oldest sister had problems, she had not felt she could come home or at least ask one of her sisters for help.

She called Peter Townley in Capitola right away and they talked for a long time. He told her all he knew about Mamie and her debilitating illness. He wasn't far into describing Mamie's condition when Angie realized he was describing the same illness that had killed Palmeda. The memories of how difficult it had been to watch Palmeda's struggles, made it hard to imagine how overwhelming Mamie's life must have been with two young boys. She felt heartsick, nauseous—unable to stop the silent tears flowing down her cheeks.

After listening to Peter, Angie understood why Mamie had not allowed Leonard and Luke to return to the care of their father Wally. She was not surprised.

Angie pulled herself together and started to explain to Peter about Mamie's will. He already knew about it, informing her that he had helped Mamie find an attorney to draw it up. He had handled everything after her death, including her burial and the article in the newspaper, and was aware of Mamie's intention for the boys. She told Peter that she and her husband George would drive to Capitola and pick up Leonard and Luke the next day.

Neither Leonard, a good-looking fifteen—soon to be sixteen-year-old boy—nor Luke, thirteen, took the news that they would be leaving Capitola high school well. Angie had not spent a lot of time around young people, except Annie; nevertheless, she had no trouble recognizing a couple of teen-age rebels when she looked at them. Her anxiety level went up several notches.

In a moment of privacy, Peter Townley told Angie what Mamie had told him—that Leonard had his dad's easy, infectious smile, wavy hair, and twinkly eyes. Angie would later learn from Luke that his older brother always had a constant stream of girl friends.

Grieving for their mother, Leonard and Luke demonstrated a combination of disbelief and anger. They were upset that after all these difficult years taking care of their sick mother, one of their mother's sisters, their aunt, would suddenly turn up, and they would have to pick up and go live with her and her husband. They made it clear they didn't like it.

The boys stood in the yard glaring at Angie. They were different in looks—Luke's eyes larger, darker, and more intense. Angie felt those eyes studying her. Both were thin, though Luke, the younger, had the more athletic build. Standing side by side, they sullenly stared down at their diminutive aunt.

Luke was silent as his older brother spoke, but Angie knew she and George would hear plenty from this younger one soon. With George standing a few feet behind her, Angie met their icy stares with unreadable looks of her own. Though small, their Aunt Angie was wiry and stood firmly planted in front of them. The look on her face made it clear this was a plan they would have to live with.

Together Leonard and Luke lashed out at Peter for letting this happen. The boys had mixed feelings about leaving Peter. He had been nice enough and treated them okay. After they had moved in with Peter their mother's illness had

become increasingly worse. She demanded all of Peter's attention. They complained to each other in private that this wasn't
fair either. They were on their own most of the time in those
three years. Peter was not a wealthy man. He managed to keep
food on the table and buy them clothes when needed. On a
few occasions he had loaded the boys into the back seat of
his car, lifted Mamie into the front passenger seat, and driven
them down the hill to the Capitola Movie Theater. Having pre-
arranged with the manager of the theater, he drove up alongside the theater and sent the boys in to open up the side door.
This allowed him to lift Mamie and carry her inside the theater
to watch the movie. The boys thought it was fantastic to get
to see any movie. Mamie was completely overwhelmed by the
goodness of this man Peter. The rare treat of going to a movie
re-confirmed her belief that Peter was their Guardian Angel.

Angie and George packed the two angry boys and their
modest belongings into their car and headed back to Arcadia.
Following George into the house and seeing ten cats roaming about and plastic coverings on the living room furniture,
Leonard said "My God, we've gone to hell."

Luke blew out some air and muttered, "No shit."

George looked at the two boys, shrugged his shoulders in
a manner that said, *Get used to it*, and lead them down a hallway
to the bedroom they would share.

Angie's first act, filling in as the boys' guardian, was to
enroll them in the Monrovia, Arcadia, Duarte Union High

School. Both boys were likeable and readily accepted by the other teenagers. Leonard was not a great student but managed to get passing grades. Luke, without much studying, managed to get A's in those classes he found interesting and C's in his other classes. Academics aside, Luke, though two years younger, successfully kept up with Leonard on the social scene. He preferred hanging out with Leonard's friends rather than classmates his own age. For some reason, Leonard not only tolerated this, but, most of the time, encouraged it. During their earlier childhood years, a solid bond built out of necessity had been formed. Leonard would say terrible things to and about Luke but others who tried to do so found themselves on the pavement looking up at Leonard whose wiry body and flailing fists posed an immediate threat to their looks. Leonard demanded they say they were sorry and convince him they really meant it or there would be consequences to pay!

Luke chose to play a supporting role with all of Leonard's girlfriends. Stringing several girls along at the same time was Leonard's norm. There had hardly been a break in his youthful amorous stride since arriving from Capitola. Girls found the younger Luke very witty and fun to be around. Using Leonard as his role model, Luke was a quick learner, tucking away all he observed for use later. Letting Luke hang around all the time made the girls think Leonard was a nicer person than he actually was. He wrongly considered Luke too young to be a rival for the older girls' attention. Luke thought Leonard often treated the girls shabbily, using them for a while for his amusement and then discarding them. Luke used his quick humor and likeability to keep the girls from getting hurt too badly. It didn't always work.

Often in the evenings Leonard crept out the bedroom window with Luke right behind him. They sneaked into pool halls and bars unnoticed—thanking their dad for teaching them in the ins and outs of that lifestyle. Leonard found ways to get beer and cigarettes and liked prowling around, checking out anything interesting happening at the moment.

When Angie received the notice from the high school telling her Leonard would actually graduate, she was both ecstatic and relieved. She wondered how he managed to get a diploma but prudently decided to thank God and not ask questions. Following graduation, Leonard, now old enough to be an independent young man, stayed on with Angie and George. Angie knew he did this only so he would be with Luke. He worked at odd jobs, saying he didn't know what he wanted to do with the rest of his life. One day, seeing a recruiter's office, he enlisted in the Army. He returned home and told Luke, Angie, and George that he would be leaving within days for boot camp. Not knowing anything better to suggest, Angie and George agreed this was probably a smart thing for Leonard to do.

Hearing Leonard's announcement, Luke's look was totally unreadable. Angie could only imagine that, once again, his world had tumbled down. Without saying anything, he went into his and Leonard's room banging the door behind him. Angie and George wondered how they would keep Luke in line without Leonard around. They need not have worried. Following Leonard's departure on an early fall evening in 1940, sixteen-year-old Luke wrote a note to Aunt Angie and George telling them not to worry, crawled out the window, and boarded a bus to Los Angeles.

Luke, who could talk most anyone into anything, sought out an Army recruiting office, claimed he was 18, and signed up.

After reading Luke's note, Angie and George decided not to call the police to search for him. They had learned the two brothers were not only determined to, but capable of, being on their own. Angie wrote to Flora to tell her what had happened. At night they each prayed for the boys' safety. George reassured her that she would hear from Luke later when he was ready. The truant officer from the high school who had come to know Leonard and Luke well, was not so accepting, letting them know he was continuing to search for Luke. To compensate for two fewer mouths to feed, as well as to soothe her guilt, Angie brought home Lucky and Lucy, two scruffy long-haired kittens found dumped in a sack by the side of the road.

1913

ANNIE MARGARIDA SALVADOR

SANTA CRUZ, CALIFORNIA

Michael steeled himself, squared his shoulders, and settled into an empty seat in the waiting room at Santa Cruz General Hospital. A nurse had already taken Maria Luísa into the delivery room. He looked around at the three other men sitting there, wondering about them. *Are they first time fathers? Do they have sons? Do they know what it's like to have five girls?* His sigh was audible. The others looked at him. He was used to people staring at him. He knew they were surprised when they first saw his mustache—thick and black on one side, thick and almost white on the other.

He gave them a bleak smile. His thoughts turned first toward his family, then ardently, as had been the case five times before, to God. He thought about what he could possibly say to God this time that he had not already said over these past seventeen years to get his attention. *Have I not been a faithful servant? Have I not been a good man? Have I not been a good father? Have I not been a generous and fair man? Don't I deserve to have a son?* He sighed more deeply. This time no one looked up.

It barely registered with Michael when the nurses came out and called each of the men who were there before him. He was startled when he finally heard his own name and felt a hand on his shoulder. "Mr. Salvador?" The nurse had a broad, happy smile on her face. "Your wife and baby are ready for you." She turned on her heel expecting him to follow.

Entering the room, he saw Maria Luísa looking tired but beautiful as she always did after giving birth. Once again she held a little wrapped bundle in her arms high on her chest over her heart. He looked pleadingly into her eyes. "It's Annie," she said, holding the little bundle in one arm so he could see the baby's face. She squeezed Michael's hand with her free one. She heard him inhale deeply. Then he gave her the smallest of smiles, bent over, and, as he had done five times in the past, kissed her forehead. He gently touched his sixth daughter's head and looked into Maria Luísa's eyes. "God has certainly given me his final answer, hasn't he? There will be no more babies." He returned the squeeze to Maria Luísa's hand and left the room. It was then Maria Luísa gave her own fervent thanks to God.

Annie Margarida Salvador, called *Annie* or, sometimes, *Babe* by her family, was, like Flora, a very observant child. She watched everyone, saw everything, and delighted in it all. She adored her older sisters. She seemed to be a composite of each of them, as well as her parents.

If Mamie was the romantic, Flora the explorer, Palmeda the homemaker, Angie the realist, and Alice the risk-taker, it soon became obvious that Annie was the artist. At a very early age, she translated her powers of observation into things of beauty. She not only painted and created objects out of any mud or clay she could find, she wrote poetry so beautiful her words made the reader weep. Her voice was like an angel. Many faithful parishioners came to the church at Christmas just for the joy of hearing Annie sing *Ave Maria*. At the family's Sunday beach outings, her sand sculptures attracted crowds "oohing" and "aahing" at how clever and detailed they were. On one occasion, she carved a particularly intricate sculpture. It was a beautiful rose surrounded by six angels, each different. With a smile, Maria Luísa noted that the angels bore a definite resemblance to the six Salvador sisters. She was sorry when the tide came in and swept it out to sea. At the age of twelve, Annie carved a small box out of rosewood scraps given to her by one of the town wood carvers for a school art project. A beautiful rose adorned the lid.

As she grew older, Annie continued to enjoy creating new pieces in various mediums, but painting became her passion. Each new painting showed the beauty, humor, earthiness and wonder of something joyous she had seen.

Many pundits said artists were better if they had endured a life of suffering—some of Annie's neighbors among them.

Amidst the joy of her young life, Annie had certainly experienced great losses and sorrow. Many whom she had loved so dearly were lost in the very early years of her life. Each of these losses had touched her deeply. Though just three when Flora's first husband, Joe, died, she could recall feeling Flora's deep sadness as though it were her own. Only seven when her father died, Annie was left with a gaping hole in her heart to be filled with the many memories of him captured through fantastic stories shared by her older sisters. She often gazed for long periods of time at the photograph of him on the stairwell wall showing his dark, piercing eyes and formidable black and white mustache. Though dead, to Annie he was always bigger than life. She sometimes stood in front of his picture reading him her poetry, frequently looking up to see what he thought. On the back of many of her own childhood paintings, the words "I love you, Papa" were scrawled in her childish hand.

The same year Papa died, Mamie ran away. In Annie's mind, Mamie's story would remain forever the story of a princess' broken heart, and love gone wrong. Watching Palmeda suffer the agonies of a horrible, mysterious, strange, cruel, and unbearable condition had deeply impacted Annie. She was twenty-three when Meda died.

Annie's pre-teen years spanned the enthusiastically wild and Roaring Twenties with its jazz, prohibition, and unending parade of flappers, speakeasies, barnstorming, and flying circuses. When she should have been delighting in turning sweet sixteen, her life was swiftly changed by the devastating crash of the stock market sinking all Americans into the Great Depression. Although Santa Cruz fared far better than other places throughout the country, its residents were affected by the economic downturn as well.

By then her father was no longer living, Flora was living in Alaska, and Mamie was who-knew-where. Her three other older sisters were working to contribute to the family's survival. After school, she hurried home to help her mother. The times were difficult for everyone—the Salvador girls included.

The eternal optimist, Annie relied on her art to counter each staggering problem as it swirled around her. Life's bleakness could not still the beauty she found in nature and created in her imagination. With the Depression in full force, Annie and her classmates graduated from high school in 1931.

Even the Depression was not great enough to daunt Annie's love for art—her passion. Letters from Flora were like life preservers encouraging her to follow her heart and not lose sight of the talents God had given her. Annie set goals for herself. One of these was to move north to San Francisco to explore the art world. She had heard and read about the famous art colonies in the San Francisco area. Feeling so sure the big city would inspire her, she told her mother that San Francisco was calling her.

During Palmeda's struggles, Annie stayed close to home to help her mother take care of her older sister. As the youngest daughter assigned to work outside, she, like her other sisters, had a love-hate relationship with the garden. They loved the food, the smells, and the good cheer of the flowers and they hated the hard work it took to maintain it. Annie found the earth dark, warm, and comforting. The colors and the smells invigorated her creativity. As a very young child with pain and sorrow moving in and out of her life, she found solace in the garden.

One day Annie, twenty-six, was working in the garden and wondering how on earth she was going to accomplish her goals. She looked down at the handful of dirt she held in her hand and thought, *I own a parcel of land.* She remembered Palmeda had sold her share to Flora. A wave of sadness passed over her as she recalled the sad ending of Palmeda's life. The parcel of land Papa had left her older sister never did go to Meda's dreams; instead it had been used to take care of her as death embraced her. She wondered if Papa, wherever in the universe his soul rested, could even imagine how the land had provided for his third daughter.

With these thoughts about the Salvador's Bonny Doon land swirling in her head, Annie left the garden and retreated to her room where she settled down on her bed to begin a letter to Flora. She wanted her sister to know how very much she wished to go to San Francisco to pursue her dream of being a *real* artist. She wanted to tell Flora that people said she had talent, yet she knew there was so much more she needed to learn.

Dear Flora,

Would you please, please buy the parcel of the Bonny Doon land Papa left me so I can have money to move to San Francisco and become a <u>real</u> artist? You see, San Francisco is <u>My Alaska</u>." She added a sketch of an airplane with a woman pilot flying over a girl standing at an easel, paintbrush at hand, looking up waving. She signed the letter,

With love to my Alaskan Guardian Angel.
Babe

Soon another Quit Claim Deed changed hands and, at the age of twenty-seven, Annie Margarida Salvador moved north.

San Francisco turned out to be merely a stepping stone for Annie. In San Francisco she was fortunate to find a job waiting tables at a small café, no small feat with jobs hard to find. The Bay Leaf Café was located on Chestnut Street not far from where she had found a room to rent. A gregarious and likeable person, Annie easily made friends.

A few months later on Labor Day weekend, one of these friends, Gina, invited Annie and a couple of other girl friends, Priscilla and Paula, to drive to Sausalito, a glorious community located north of San Francisco. They drove across the already famous Golden Gate Bridge which had opened to vehicles the year before, pooling their money to pay the dollar plus five cent round trip ticket—the five cents being a surcharge for more than three travelers. Sausalito was a haven for artists who had flocked there for years. The city's amazingly beautiful bay, dotted with ships, and surrounded by a gorgeous natural habitat, provided plenty of inspiration for its resident artists.

Annie felt like she had arrived in heaven. She and her friends joined the scores of others wandering through the town. San Francisco had many artists scattered throughout the city, yet Sausalito was different—everywhere she turned artists were either painting, sculpting, making jewelry, or creating other art forms that dazzled her. At times Annie saw paintings or ceramic pieces she thought to be weird or crazy, and she wondered whether the artist needed, or perhaps was already in, therapy. Some of the offerings caused her to laugh in pure delight. Throughout the afternoon she stopped and chatted with many artists—all eager to talk about their work.

Annie and her friends stayed in Sausalito well into the evening. The town didn't lack in small cafes and bars and she smiled as she watched people eating, drinking and, she thought, *definitely being merry*. The revelry of the customers overflowing the numerous eateries was contagious. When it came time to head back to San Francisco, Annie didn't want to leave. She had fallen under the spell of Sausalito. She felt magic in the air. Once they were in the car heading back across the bridge she told her friends, "I feel like I belong in Sausalito—some force is pulling me there." They all laughed, yet Annie knew in her heart it was true.

Once back in San Francisco, Annie immediately began executing her new plan. She worked hard, putting in as many hours at the café as the owner would allow. Borrowing newspapers from her friends, or picking up those left by customers in the café, Annie looked for ads listing Sausalito rooms to rent. She knew her Bonny Doon property money wouldn't last very long. Much to her chagrin, she discovered Sausalito to be as expensive as San Francisco. She found very few ads for small studio apartments or rooms to rent which met both her needs and her budget.

In 1940, Annie returned to Santa Cruz to attend her sister Alice's wedding. She had not been surprised to learn about the wedding taking place so soon after Alice met Nathan. *After all*, Annie thought, *that's exactly the kind of thing Alice would do.* As did the rest of the family, Annie liked Nathan immediately. She thought he was the perfect match for Alice and felt happy for her sister.

Arriving home, she was shocked when she saw her mother. She had received notes from Angie who said Mama was looking frail. At the wedding, Annie pulled Angie aside and said, "Frail! What do you mean *frail*? She looks like if someone sneezes, it will blow her over."

Following the wedding, Angie and her husband, George, returned to their home in Arcadia leaving Annie to stay with her mother until Alice and Nathan returned from their honeymoon. Once they were back, she returned to Sausalito only to come back home less than two months later after receiving a call from Alice saying Maria Luísa had collapsed and died.

Annie was seven when her papa died. She thought about how she had spent every day after that looking at pictures of her family. After her mother's funeral, Annie returned to Sausalito and painted a small beautiful picture of a young Maria Luísa wearing a crown of yellow and white flowers on top of her dark hair. Annie told herself she would pass it on to her daughter, if she ever had one so she, too, would know how beautiful her grandmother had been.

Nine months later, Annie managed to make her move and settle in Sausalito. She found a small studio apartment located above one of the many art galleries. Once again, she felt fortunate when the owner of a small café and bar, *Angelos*, hired her. She worked evenings, leaving the days for sleeping, painting, and visiting the numerous art galleries in the city. She talked with an endless number of artists and other people involved in the art world. Annie soon felt she had arrived "home."

Gradually, she came to be accepted as one of the Sausalito art community in-crowd. When asked how she had managed that, she laughed and said it was because her own work was not a threat to the other artists. They accepted her as a kindred spirit who loved and appreciated art, artists, and their beloved Sausalito. She frequented the galleries and attended more artist openings than she could count—developing close personal friendships along the way, thriving on the entire Sausalito art scene.

Annie was good looking with straight dark hair, olive skin, and large sparkling eyes. She was not only vivacious but affable and a welcome addition to any gathering. Her deep laughter always seemed to lie beneath the surface ready to bubble up at any moment. Never vying for acclaim for her own art work over theirs, she was accepted by most of the other artists. When groups of artists gathered viewing each other's work, Annie's nature was to be honest and kind—most always managing to find something in the other artist's work to praise. When she felt compelled to point out something negative, she had a talent for turning the conversation so the artist eventually saw the same thing, thinking it was his or her own observation. If she simply could not see anything at all redeeming in the work, she artfully swung the conversation towards something else of mutual interest.

Occasionally, a fellow artist or art lover was less than excited about Annie. These were usually women who feared their current boyfriends or lovers found Annie far too interesting. When their men were not around, these women, too, appeared to enjoy Annie's company.

By reading the daily newspaper and scanning the flyers she found posted everywhere, Annie discovered many free demonstrations and other offerings of watercolor painting techniques—managing to take a few paid classes along the way. She sold some of her paintings at *The Bay Gallery* when a friend of hers, Madelyn Olivera, who owned the gallery, allowed her to bring in her work with a discounted consignment fee.

A year after WWII ended—five years after moving to Sausalito— Annie attended a Sausalito Art Gala at the home of her very good friend, Miriam Ledos, Madelyn Olivera's sister. The Art Gala was being held to introduce the paintings of Zico Carvalho, a bright young painter from Brazil. Annie had not seen any of Carvalho's work, or even heard much about him when Miriam called to invite her. Having worked late at the Gallery the day of the Gala, Annie hurried home, changed her clothes, and rushed to get herself across town.

The party was already in full swing when she arrived. Annie dashed up the stairs to the bedroom to deposit her poncho and purse. Once back downstairs, she noted the table laden with a delectable variety of beautifully presented foods, including an assortment of her favorite, chocolate. A pleasant looking young man—one of the caterers—asked Annie what she would care to drink. She requested a daiquiri, her personal current favorite. The server scurried away and within minutes returned to hand Annie a chilled glass.

Annie, suddenly feeling like she was starving, could barely recall what she had for lunch—if anything. She was juggling a small plate, a napkin, and her drink glass while trying to decide how best to get a few more of the hors'd'oeuvres onto the plate, when a deep, heavily-accented voice from behind her said, "'Scuse me, Miss. It looks like you could use some help. Please. Let me hold your glass."

"That would be...," she didn't finish her comment as she turned to stare into the most intense dark eyes she'd ever seen. She wasn't sure if they were dark brown or totally black. The man's full black eyebrows arched slightly as he returned her stare with an amused quizzical look. Thick black hair, uncontrolled around his face and ears, brushed the collar of the bright blue and white striped shirt showing beneath his khaki jacket. A generous smile of straight white teeth set off by his dark golden-brown skin, gleamed. Though not classically handsome, Annie liked his face—deciding it looked like he had traveled through many adventures in life—each adding character. His smile and eyes sparkled with a gentle humor, leading her to believe he must be a caring soul. Realizing how intently she had been looking at him, she blushed, struggling to regain her composure.

He lifted her glass out of one hand, freeing her to select what she wanted from the array of foods before them. "Thank you," she said, smiling back. She selected a few hors d'oeuvres. Realizing just how hungry she felt, she added more until a small mound of assorted tidbits covered the plate. She saw her new acquaintance's amused look. Again she blushed slightly, lamely explaining, "Uh, I skipped lunch."

Giving a low chuckle and without handing back her glass, he motioned her to follow him. They went out into a very large room filled with people. Display easels had been placed around the outer circle of the room. Bright colored paintings were arranged on the mantle and the many book shelves. Several people caught her eye, calling out "Hey, Annie, glad you're here!" or, "Annie, are you at the gallery tomorrow?" or

just "Annie" with a smile and a wave. She waved and nodded as she continued following the khaki-colored jacket, dark
tousled hair, and her drink across the room. The man carrying
the drink stepped through open doors out onto a large deck
swarming with people.

It was a lovely, late summer evening and Annie took in a
deep breath of the fresh air, wondering when her guide would
stop walking.

As though reading her mind, he abruptly stopped. She
nearly ran into his back having to juggle her plate while stopping just short of a collision. She thought how horribly ironic
it would be if this nice man who had rescued her at the table
ended up wearing the foods she had selected. He turned,
waited for her to reposition her plate, and handed her back
her glass. She accepted it but then looked between glass, fork,
and the man. Once again he chuckled and said, "Take a sip. I'll
hold it while you enjoy your food."

Annie returned his smile and gobbled down the food. As
she looked around for a place to get rid of the plate, a server
passed by and took it.

Her companion gave her back her glass then lifted his
own in a silent toast. They stood for a few moments enjoying the summer air and watching the people on the deck who
were chatting in small groups. Annie recognized several of
Sausalito's better-known artists and noticed many who were
newcomers. She watched the man beside her gazing at the

people and gardens surrounding the deck. "So you are Annie," he said amicably.

Annie was surprised. "Yes I am. The way you said my name makes it sounds as though you know me, but I don't know your name."

Chuckling, he responded, "How could I not know your name? Everyone we walked by on the way out here called out the name 'Annie' and you answered or waved. It was not exactly difficult on my part." Annie heard the thick accent reminding her of her father. "Well, it's a good guess. I'm Annie Salvador." She held out her hand.

"Please call me Zee," he said. Before he could go on, Miriam Ledos, their hostess, stepped up and took hold of the man's arm.

Staring at Annie's companion, she said, "I've been looking all over for you. I see you met Annie." With that she gave Annie a warm hug and turned back to Annie's companion. "Come with me. There's someone I want you to meet." She smiled at Annie and pulled the man with her, heading back into the house.

Annie laughed and waved them off. She walked about chatting with friends. Her friend Vivian joined her to look at the art displayed around the deck and throughout the house. The colors of the paintings were bright and bold—their vibrancy and humor made her smile. Hard-edged contemporary was her favorite style and she liked most of the paintings she saw. She came to an abrupt stop in front of one displayed in the library. Vivian spotted someone else she knew and moved on leaving Annie to enjoy the artist's work on her own.

The painting drew her in. The artist, Carvalho, had painted two birds sitting on a branch filled with jungle-like heart-shaped leaves—the birds clearly seeing nothing but each other. The vibrant colors—blue, red, purple, and pink—emitted an inescapable energy. The birds were simple and graphic in line, with the larger, two-toned turquoise and white bird, presumably the male, sitting on the left leaning towards a slightly smaller two-toned magenta bird—their beaks almost touching. The large wing of the male bird extended forward and around the smaller bird as though embracing it. The background was emblazoned with multiple circles of color—a partial circle of gold in the upper left hand corner depicting a hot tropical sun.

What amazing doves, Annie thought—*So simple and yet bursting with such passion for life and love for each other.* While the painting made Annie smile happily, as she looked at it, she felt a surge of melancholy and regret. She wondered if the regret stemmed from the fact that she, herself, had not yet found her own life partner.

With a heavy sigh, she leaned forward to read the simple white tag posted on the wall behind the mantle where the painting sat. The title read *Two Birds* with the artist's name, *Zico Carvalho*, printed beneath it. The price seized her attention. It read $750. "Yikes!" She said under her breath.

A familiar deep voice said, "You like it, then, if you are checking out the price?"

Glancing up she saw Zee. Looking back at the painting, she said, "I love it. It's so refreshing—cheery and at the same time— passionate. If those two birds are as in love as they appear, how could it do anything other than make me wish for the same?" She paused, then said, "And you? How does it make you feel?"

Zee studied the painting. Thoughtfully he answered, "Yes. You are right. The birds—each different from the other yet sharing the same spirit and vitality—know they have found the love they have been looking for."

Again Miriam Ledos interrupted, this time taking hold of Zee's arm on one side and Annie's on her other. "Come you two. Join me as I introduce my new Brazilian star."

Annie was eager to finally see the artist Zico Carvalho. It was unusual for her to be attending a gala for an artist she had heard so little of before. She knew Miriam had been out and about town discussing how talented her new-found Brazilian discovery was and how eager she was to introduce him to Sausalito. Carvalho was well known in his own country but not yet in the United States. Earlier in the year, Miriam had visited Sao Paulo, Brazil, where she had seen his paintings. Thinking they were incredible, she had talked him into bringing some of his work to California. Miriam, very influential in the art community, had found and launched other talented artists in past years. Having been busy on a project, Annie had not seen Miriam since her return from Brazil.

Once in The Great Room, as she loved to call it, Miriam led them towards a massive fireplace where a small beautifully crafted black Mexican bell sat on the mantelpiece. Miriam picked it up and rang it—gaining the attention of her guests. The once-dispersed crowd now flowed into The Great Room.

"What a beautiful summer evening," Miriam began, "for having friends get together, have a few drinks, break a little bread, and best of all, to share in new and beautiful treasures for our eyes and for our souls." A pleasant murmur of agreement spread throughout the room. "While I think I've managed to get around to many of you introducing this extraordinary talent and my new friend, known to his Brazilian friends as Zee, I want to take a minute to formally introduce him so all of you can know Zico Carvalho—the man as well as his work."

When Miriam said "Zee" Annie's face turned red. She lowered her gaze, hoping she wasn't glowing like a pink candle. *How could I have been so stupid? Zico. Zee. How many Z names do I know? None. How could I have not put it together? The dark Brazilian good looks. The accent. The name Carvalho. Good God!* She, who prided herself on learning as much about the artists in or coming to Sausalito closed her eyes. *How could I have not known!*

Looking up, Annie was relieved to notice the crowd's attention completely focused on Zico "Zee" Carvalho. Adding to her embarrassment, Annie realized that while she was chastising herself, she had missed hearing what Miriam was saying about him. Wishing she could disappear, Annie edged closer to the side of the mantle so she could, she hoped, fade away into the crowd. At that moment a pair of arms circled her waist from behind and a tall blond good looking guy bent his head down beside her cheek. "My Annie," he whispered, "You look a bit flustered. Are you okay?"

Annie recognized her good friend Richard Wize—Richie. She let her left hand drift up, patted him on the cheek, and nodded. Richie straightened but kept his arms around her waist. Annie noticed Zee looking her way. He was smiling and she shyly returned his smile.

With Miriam's introduction ended, the crowd enveloped Zico Carvalho. Annie drifted off with Richie to find their friend—his love of the moment, Theodore. The trio chatted and moved about the rooms looking at more of the paintings. Annie loved the way Miriam had displayed them. Some hung on the walls, some were on easels, some were simply placed on tables and shelves—all brightening the décor. Miriam had marvelous lighting in her lavish home and each painting was illuminated as though it alone was the star of the evening. Theodore and Annie admired Carvalho's use of the extraordinarily vibrant colors. Richie, whose paintings tended to be stuck in the varied colors of sand, made remarks indicating he was not at all envious of the newcomer's obvious talents and, moreover, could not understand why the crowd was so enthralled.

Later in the evening, Richie and Theodore said their goodbyes to Annie, each giving her a warm embrace before departing. Annie found her way back into the library where she wanted to take one more look at *Two Birds*. She again found it uplifting. It made her smile. What didn't make her smile was seeing the red dot on the tag indicating the painting was sold.

Ah well, it's not as though I have $750 hidden under my mattress.

She wove her way upstairs to retrieve her poncho and purse. Downstairs, she spotted Miriam surrounded by many guests, and moved in to say thank you and tell her how delighted she was to see such remarkable paintings. She gave her friend a big hug and said her good night. She looked around for Zee to apologize and tell him she thought his work was outstanding. He was nowhere to be seen.

It was the end of August, a few days after the gala and a week before the local galleries were to hold an Art Extravaganza, when Annie invited about thirty of her good friends to come by her house for drinks and to enjoy another glorious day of summer. Everyone in the art community had been arduously working on the Extravaganza. If asked, most would have agreed that Annie's get-together would be a fun way to celebrate the *glorious daze* of summer. Annie's friends, tired, though in good spirits, looked forward to her party.

Annie's parties were spur-of-the-moment and were always casual. Invitations were by word of mouth—friends telling other friends—with anyone who got the word welcome to come. Annie made a huge pot of *Caldeirada á Moda do Pescador da Maria Luísa* and *Pão Estendido* thinking, as she always did when she made it, about her parents and her sisters. Most of Annie's friends arrived with food or drink in hand to contribute to the evening's offerings. The result was a worldly and eclectic collection of foods.

Three years prior, Annie had been delighted to find a small house on the side of the hill. She bravely decided to buy it, although, at the time, she felt like she was signing away her life. She smiled when she first saw the tiny front yard surrounded by a short wooden fence. In the tradition of the Salvador family, she intended to plant lots of flowers in the yard. Now, already, there were several flowering bushes near the entry way, creating a welcoming effect. A winding path and a few stairs led the way to a porch circling around the house where a front door, painted bright red awaited.

A playful ceramic figurine of a mermaid holding a bouquet of flowers hung to one side of the door. Annie had made it soon after her arrival in Sausalito. Her friends had come to expect some new art piece, painting, ceramic, or sculpture added for each party—this night a tiny angel holding a single yellow rose sat on the tail of the mermaid.

Inside the small house, the lighting was dim. Numerous candles were placed on almost all available flat surfaces, giving a warm glow to each room. As always, six round white candles, each a different height, were spread out in a line down the middle of the old wooden dining table. Tonight, sitting closer to the walls were the dining room chairs, each painted a different bright color.

The walls of the living room, painted a light sand color, provided a welcoming background for the many colorful paintings and ceramic pieces Annie displayed. Everywhere her friends looked they discovered some visual and, most often, whimsical surprise. The rugs on the dark wood floors added warmth to the rooms—each simple hand-woven design composed of different and colorful geometric patterns. The furniture was a conglomeration of dark wood pieces Annie had found at thrift shops and re-stained. A multitude of colorful stuffed cushions and pillows tossed about invited guests to settle in.

A small kitchen had been tucked into a corner at the back of the house. Someone who had lived there before Annie had been into carpentry and cabinetry and had taken out one square corner of the house and replaced it with a circular space. The space held a small round table with a built-in curved bench. Large windows drew all who entered to look out on a small garden filled with wildflowers and a central birdbath designed by Annie, herself. At night, a few lanterns interspersed throughout the greenery, lent a mystical quality. While there was not much room in the kitchen, the central cabinetry channeled people in a circular flow around the kitchen and back into the dining room the way they had entered. The walls were covered with shelves filled with Portuguese cook books, interspersed with ceramic or wood-carved treasures. Nothing shouted *expensive* or *elegant*, but all had been put together with

Annie's artistic eye ensuring the viewer a smile. *Whimsical is good*, she often thought.

All first-time visitors remarked on Annie's bathroom—a red claw- footed tub was the center of attention. The walls and floor were painted a Mediterranean blue while the single small cabinet holding two sinks below the mirror was bright purple. It was at a rummage sale that Annie had found two rose-shaped sconces to hold the lamps displayed on either side of the mirror. A small rug woven of the same colors covered almost the entire floor. On the wall over the commode hung another of Annie's whimsical paintings—this one an angel.

Entering Annie's bedroom, the first thing one noticed was the huge bed which almost filled the room. Behind the brass headboard, the purple wall held Annie's newest works—six paintings of flowers displayed three to a row. Each square frame was filled with a bright flower—all different in kind and color—inspired by each of the six Salvador sisters. Annie had selected a purple and white daisy for Mamie, a red bougainvillea for Flora, and a white Madonna lily for Meda. She thought a bright yellow-orange sunflower was fitting for Alice, a blue hydrangea for Angie, and for herself—a single yellow rose.

A long, hand-crafted rosewood dresser filled the opposite wall. On each side of the bed, small tables sat holding lamps with colorful stained glass shades. The wall facing the bed was blank. Annie was trying to decide what she wanted to paint next. Whatever it turned out to be would go in that space.

Richie and Theodore, the first to arrive, helped Annie set the food on the table and the drinks on the kitchen counter. When Annie's other friends arrived, they were all soon helping themselves to food, wine, or other drinks, while roaming about chatting. The party was quiet in comparison with Annie's past parties. People came and went. Most talked enthusiastically about the anticipated Art Extravaganza—conversation focused on what remained to be done in less than a week-pieces of art to be completed; transportation of larger sculptures, paintings, ceramic pieces; and a myriad of other details. Everyone, with the exception of Miriam, left early.

Once they were alone, Miriam said, "Annie, I brought you something, but I didn't want to bring it in when everyone was here. It's in my car." She smiled.

"What is it?" Annie said, puzzled.

Together they walked arm in arm to where Miriam's Woody Wagon was parked. Opening the back door, Annie saw a large wrapped package. By its shape, she assumed it to be a framed painting. "What's this?" she asked?

Miriam ignored the question and said, "Let's carry it into the house." The piece was about four feet by four feet. The women each grabbed an opposite side and carried it back to the house, up the stairs, and into Annie's living room, once there, leaning it against the bookcase.

"I've got to rush, Annie. I have a zillion things to do tomorrow. Nice party as usual." And with that, Miriam gave Annie a quick hug, hurried out the door, waving as she skipped down the stairs and out to the street.

Annie closed the door and locked up. She was curious about the package but noticed a couple of the candles on the shelves were burning low. She blew them out then moved through the rest of the house extinguishing all other candles except the six large ones on the dining room table. She always saved those for last. Happy for their golden glow, Annie picked up her wine glass, went into the bedroom, undressed, and slipped into her soft blue, well-worn lounging pajamas.

She padded barefoot back into the living room and stood in front of the wrapped package teasing herself by delaying the opening. She stared at the package, wondering what Miriam had given her. Finally she could stand it no more and undid the tape and lifted away the brown paper wrapping. She gasped in disbelief at what she saw.

Staring back at her were the two *Amazing Doves* painted by Zico Carvalho. The candlelight glow lent softness to the bright colors, yet she could feel the Dove's passionate energy. She flopped down on the sofa across from the painting, soaking it in. It took a minute for her to notice a very small white envelope taped to the outer lower edge of the frame. She carefully removed it and sat down on the sofa. Opening the card, she read,

When I was painting this, I felt in my soul that it was meant for someone very special. I now know that someone is you. May it always bring you happiness. It was signed *Zee.*

Annie picked up the painting and carefully carried it to her bedroom. She set it on top of the long dresser across from her bed. She hurried back into the dining room to blow out the six candles and followed her usual ritual by reciting, "Boa noite Flora Estelle—then repeating the phrase from her childhood to each sister— Terezinha Palmeda—Mamie Antónia—Angelina Gabriela—Alice Efigeria." This was followed by "Boa noite Mama and Papa. Minha familia, eu vos amo todos."

Annie returned to her room and crawled under her comforter to gaze happily at the two doves basking in the soft glow of one of her bedside lamps. As Annie fell asleep she was sure she saw the turquoise dove's dark eye wink at her.

The next morning Annie called Miriam. Miriam didn't know which painting Zee had sent because the day after the gala at her home, the unsold paintings and those to be picked up later by their new owners went to the Bayshore Gallery which Miriam's sister Madelyn owned. They were to be held until picked up by the new owners or sent elsewhere to be displayed. Zico Carvalho had asked Madelyn to wrap it up with the envelope attached and to have it delivered to Annie's house, then he had returned to Brazil. Madelyn, knowing Miriam was going to be coming into the Gallery that day and later going to Annie's party, asked her to deliver it. Miriam gave Annie Zee's business address in Sao Paulo.

Annie sent him a note reading,

Dear Zee. I will think of your kind heart, tender soul, and over-whelming generosity each morning when I awaken to be greeted by the Amazing Doves. Seeing them will remind me that today will surely be my best yet. Each night in return I will share with them the wonders of the moments the day did bring! Muitissimo obrigado. She signed, *Annie.*

Five months later in early January, Annie picked up her phone to hear the deep accented voice say, "Annie. It's Zee."

Annie had not realized how much she had hoped some-day they would meet again. Though he was far away in Brazil, he was in her life each day as she awakened to the *Amazing Doves* and went to sleep feeling safe as they watched over her. They brought her feelings of overwhelming happiness, joy, good cheer, hope, peace, and safety. From their arrival, she realized how empty her life had been without them. The *Amazing Doves* showed passion. She knew they exemplified the passion for life she wanted to bring to each of her own paintings. She wanted to learn how to do what Zico Carvalho did—give those people who saw her paintings a glimpse of her own passion.

After a second, Annie recovered and said, "Zee-Zico. How wonderful to hear from you. You will never know how very much I love *The Amazing Doves*. I was so overwhelmed to receive them."

She heard his deep chuckle "*The Amazing Doves?* That is what you called them in your note. You still call them that?"

"Oh yes. Because they are simply amazing, you know!" And then without thinking she added, "Will you teach me how to paint with such passion!"

"I would love to teach you, Annie. Thank you."

"Thank you?"

Again he chuckled. "Yes, thank you. I was going to invite you to have dinner with me somewhere, but instead you have asked me to teach you passion. So I thank you."

It was her turn to laugh. After confirming he really was in Sausalito, she said, "Do you like Portuguese food?"

This time, his was a deep and enthusiastic laugh. "I am from Brazil—of course I like Portuguese food. Long ago my family came to Brazil from Portugal."

She invited him to come to her home and join her for dinner. He did and together they enjoyed her *Carne Assada Açoreana, Salada de tomate com queijos, and Pão, with Pasteis de Nata* for dessert. They drank one bottle of *Basalto* and had barely started on the second when she received her first lesson in passion.

Annie had enjoyed a few lovers in the course of her young life— each was fun, and some were delightful. She could truthfully say none made love as passionately and tenderly as Zico. She loved the touch, the feel, and the smell of him. Hearing the raw, sexy sounds he made in the throes of his passion gave her satisfaction, bringing her more joy. She learned he was as talented in his lovemaking as he was in his art. Later, when they were speaking of his art, Zico told her he found few happier moments then when he observed a viewer or potential buyer respond with true joy when viewing his paintings. This is how he had felt when he had first seen her looking at the *Two Birds* at Miriam's gala.

The next morning following their first night together, Annie learned Zico had a wife. When he told her this at breakfast, she felt a stab in her heart and an overwhelming sense of betrayal. A strange sense of relief swept over her when she realized they were not in front of the *Amazing Doves* when he told her. She started to pull away from him but Zico, holding tightly to her hand, rushed on to say he and his wife had separated right after Christmas. "We will never be together again. Brazil does not allow anyone to divorce or I would have filed before I came back to Sausalito." He held her small hands in his large ones and looked deeply into her eyes willing her to believe him as he said, "I will never be in her house or her bed again. You are my only love and have been since the moment we met."

Annie looked in his eyes and saw a thousand emotions—the strongest was hope.

Very softly she said, *"Oh meu Deus; Diz-me que e verdade."* Never in her life had she wanted God to tell her something was true than she did right now.

Without saying anything further, she cleared the breakfast table, picked up their coffee mugs, and led him back into the bedroom. She got in her side and beckoned him to the other. She propped up her several pillows so they could each sit side by side. They sat close together quietly gazing at the *Amazing Doves*. Finally she set her coffee cup on the table beside her and took his hand. Turning to him, she said "If you move in, you must promise to stay forever."

He promised—moving in that day—beginning their journey towards forever. Each morning, *The Amazing Doves* greeted them—each night, Annie and Zico told them tales of their busy day. Not wishing to move from Annie's house, they remodeled the back, creating a smaller yard in order to add a studio. They put in as much glass as possible to allow the northern light to bathe the room as they painted.

Zico was an inspiring teacher—showing her how to use color to its full advantage. Influenced by him, Annie's painting techniques improved. She didn't believe she would ever become as accomplished an artist as he, yet she felt her paintings were good. Often they were whimsical making Annie and Zee smile. Their styles of painting were individual and distinctive, engaging different audiences.

Annie would later tell her friends she knew the moment she became pregnant. Zico was as excited as Annie. Never having children in his first marriage, he had long ago resigned himself to the fact it was not to be. When he fell in love with, and moved in with Annie, it never occurred to him to think about starting a family. Annie had already filled his world with joy. When Annie was eight months along and feeling it, Zico told her she was more beautiful than the day they met, and confessed that he would like to have a daughter.

He didn't understand why Annie found this so amusing. She chuckled about it off and on all day. At dinner she lit the six candles while telling him the story of her father and his unfulfilled desire to have a son.

Annie and Zee occasionally spoke with each other about the marriages they had seen fail, and the bitterness that had destroyed families they knew. They agreed they were very happy and decided that the fact the church would not allow them to marry turned out to be fine for them. On the days they found things to argue about, they held to their vow to resolve the situation before going to sleep. "After all," they said, "how could one go to sleep angry with the *Amazing Doves* staring at them, with their all-knowing, soul-searching, eyes?"

1950

Rose Salvador Carvalho was born at 6:45 a.m. on October 24, 1950. Annie and Zee agreed she was the most beautiful baby on earth making them extremely happy.

Rose grew up adoring and being adored by her parents. One day, when she was five, she appeared at the breakfast table and held out her arms to her father for his morning hug. Then spontaneously she said, "Good morning Mama Annie. Good morning Papa Zee." She watched to see her parent's reaction. Their grins and loving response told her they liked it. From then on, she addressed them this way on special occasions or whenever she felt in need of a hug.

Rose lived happily with her parents in Sausalito until she graduated with top honors from Tamalpais Union High School in 1968. Her graduation thrust her squarely into the midst of the social turmoil known as "the sixties."

Rose graduated from UC, Berkeley. By the end of her first four years, she had decided to pursue a career in law. This, she decided, would lead her to a seat at the table of social justice. Her graduation, summa cum laude, secured her scholarships to be admitted to Stanford Law School.

In her final year of law school, on a Saturday morning, Rose was in her room at the house she shared with four other law students when she was called to the phone.

Placing the receiver to her ear, Rose could barely hear anything. She felt more than heard, agonizing sobs. While the words were hard to make out, Rose heard her mother, between sobs, tell her she had just returned from the emergency room at UCSF Medical Center. Papa Zee was dead. Her Mother told her how her father had awakened that morning and was heading toward the bathroom to shower when he collapsed. Annie heard him fall and ran into the bedroom and found him on the floor at the foot of the bed. He was on his back on the floor, his eyes staring blankly up at the painting of *The Amazing Doves*. She called 911 and started CPR. "It didn't work," she sobbed. "Emergency technicians performed CPR on the way to the hospital. They couldn't revive him." Her mother's sobs continued. Rose, feeling like her heart was breaking, said, "I'm coming home."

Less than three hours later, Rose Salvador Carvalho sat on her parent's bed hugging her mother. The only comfort in the room was provided by the presence of *The Amazing Doves*.

Years before Zico Carvalho's death, he and Annie had discussed what they wanted to have happen if they were the first to pass on. In keeping with Zee's wishes, Annie arranged for his cremation and asked the funeral home director to place his ashes in a simple black Portuguese ceramic urn she had made and which Zee had admired.

After retrieving the urn, Annie and Rose headed into San Francisco. They found their way to Telegraph Hill and walked until they found the area Annie was seeking, a place she and Zee had been often. Parrots chattered in the trees and flew back and forth. Annie and Rose pointed out ones they knew Papa Zee would have loved to have painted. They sat down and placed the black urn between them. They ate their lunch and talked—sometimes to each other and sometimes to the urn-telling stories about Zico, the artist, and Papa Zee. They laughed. They cried. Holding up the urn they each described for Zee what they were seeing, each selecting some parrot of unique character and color and making it stand out from the vast number of solid green birds. Later in the afternoon, the breeze picked up and they accepted this as their signal. It was time to carry the urn to the edge of a ridge where they could look down on trees where there were many parrots and other birds. They each kissed the urn before Annie, giving it a last caring hug, opened it, and with a wide swoop of her arm, let its contents be carried away in the wind. The volume of the parrots' screeches rose, perhaps welcoming Zee. Arms about each other's waists, tears flowing down their cheeks, and sad smiles on their faces, mother and daughter found their way back to their car.

Rose stayed with her mother through the next weekend. Miriam, Richie, and Theodore helped Annie and Rose host a "Celebration of Zico." Annie wanted it to be at their home. That was not possible as Zico had become so beloved by the entire Sausalito art community that the small house could not accommodate everyone who wanted to remember him. Instead Miriam invited everyone to her large home and garden. Since this was where they had first met, Annie thought Zee would not only approve of but love the setting. The house overflowed. Annie and Rose lost track of the number of toasts, stories of remembrance, and celebration of Zico his many friends shared. After the celebration, Annie and Rose retreated home spending the rest of the night in silence and in tears holding on to one another.

In the days following Zee's death, her mother gave Rose explicit instructions about what she wanted Rose to make happen when she, Annie, died.

Rose's inevitable departure left Annie feeling bereft. She, who had been so independent and had a vibrant life so full of friends and paintings, soon found she could hardly bear to get out of bed in the morning. She thought about her darling Rose, so bright and capable. She knew that her daughter was well launched towards a successful career and was sure life's wondrous adventures awaited her.

Annie wanted only to pull the covers over her head and die. Death would take her to Zee. She took leave from Madelyn's gallery. Friends checked on her or brought food. Those who did reported that the person who had answered the Carvalho's door was not "their Annie."

After Zee's death, Annie felt a big gaping hole in her universe. She felt overwhelmed by the sadness. She had been happy all of her life. Her Mama and Papa had always told her she was an optimist. When Zee came into her life, she didn't quit being an optimist—she simply made a shift. She was no longer "one." She was half of this new entity, "Annie and Zee." Together they had happily shared and celebrated the joys of life.

Rose's birth brought them even closer together. Annie did not know when it had happened, but somewhere along the line, she and Zee had become inseparable in life and in spirit. Now he was gone. Painting, once her passion, suddenly became a less brilliant star in her world. At first she tried, only to find her heart no longer in it. Her loving circle of friends could not pull her back from the dark abyss. Her heart was now only half a heart, she not only didn't know how, but didn't want to know how to heal it.

Annie spent each day praying to God to let her to be with her beloved Zee—her soul mate. She believed she could feel Zee pulling her towards him.

It was Christmas break when Rose returned home for her holiday visit. Her law studies being demanding and graduation not far off, Rose had only been able to make phone calls to check on her mother. She had no idea her mother's depression was so deep. Once she arrived in Sausalito, she was shocked to see the person lying in her mother's bed. Her mother appeared so thin she looked as if she would snap if anyone touched her. Her hair, once so beautiful, was badly in need of washing and, though she never used much make-up, it was obvious she hadn't even considered it for weeks or maybe months. Rose lavished tender, loving care on her mother and tried desperately to convince her to return with her to Palo Alto. Annie refused to leave saying she needed to stay by *The Amazing Doves* so she could feel closer to Zee. Rose was convinced her mother was willing herself to die.

In a little less than one year, Annie succeeded. Rose carried out her promise to scatter Mama Annie's ashes from the same urn and from the same place where they had scattered Papa Zee's. As Rose sat in the same place she had shared earlier with Annie, she remembered her mother saying to her, *I know in my heart Zee is waiting for me to join him. When I do, we will return to earth together in our next life as The Amazing Doves.*

1956

Flora could think of no place she would rather be than in Alaska with Mickey. The first day she stepped foot on Alaskan soil, she knew it was the most magnificent place in the world—even more so than Montana. She found living in a state where nature constantly presented new discoveries daily, thrilling. She was in awe of the land's ruggedness which drew her to it, then was unforgiving in its hold on her soul.

Before Flora arrived in Alaska, Mickey Mickens and his partner, Jeff Barlow, purchased their first airplane—a Stinson bi-plane. They set up their company, *Brave Eagles,* and took hunters, fishermen, and mountain climbers to destinations throughout the vast state.

Flora's first act in Alaska was to become Mrs. Mickey Mickens. Once Flora and Mickey were married, Flora was eager to start learning everything about his work. They had barely settled into their home in Anchorage when she began begging him to teach her how to fly. To stave off her request as long as he could, Mickey and Jeff insisted on teaching her about the rest of the business first. Soon Flora was capable of handling the reservation and bookkeeping aspects of the business. Having demonstrated her proficiency in those things, Mickey and Jeff began teaching her the ins and outs of the mechanical maintenance required to keep the plane running. Following that, Mickey was no longer able to deter Flora's determination to pilot the plane. Finally he gave in and began giving her lessons. To no one's surprise, she was a quick learner.

Five years after Flora had moved to Anchorage and married Mickey, Jeff Barlow became ill. His doctor diagnosed a heart condition and said it wasn't safe for Jeff to fly anymore. Jeff was devastated. Being forced to stay grounded, he helped Flora with the business side of *Brave Eagles*. Flora continued her flying lessons, soon demonstrating to Mickey's satisfaction, that she was capable of flying solo. After passing all required examinations, she left the office to Jeff, replacing him as Mickey's co-pilot. The result of Jeff and Flora switching positions turned out to be positive for the company. Jeff was able to expand the business considerably, soon turning what had started as a good business into a very successful one.

Once forced to stay on the ground, Jeff discovered that he actually enjoyed the business end of things. He admitted privately to his wife, Norah that he never had loved flying as much as Mickey—then added he wasn't sure if either of them loved it as much as Flora did. Partly due to his efforts, the partnership of Barlow and Mickens profited. Bringing in new business allowed them to purchase their second plane, a de Havilland Twin Otter.

Mickey and Flora were soon flying mail to the outlying areas of Sitka, Homer, Kenai, Palmer, and Kotzebue, and often made to other areas. The business grew as word of mouth advertising brought more hunters and fisherman their way. The company also responded to emergency calls wherever they happened to be, often aiding those, like State Troopers, attempting to find persons who had lost their way. It was a very exciting life and Flora couldn't imagine having a different one.

Early in August of 1958, the flu was running rampant in the Anchorage area and did not let the usually hearty Flora escape. She had rarely been ill, but this flu bug hit her with a vengeance—leaving her barely able to get out of bed. Her fever was high and she and Mickey acknowledged she was in no condition to pilot anything. This left Mickey to fly solo out to the Kenai area to pick up four fishermen they had dropped off six days earlier.

Mickey tucked Flora into bed with a hot cup of tea at her side, gave her a big hug, and planting a kiss on her forehead, he put on his leather jacket and headed out the door.

It took a while for Flora to settle down. She was mad at herself and at the flu. She hated anything interrupting her plans. To do so was like giving over control of her world—something she neither wanted to do, and in those rare times when forced to do so, did not do gracefully. She loved to fly and it upset her that Mickey had to take over her job while trying to focus on his own. *Dear sweet Mickey*. The thought of him and his wonderful crooked grin led her muddled thoughts drift back over their life together and the good and fun times they had enjoyed ever since meeting so long ago.

There was no question that Mickey had presented her with incredible adventures since walking into her life. *Being with him has been the best adventure of all*, she thought. The state of Alaska took second place, and flying the plane was icing on the cake. They could not have been happier. Her thoughts turned into dreams and Flora finally nestled deeper into the warm quilt letting sleep embrace her.

By the time Mickey reached the airfield, his thoughts had shifted from concern for Flora to the tasks at hand. The weather was not good. With a sizeable storm predicted to hit the area within the next 48 hours, Mickey was thinking that the sooner he took off, the sooner he could return. If not for his concern for the lives of the four fishermen, he would have cancelled the flight.

The flight, frequently bumpy at this time of year, was much more difficult today. Visibility changed moment-to-moment—from not- so-good, to bad, and on to worse. Between few precious breaks of clearing, Mickey alternately swore, and then, though not a religious man, fervently thanked God for his dependable Twin Otter, *Brave Eagles*. While the plane had the best communication system and up-to- date technology, he prayed it would be good enough to get him through this mess. Looking at the empty seat beside him, he thanked God Flora was at home safely tucked into their bed. The thought he would be smart to turn back crossed his mind—Mickey dismissing it immediately, unable to bring himself to abandon the fishermen who he was sure nervously awaited his arrival.

From past experience, Mickey knew exactly where on the lake he would need to touch down. As the wind began to swirl snow around him, he pictured the landing in his mind and hoped he would be able to spot the landmarks he normally relied on. He worried about having enough room to maneuver if there should be an unexpected wind burst. He hoped the men he was picking up were on the dock and ready to leap on board so they could get out of there quickly. He also hoped the men realized they would have to leave *everything* except the clothes on their backs in order to quickly jump aboard the plane—assuming he could get to them.

He circled the lake, lining up his approach. His worst fear was realized as a huge gust of wind suddenly caught him broadside. *Brave Eagles* flipped and fell rapidly down toward the choppy water below. The plane barely touched the water's surface when an even stronger wind gust struck again from the north, this time thrusting *Brave Eagles* upward and forward. The plane erratically jerked up and down over the water and, finally, a third wild gust mercilessly hurled the battered plane into a stand of sitka spruce. The plane exploded sending a large ball of fire and pillar of smoke into the air while violently throwing the fiery remnants of *Brave Eagles* into the trees. The fishermen, who had been anxiously waiting at the dock, helplessly watched in horror. A large moose standing in the trees behind the men looked up, let out a terrified roar, turned around, and tore backward, disappearing through the dense trees behind him.

At the same instant, at home in Anchorage, Flora awakened with a start. Sitting upright, her aches and pains momentarily forgotten, she experienced an overwhelming feeling of foreboding. A chill settled into her bones telling her something was terribly wrong. She pulled the heavy quilt securely around her. Depending on whether she felt feverish or chilled, she had been taking off and putting on her wool socks. She pulled them on now and, trying to ignore her aches and chills, forced herself to walk across the room into the kitchen to grab the telephone. Hearing the howling of the wind outside, she hoped the telephone would work—it didn't, leaving her unable to reach Jeff at the office to learn what he was hearing from Mickey. Feeling weak in the knees and shaking from the cold, she trudged back to her bed, crawled in, and pulled the quilt more tightly around her. She looked to confirm there was still wood burning in the fireplace as the coldness filling the room was overwhelming. Sleep would not come. No matter how tightly Flora squeezed her eyelids closed and pulled the quilt around her ears to drown out the sound of the wind, she could not suppress the fear she felt inside.

Hours later, loud pounding on the door startled Flora. Tugging the quilt around her and thankful her wool socks were already on her feet, she hurried to the door. Pulling it open, she saw her friend, State Trooper Ted Wallins, standing there. He looked uncharacteristically hesitant. In that instant she knew what he had come to tell her.

For the next month with Mickey's fatal accident weighing heavily on her heart and the flu not wanting to let go of her body, Flora had a hard time coping with anything—even the simple act of getting out of bed. Jeff and Norah, checked in with her frequently, bringing her food and making sure there was enough wood for the fireplace. They asked if she wanted them to stay with her, or better yet, if she would come home with them. She said no and they could not convince her to change her mind.

Flora didn't have to worry about a lack of food. Friends kept her refrigerator bulging with lovingly prepared moose stews, soups, and other foods, though the food supply far exceeded her appetite. At first she felt numb and could barely acknowledge their kindness. Later she could express her deep gratitude for the supporting community of friends in her adopted hometown.

Without Mickey, Anchorage became a bleak and empty town for Flora. Where she had once seen only the beauty of Alaska, now she saw only its hidden dangers. Flora could not find it in her heart to forgive Alaska for the loss of her beloved Mickey. For the second time in the past several weeks—the first to notify her of Mickey's death—Flora called her sister Angie.

Angie, who had gone through the pain of losing *her* husband, George, two years earlier, felt great empathy for her older sister. Calling weekly after Mickey's death, she begged her to return to California. This day Flora announced on hearing her sister's voice, "Angie. It's me. I'm coming home to California."

1975

Angie's first response was to tell her sister she could live with her. Flora snorted. "Angie, Dear. You know I love you, but you and those thousand cats of yours would drive me crazy in less than a week. Here's what I want you to do."

Angie listened, and after hanging up, set about her assignment. She phoned a local realtor and told him what she wanted. In less than a month, Alaska Airlines having made only one brief stop in Seattle, delivered Flora from Anchorage to the Burbank airport.

Angie met her older sister at the airport and drove her to the small house she and the realtor had found for Flora— located exactly 2.6 miles from Angie's house in Arcadia. It was a simple adobe house, located in an unassuming neighborhood filled with similar-looking adobe homes. A short path led to the front door. Angie and Flora climbed the two steps, admiring the rose bush beside them, and stepped into a small furnished living room.

Angie showed her sister the rest of the house finishing with a small dining area where Angie had lovingly covered the table with one of the lace tablecloths which Palmeda had made. A small vase of red roses, cut from the bush by the front door, sat in the middle. Flora, who looked pale and tired from her trip, hugged her sister, looked her in the eye and said, "Ange, this is perfect." The words were barely out of her mouth before she turned and headed into the bedroom declaring she needed to take a nap.

The next day, Angie checked in on her older sister. They ate lunch together at the dining table—a pattern that continued the rest of their lives. Though she had her own car, Flora rarely went to Angie's place. While she loved animals and thought one or two cats to be sweet, she felt overwhelmed by the horde of cats roaming Angie's house. She always called them *those thousand cats of yours* though, in fact, the number at the time Flora returned to California was only twenty. Flora laughed at how Angie had carefully covered her sofa and stuffed chairs with plastic *so they would stay clean*. Flora kidded her about this for weeks and then finally gave up.

By the end of the year, Flora had given in to her younger sister and adopted Bear, a large long-haired white cat Angie had found walking along an isolated road. Flora would never admit it to her sister, but she soon became attached to Bear—so much so, she let him sleep on her bed. Angie noticed this, but knew better than to say anything—content knowing another stray cat had a good home.

Flora settled back into California life. A few years later during one of their daily conversations, the sisters discussed the fact that between the two of them, they owned 5/6 of the 120 Bonny Doon acres in Santa Cruz that Papa had originally left the sisters. Flora had Palmeda's and Annie's parcels as well as her own. Angie had her own parcel, as well as Alice's. Mamie, they knew from the will Flora had received, had left hers to her sons, Leonard and Luke.

Neither Flora nor Angie had ever gone to actually see or walk on the Bonny Doon land. They could recall Papa talking about its beautiful location and how someday it would have great value or they could farm it—that thought causing them to burst into laughter. They drifted into a discussion about what Papa would have to say if he had known how his daughters had actually chosen to *use* the land. "What should *we* do with the land after *we* are gone?" Angie asked.

They agreed that whichever of them went first would leave it to the other. Flora said, "You know, Ange, I would like Annie's parcel to go back to her daughter, Rose." Angie agreed that would be a good thing to do. "Mamie's boys have hers," Flora continued.

Angie thought for a moment and said, "Well, if I go after you do..." Flora, twelve years older than her sister, rolled her eyes. Angie ignored her. "If I go after you do, I want to leave whatever I have to the boys as well. I know they weren't with me long, but it was the closest thing to being a mother I ever was or will be."

Flora couldn't resist and said, "Thank God, Ange. I was sure you would leave it to the cats—let them go roam around out there in the hills of Bonny Doon." Angie glared.

Through the years, Angie and Flora often reminisced about their family. Sometimes their stories left them feeling overwhelmed by the tragedies that had befallen Mama, Papa, Mamie, Joe, Palmeda, Alice, and Mickey. Whenever they talked about this, they first felt sad, and then became quiet until one or the other would think of something funny, and they would giggle about it for the rest of the day.

Angie researched the disease that so tragically killed Mamie, Palmeda and, as they would later learn, Mamie's oldest son, Leonard. Angie shared everything she learned with Flora and sent copies of the information to Mamie's remaining son, Luke.

She learned that the inherited neurological disease, was called Joseph's Disease after a Portuguese sailor from their parent's beloved Island of Flores. Medical researchers had fairly recently identified him as the source. There was no way to know how many children the sailor, Joseph, had fathered. He had left Flores and came to the United States in the early 1800s. The Salvador family were some of his descendants. Flora and Angie remembered their father telling stories of having to help his father sit upright on the boat when they went out fishing not long before his father died and Angie was sure he, too, must have had Joseph's Disease.

As Angie was telling Flora about Joseph's Disease, she said, "I think it was really the Devil just hiding in the form of Joseph so he wouldn't be discovered." Flora rolled her eyes upward.

As she learned more about the agonizing symptoms of the disease and the suffering of those who had it, Angie, who seldom cried, was brought to tears. She cried for her father, her sisters, Mamie, and Palmeda, and for her young nephew, Leonard, whom she had so fleetingly cared for in her home. It was after Leonard's death that Luke had written to Aunt Angie describing the agonies his brother had endured.

Luke described how Leonard, like their mother, had started showing the symptoms early in his adult life. He became clumsy and weak, always stumbling and dropping things. He had double vision and his body twisted in agony. His face and tongue twitched and his eyes bulged. He had difficulty talking and swallowing. And yet, Luke wrote, his wife Gladys said he never lost his mental faculties. At least, she said, she hadn't thought so. It had been so difficult for him to communicate, she really was not sure. From what Angie had read, the physicians who were studying the disease said this was true. The sad part was that people around them had a hard time knowing what the person's mental status was and often treated them like they were retarded or crazy.

When Angie read the letter to Flora, their thoughts turned to Meda and Mamie bringing an overwhelming feeling of sadness for their sisters. Angie said, "I think it was God's answer to give Palmeda pneumonia and Leonard the severe lung infection that killed him."

"He was only 42," Flora responded. "You're right, though, while it was an awful way to die, it was a more horrible way to live."

Angie continued to share all she learned about the disease with Flora. "There's a fifty-fifty chance of inheriting it. That means about half of someone's children die from it. Think about that. It means there might have been three of us who got it. We know Mamie and Palmeda had it. Do you think Alice would have had it if she hadn't developed cancer when she was so young? What about Annie?"

At some point in their discussions, they agreed that while cancer was a terrible way to die, they would rather have cancer then the horrors they had learned, Joseph's Disease inflicted on its victims. They thanked God each of them and dear, sweet Annie had not displayed any signs of the disease. They were thankful that, so far, Leonard's brother, Luke, didn't have it. They were glad neither of the boys had any children.

The years passed, and in spite of their age difference, Flora and Angie grew closer. Silently and with neither sister realizing it, an insidious visitor found Flora. She began having problems with stomach pains. In order to stop Angie's nagging, she finally agreed to visit a doctor. He said she might have a polyp. She accepted what he told her and left it at that. Months later when the pain became too great to ignore any more, she returned to the doctor. He informed her she had a grapefruit sized malignant tumor in her uterus. The cancer had spread to her lymph nodes. She insisted Angie not let Annie know until after her death. She died five months later, her sister Angie by her side.

Angie notified Annie, who immediately came from Sausalito to Santa Cruz to be with Angie for Flora's funeral. It was a small service—one Angie knew Flora would like. After all, Flora had planned every detail and from her hospital bed had quizzed Angie relentlessly to be sure her sister had memorized every detail and wish.

The casket, simple in design, was made of dark gleaming wood with shining gold handles on the sides. The dress Flora had selected was her favorite color—red. Even though Angie teased her sister saying she would be too hot, she respected Flora's wish and had the funeral home put her favorite Alaska parka on her sister over the red dress. The parka had white fur around the hood and had been pulled up around her head and softly touched her cheeks. The parka, Flora explained to Angie, had been a gift from Mickey. "He gave it to me the day I arrived in Anchorage," she said. She looked forward to wearing it throughout all eternity. The funeral flowers were white, representing the snows of Alaska, and positioned carefully in her hands was a picture of Flora and Mickey standing beside *Brave Eagles* on the dock at Beaver Lake—their arms wrapped around each other. When she saw Flora in the casket holding the picture, Annie said she could feel their love radiating from the photo. Had she been able to recover any of Mickey's ashes from the crash, Flora's instructions would have included cremation with her ashes strewn with his over Beaver Lake. Under the circumstances that had been impossible, instead, Flora had asked to be buried in Santa Cruz next to Mama, Papa, Mamie, and Palmeda.

Following Flora's death, Angie remained in her Arcadia home surrounded by her cats. The sheer number of cats—twenty—kept her busy. She would often sit outside in her casita petting whichever cat had been the first to garner her lap and think back about her life growing up with her family in Santa Cruz.

She thought of Mamie dealing with a failed marriage, the agonies of Joseph's Disease, and trying to raise two active boys only to die at a young age. She thought of Palmeda who believed God would never let her down yet having gone through the same agonies. Her memories of carefree Alice made her smile—the smile fading as she thought that Alice, too, had succumbed to death at much too early an age. Then there was Flora who, after the tragic death of Joe, found happiness with Mickey until his tragic death. She was glad Annie had found happiness with Zico and had such a wonderful daughter in Rose.

Angie sighed deeply causing her lap cat to jump down and trot away like a dethroned queen—another immediately taking the first cat's place. Angie reflected on her own brief attempt at mothering—if one could call it that—with Leonard and Luke. She felt like she had hardly gotten to know Leonard. It wasn't until after his sad death that she began exchanging occasional telephone calls with her nephew, Luke. She was happy things seemed to turn out well for him. Luke would listen to her talk about the family, Joseph's Disease, her cats, California, and anything that came to her mind. He always made her laugh.

While a third and then a fourth cat traded places on her lap, Angie settled back happily and thought about George.

What a fine man you were George Brazil. I was fortunate to find you, she mused. *I miss you. I wonder what you thought up there when I named the first cat I adopted after you passed, Big George. He was so much like you in temperament and has always been here for me. Maybe you sent him to me? I'm sure you knew I would take him in*. With this thought she gave a laugh and a little snort.

Yes, she thought, *we did have a happy life.*

She began to cough again—the cough rapidly worsening—her only clue to her own condition, had she paid attention to it. Whenever she thought she should probably get it checked, she remembered that her fuzzy little Wilbur—or Jingles or Sassy—needed some medicine or a check up at the vet and took care of them instead.

Less than six months later Rose, having recently lost her own mother, returned to the same cemetery in Santa Cruz where Flora and her grandparents and aunts had been buried. She gathered there with a few of Angie's friends, including Dr.

Dorothy Darling, Angie's vet, to lay Angie to rest beside her parents and her sisters.

Following clues from her mother's paintings, Rose brought different colored flowers to place, not only on Angie's casket but on each of her other Aunt's graves as well. She left her final flowers for her parents and one for George.

Leaving Angie in her final resting place, Rose, now executor of her Aunt's estate, went to Arcadia to complete clearing out of Angie's house. Rose was relieved to learn from Dr. Darling that the first thing Angie had done when she found out she had little time left to live, was to make arrangements for good homes for her twenty cats. This was probably a good thing for Angie to do because it had occupied her time, thoughts, and remaining energies as she waited for her life to end.

Rose had agreed to take in a little black and white long-haired, female cat—the cat totally black with a circle of white in a ring around her neck, like a clown suit. Rose laughed when she learned the cat's name was Ruffles. Rose had collected Ruffles from Dr. Darling, Angie's vet and good friend, on her way to Angie's house. Dr. Darling confided that Angie had left a considerable sum of money to the Darling Veterinary Clinic to be used to care for unwanted, abused, or otherwise needy cats. Rose was happy to hear that, thinking, *That was so Aunt Angie.*

Reading Angie's will, Rose learned that she and her cousin Luke were left any personal items from her home that they might wish to keep, and that they each would receive half of any profit from the sale of her house and other unwanted furnishings or personal items. The attorney, Eugene Palmer, had given her the key to the house and said he would help her arrange a sale of the house and items once she and Luke let him know when they were ready.

Once at Angie's house, Rose did a walk-through to get a feel for what was there and how big a task she would be dealing with. She was struck with how simply it had been furnished, and in awe of how much space had been devoted to the cats. Walking to the back of the house, she came to what, obviously at one time, had been Angie and George's bedroom. She had barely stepped into the room when her eye was drawn to a dark carved wooden box sitting on a bedside table. Immediately she recognized what it was—her grandmother, Maria Luísa and her grandfather, Michael's wedding box. Her mother had told her the story about its being a gift from her grandmother's parents when she was married in the Azores so many years ago. Rose clutched it lovingly to her heart.

While looking through the house and sorting through Angie's well-organized papers which Ruffles seemed determined to disorganize, Rose found the address and phone number for her cousin Luke. She noticed that Aunt Mamie's only surviving son lived in Seattle, Washington. She added Angie's address book to the box with the family pictures and a few other small mementos and remembrances she had chosen to take with her. Before leaving, Rose paused to glance around the house again. It struck her that Angie had lived an extremely modest and uncomplicated life. She wondered if she had been happy.

The next morning, Rose, with Ruffles in the car sitting happily on top of the box which held Rose's mementos of Angie and the carved wedding box, left the motel and headed back to her fairly new home in Capitola.

1985

Once home, Rose watched Ruffles inspect the house as though she had a plan. She took her time going from room to room, selecting one corner and then methodically circled the entire room carefully sniffing each piece of furniture she encountered. After checking out each space, she discovered a bright checkered rug with a beam of sunlight floating from the living room window creating a welcoming circle. Apparently deciding she had done enough investigating, Ruffles turned around twice within the circle of sunlight, settled back on her haunches, raised a leg, and gave herself a bath. Occasionally, she looked up, checking to be sure Rose was still nearby, and then continued to the next piece of fur requiring her undivided attention. After her bath, she leapt up, looked at Rose, gave a small meow, and trotted up the stairs, looking back to be sure Rose knew she was to follow. Without any hesitation, Ruffles went directly into Rose's bedroom, hopped up, placed herself squarely in the middle of the queen-sized bed, and fell asleep. Rose wondered how she knew which room was hers. *Probably by smell*, she thought. Rose, who had not been at all sure she would like having a feline roommate, found this small furry creature sharing the bed to be comforting and amusing.

A couple weeks after her return home, Rose retrieved the box she had brought from Angie's house from the closet floor. She set it beside her on the bed as she settled down beside Ruffles. She glanced up at the "hot pink" wall behind her bed which held her favorite reminder of her parents, "*The Amazing Doves*." The birds' bright beady eyes watched her *Or maybe*, she thought, *Ruffles*.

She sorted through the box taking time to look at the family pictures. She found those of the six sisters of interest, lingering over any showing her mother. She tucked these back into the wedding box.

She found the paper she had been looking for and pulled it out. It held the address and phone number for Cousin Luke. She had never met Luke nor spoken to him though she knew he was twenty-seven years older than she. She wondered what he was like.

She remembered her mother telling her about Luke's mother, her Aunt Mamie. Rose sighed as she thought of Mamie's very short and sad life. She sat a few minutes reflecting on the fact she had never met her Aunts Mamie, Palmeda, Alice, or even Flora—except for viewing her at her funeral. She had only met Aunt Angie. It seemed odd that through her mother's stories, she felt she knew each of them. She clearly recalled her mother continuing to light the dining room candles and saying good night to each of them.

Her curiosity aroused, Rose got up and grabbed the phone. While waiting for an answer, she wondered about her *Cousin Luke*—would she be talking with a bitter old man? Her thoughts were interrupted by a chirping young female voice at the other end of the phone line, "University of Washington. How may I direct your call?" Completely taken by surprise, Rose didn't respond for a moment. Finally the now less chipper voice said, "Hello?"

Startled, Rose, replied, "Oh, I'm trying to reach Luke Kohler. I'm calling from California."

The voice, back to being chipper and sounding pleased there was someone to help, said "One moment please." Rose listened to the Jackson 5's "Dancing Machine" for a few seconds.

Another female voice, this one low and sultry, answered, "Department of Economics."

Rose, intrigued, repeated, "I'm trying to reach Luke Kohler. Would he be at this number?"

"I believe he has a class now. I'll see when Professor Kohler will be in his office. Please hold a moment." After a brief pause, *Low and Sultry* returned, "He has office hours today between two and four. Would you like to leave a message or call back at that time?"

"I'll call back," Rose responded and hung up.

That afternoon, Rose had a client meeting at her office. It was ten minutes to four by the time the client left and she had returned from the conference room to her office. She dialed the number Ms. Low and Sultry had given to bypass the switchboard and call directly into the Department of Economics. She recognized the voice as the same person she had spoken with earlier. She said, "My name is Rose Carvalho. I'm calling from California. I'd like to speak with Luke Kohler." She could hear Ms. L and S calling out "Luke, that lady from this morning—the one from California—is on the line. Do you want to take the call?"

Rose could hear other voices chattering in the background amidst lots of laughter. She couldn't make out what anyone was saying. She was intrigued, never having personally found economics that enjoyable. Ms. L and S came back on the line to inform her that Mr. Kohler would take the call in his office. She was put on hold and back to listening to music. This time John Denver was singing "Annie's Song."

A deep, booming voice cut off John Denver, "Kohler."

Surprised for a moment by the sheer vitality expressed in one word, Rose found herself staring at the phone. Recovering, she said, "Luke Kohler?"

"That would be me."

"This is Rose Carvalho calling. I'm your..."

The big voice chuckled, "My cousin Rose," he finished for her. "Aunt Annie's only daughter. This is a surprise."

Rose couldn't tell if he thought it was a good surprise or not. She hurried on. "As you know Aunt Angie passed away." There was silence at the other end. "You did know, didn't you?" she continued. "I sent you a notice of the funeral service."

She thought the voice was slightly huskier when he answered. "Yes, I got it. I wanted to come down for the services, but I couldn't." He didn't explain further.

"I'm sorry," she said, wondering if he was.

He continued, "Is there anything left for me to do? I'm sorry it fell on you to handle all the arrangements." He paused. "My God, did you have to take home a thousand cats?"

Rose laughed. She felt her cheeks turning pink. "No, only one—Ruffles. Aunt Angie was amazing, though. Would you believe she found homes for all the others before she died?" There was silence at the other end of the phone line. She waited and then a thought came to her. "Did you?" she asked.

There was an enjoyable, deep laugh, and a pause. Luke said, "Same thing. My wife and I took one—Tiny." He laughed again. "I think Tiny weighs 20 pounds. Angie had her shipped up here by a pet travel service. She arrived in the middle of one of the worst snow storms we've ever had. We'd gone to the store and it took us hours to get home. We were barely in the door when a van pulled up in front and a delivery man lugged in a huge pink pet carrier. The cat probably felt like she'd been shipped to Siberia, coming from California's sunshine to a couple feet of snow." He laughed again. "She's a good cat, though. Fits right in with our other two." Another pause and then, "In case you're curious, we don't have any plastic on *our* furniture!"

They laughed together at the shared image.

After telling him briefly about the funeral service, Rose chatted about clearing out Angie's house. She told him about the pictures and the few things she had kept. She explained there had been a delay while she arranged to fix up the house and yard and that it was soon going to be placed on the market. "I don't think there will be a problem selling it, although the house really isn't in good shape." She told him about the yard being overgrown by several fruit trees and lots of flowering bushes. They laughed as she described all of the plastic-covered furniture. Rose told Luke she had hired someone to manage the sale which would be happening in a couple of weeks. All the furniture, dishes, and other household items were to be sold. She asked him if there was anything he wanted. His answer, coming after a short silence, was not what she expected.

"My brother Leonard and I lived with Aunt Angie and George for a short time when we were teenagers. We were more than a hand-full. She and George probably thought we were incorrigible. I'm sure we were," he said sighing. "I do remember one time I bought something for Angie with my own money. I guess it was her birthday or Christmas—some special day. It was a glass juice set. Do you know what that is? There was a pitcher and some small juice glasses with oranges painted on them. I don't even know why I remember them."

He paused as though he were thinking. "Well," he laughed, "I probably remember because it was the only nice thing I ever did for her. Strange as it sounds, if you happen to see a set like that I would like to have it."

Rose, oddly touched by this sentiment, promised she would check into it. When Rose heard someone knocking on what she supposed was his office door, they ended their conversation. Before hanging up, Rose gave him her phone number and said she would call in a week or two to talk about the Bonny Doon property in which, according to Aunt Angie's will, they shared ownership. "Although," she reminded him with no envy apparent in her voice, "you have by far the greater share—almost the whole thing."

Over the next few months, Rose and Luke spoke several times. They discovered during their phone conversations, that neither was interested in keeping the Bonny Doon property, so they agreed to sell it. Since Rose was in California and had some contacts there, she offered to find a reliable real estate agent who handled undeveloped property like theirs.

Their next conversation occurred several months later. It consisted of Rose giving Luke the information about Lewis Rogers, the real estate agent she had found in Santa Cruz—one of the few realtors in the area knowledgeable about undeveloped properties. They agreed she should contact him. It was not long after the agent made a recommendation that they agreed on a listing price.

It was close to a year before Lewis Rogers notified them he had found a buyer. Rose and Luke accepted the offer. Closing was to be in a month.

Less than a week after the acceptance of the offer, Rose answered the phone to find Luke on the other end.

"I have an idea," he said. "Why don't I fly down to San Jose and meet you. We can drive up to Bonny Doon and have one look at the property before it officially leaves the Salvador family. Since neither of us has actually seen or set foot on the place, it seems only right we should see it at least once—after all, it has been part of our family since 1920."

Agreeing this was a great idea, Rose told him to let her know when he could fly into San Jose. She suggested he arrive in the evening, get a motel, and she would pick him up early the next morning and they would drive up to the property.

Two weeks later at nine o'clock on Tuesday morning, Rose pulled her white Toyota Land Cruiser into the driveway outside the office of the Vista Inn not far from the San Jose airport. She hadn't turned off the engine when the doors marked "Office" swung open and a man of medium height stepped out. He carried a cup in each hand and had a smile on his face. With keen interest, Rose studied the man—the thick dark hair hanging down around his ears touching his collar, his full black mustache, and, from where she sat behind the wheel, she could see his dark eyes twinkle. She caught her breath. It was like looking at a younger version of her grandfather in a photograph she had seen in her mother's things. She got goose bumps as she felt the same energy emanating from him as she remembered from her own father.

He strode to the Land Cruiser and stood beside her window, indicating she should roll it down. He said, "Good morning. I didn't know if you use cream or sugar, but I have a handful of both in my pockets." He handed her one of the cups.

"Uh, thanks. Black is fine."

He circled to the passenger side, opened the door, and slid inside. She stared at him while he juggled his cup and strapped himself in. Then he looked at her and said, "You're Rose, I presume."

She laughed. "Well, it might be another type of adventure if I weren't, wouldn't it?" She saw the mustache twitch as he sipped his coffee.

Reaching across him, she opened the glove box, pulled out a map, and handed it to him. "You're the navigator. This is the map Lewis gave me to show us how to get to the place. It should take us about an hour to get up there."

They chatted amiably about his flight down, his luck in finding a place to eat the night before, the comfort of his room, and then turned their attention to the drive and the surroundings as they began their climb up the hills northwest of San Jose. It was a nice, cool California morning with an occasional bit of morning fog, lightly touching the road. They agreed this was a perfect day for their trip to Bonny Doon.

They commented that the map was as precise as Lewis himself. Following it to Scott's Valley and Felton, they turned onto Highway 9. They passed a small community, Ben Lomond, and took the Alba Road. It was steep and winding, leaving Rose glad she was driving because when she was the passenger she often felt nauseous on seriously winding roads. The road was lined with tall fir, cedar, and very large redwood trees—all creating alternating stripes of sun and shade across the road. Arriving at the top of Empire Grade, they saw a sign indicating they were entering the area of Bonny Doon. "I can't read the name *Bonny Doon* without feeling like I've entered a scene from *Brigadoon*," Rose said, giggling. She heard a chuckle and saw Luke's mustache twitch.

A short time later after referring to Lewis' map, Luke directed Rose to turn off the main road. Winding their way down a less well maintained road, they reached a dirt turn-out area beside a fence and gate. A hand-written sign with large letters reading "Latter Day Saints Summer Camp" hung off the fence. The gate sported several locks. Rose maneuvered the Land Cruiser into a parking area. Digging through her purse, Rose pulled out a paper and waved it towards Luke. "Lewis gave me the combination we'll need to get through the gate."

Taking the paper, Luke headed towards the gate. Rose said, "I'll get our stuff." Luke paused, looked back at her curiously, wondering what *stuff* that would be. Giving a small shrug, he turned back to the gate to face several locks. Finding the one Lewis had indicated, he tried the combination three times before it opened. Turning to tell her it was open, he discovered Rose right behind him. She now wore a good-sized blue backpack and was carrying a large red and white picnic basket.

Taking the basket from her, he said with a laugh, "Well, this *is* going to be a real adventure, isn't it?" The basket felt so heavy he wondered what was inside. They passed through the gate and Rose closed it behind them. Following a dirt pathway, they headed down a small hill toward some cabins. The first one was the largest with a small grassy knoll surrounding it and two other cabins beyond. A woman appeared and crossed the path to meet them—her stance clearly indicating her intention to block their entry. "Morning," she said, crisply. "Where you folks headed?"

She was not tall, yet her crossed arms and stern look made her appear larger.

She continued, "My husband and I are caretakers for the camp. Not many folks show up once summer is over." She said this like it was an accusation.

Luke spoke up. "I'm Luke Kohler and this is Rose Carvalho. We own some land out there." Having set his basket down, he swung his arms vaguely towards what he hoped was the direction of the ocean.

Not being able to tell if the woman was satisfied with Luke's answer, Rose hurried on. "Our realtor, Lewis Rogers, said to follow the path around and down the hill. He said the path was really rough but a couple miles down there, we should see a cabin on the left." Realizing she was speaking rapidly, Rose slowed down. She glanced at Luke—taking in the twinkle in his eyes.

The woman had glanced at Luke. The two women looked back at each other, and Rose noticed a softening in the woman's look. Rose continued. "He said the cabin is deserted. Once we go about twenty yards past it, we'll be on the Salvador land, our land."

Hearing this, the woman uncrossed her arms and gave them what Rose thought was an attempt at a smile. She said she had met the real estate agent who had hiked in with a couple earlier in the year. After clarifying for Rose and Luke the best way to get there, she waved them on their way. Luke picked up the picnic basket and took the lead.

They were glad they had dressed for hiking because it was not an easy walk. They had gone about a mile carefully avoiding ruts, holes, and rocks when they spotted an abandoned school bus. Luke said, "Looks like it might have been home for some hippies." Noting the broken windows, the graffiti scrawled on the sides, and all the tires missing, he added, "It certainly hasn't been occupied for a while."

Looking out over the tree-covered ridges of the hillside, Luke noticed one cabin at a distance far out on one of the points in the direction of the ocean. He might have missed it if not for a bit of smoke swirling upwards which he pointed out to Rose. "Thank God that's not a forest fire," Rose said and fervently meant it. Fires were something forested ridges in all of southern and central California experienced almost every year. Sadly the dreaded fires were increasing in numbers, intensity, and damage.

Luke was first to spot the small cabin. Taking Lewis' word that it was deserted, they continued toward it and climbed the stairs and entered. Rose, remembering the abandoned old school bus, hoped they wouldn't find any squatters in the cabin. She gave a sigh of relief when she saw it was empty.

Virtually one room, the cabin had one wall, facing out over the hillside—the glass from its windows long gone. Selecting what appeared to be the cleanest part of the aging wood floor, Rose dropped her backpack and Luke set the picnic basket beside it. Once unencumbered, they stepped out on a small, questionably stable porch to look out over what they were ninety percent sure was the Salvador land. They were struck with the beauty presented by the montage of greens, blues, and blacks of the forest covering the ridges and splashing down the hillside before them. They could see what might be old redwood trees, mixed conifers, and oak with lots of ferns and chaparral below.

They trooped down a steep incline and started to hike across the ridge but were prevented from going too far by thick trees and undergrowth. Neither was interested in a serious mountain hike—they just wanted to *see* their land—so they stood looking out over the tree-covered ridge. Rose suggested they return to the cabin. "Even though the cabin actually isn't on *our* property," Rose said, "it sits up higher and we can see our land better from there."

They climbed back up the hillside and, before going inside the cabin, stood on the rickety porch taking in a marvelous view of the whole area. Looking straight out towards their property, they could see the shape of the terrain better—the ridge falling steeply from east to west down the hillside toward the ocean. Slightly to the left they saw a slight bump in the trees near the top of the ridge. From Lewis Roger's map they decided the bump was probably the highest boundary of their land. Lewis' map showed that further up the ridge, beyond their land and where they could see, Lockheed had a facility.

From the other end of the porch, Rose called Luke. "Look!" she pointed. "The fog has lifted and you can actually see the Pacific Ocean. Look that way." Their eyes followed the sloping hillside of trees west all the way to the ocean.

For a while, they stood quietly enjoying the rugged beauty before them. They talked about what kind of people would want to live in this area—deciding they were people who, for whatever reasons, didn't want to be close to other people. "Perhaps some are old hippies and Vietnam Vets who can't tolerate living in the cities," Luke said.

"Or," Rose suggested, "there are probably a few pot growers out there. I hope not, though. Lewis told me the man who is buying the property has a family and wants to bring his kids out hiking so they can experience the outdoors."

Discussing what type of wildlife might live among all those trees, Luke suggested there might be coyotes or maybe mountain lions, although, in truth, he hadn't a clue. They agreed the chaparral looked thick and might prove to be hard for large animals to get through. They laughed when Rose suggested that the wild, anti-people types one might encounter in the area would be far more dangerous than the wildlife. Luke took out his camera and shot some pictures, promising to send copies to Rose. Then they took turns taking pictures of each other with the Salvador land as the backdrop.

Satisfied they had now seen and walked, albeit not too far, on their family's land, they re-entered the cabin. Rose crossed the small room to retrieve her backpack. She pulled out a rolled up royal blue blanket, selected a sunny spot on the floor, and spread it out. Picking up the basket, she emptied the contents onto the center of the blanket. Amazed at the number of items appearing, Luke commented that the basket resembled those little Volkswagen Beetles filled with clowns that one saw in the circus.

As she unpacked the basket, Rose explained that her mother, his Aunt Annie, had given it to her. It was the same picnic basket in which their grandmother, Maria Luísa, had packed the family picnics when their grandfather, Michael, and all six Salvador sisters went to the Santa Cruz beach on Sunday afternoons. Rose had brought along some *papos secos* from a recipe her mother had learned from their grandmother.

There were *Tortas da Flores, Linguiça, Empadas, Pimentas Assadas, Favas frescas em salada, and Rosquilhas Secas.*

Rose asked Luke to open the wine. "And yes," she answered his unspoken question, "I did pack a corkscrew."

The wine was *Bucelas*, a favorite Portuguese wine of her mother and father she explained. Luke was not familiar with it. When the wine was open, Luke, with eyebrows raised, asked the question, "Glasses?"

Rose's eyes sparkled as, with great flair, she reached into the basket and pulled out two small juice glasses sporting painted oranges on their sides. "Ta Da," she said, laughing at his look of surprise.

"You found them," he said, his voice slightly husky.

"I did," she said happily. "The rest of the glasses and the pitcher are, as we speak, in a box in the back of my car.

Luke poured the wine and offered a toast. "To Aunt Angie."

Rose insisted they take their charming wine glasses to the porch to make another toast to each of the Salvador sisters and their Bonny Doon property. Looking amused, Luke followed her outside.

Toasts completed, they returned to sit on the blanket, enjoying the rest of the food and wine as they exchanged information and stories about their family. They shared stories about their Grandparents' journey from the Azores to America. They each knew different tidbits of information about the six sisters and Rose asked Luke to tell her more about his mother, Mamie.

At first he hesitated. After a minute, he began. He said that other than with his first wife, Clair, and his current wife, Lena, he had not talked much about his childhood. He told how he and his brother, Leonard, lived when they were children. He admitted they were pretty much on their own from the time his mother, Mamie, became ill. He talked about how much he and Leonard loved to swim. "We could always find a place to swim. I was a very good swimmer then," he added immodestly. "I remember going to the natatorium in Santa Cruz. There was an extremely high ceiling with a beam extending across the length of the building. There were stairs going up so repair people could get up to the ceiling. I would climb up and then dive into the deep end of the pool. The people in the pool and on the sides would applaud." He chuckled. Demonstrating, he cupped his hands around his mouth like a megaphone and continued, "The manager would yell. 'Hey! Kid, stay off the rafters! You're going to kill yourself!'" At the memory, Luke laughed heartily—a deep belly laugh. Rose imagined that he sounded like her grandfather, Miguel Salvador, would have if he were alive.

Luke talked about his mother being ill most of the time he had been with her. "Of course, as a kid I had no idea what was wrong with her. She became less able to do things for herself and it embarrassed me. Leonard was already a teenager and I tried to act like I was. I had things I wanted to do. I resented her being ill because it meant instead of her taking care of us, we had to take care of her. Leonard was older than I was, so he had more things he had to do after school; or at least that's what he told Mom. Truthfulness wasn't Leonard's long suit. That left the home chores, like cooking and cleaning, up to me." He shook his head as he remembered. He sighed. Rose saw the sadness in his dark eyes and knew he still carried guilt over those feelings.

His father, he said, left before his mother began to show the really serious signs of her illness. He believed they split up over something else, not the fact she was sick. He wasn't sure what. He and Leonard had been too little to know what was going on when his parents were together. Luke couldn't recall exactly how it had happened, but later, one time—after his Mom began having real problems taking care of the boys—she sent them to live with their father in San Francisco. He remembered his mother was very worried and unhappy about having to do this. She hated the fact his father owned a bar. Luke laughed saying, "She would have been even more unhappy had she known the real story. The truth was," he said, "it was a strip bar. Several strippers worked there." Noticing Rose's curious look, Luke said, "They were *very* nice." Wiggling his eyebrows, he chuckled and continued. "Really, they really were nice people. They were kind to Leonard and me and tried to keep us out of trouble." He paused and took a sip of wine, holding the glass out so he could see the small oranges.

"Naturally, Leonard and I often sneaked into the bar at night when we were supposed to be sleeping. We liked to watch the show. Yeah," he said, pausing to reflect, "Leonard and I learned a lot when we were with my father." When Rose looked at Luke his eyes were twinkling and mischievous. She could only imagine what he was remembering. It had not escaped her notice that Luke, in spite of being 27 years her senior, was a very sexy man.

Luke continued, "My father was fun to be around. Everyone liked him. He was easy-going, and we had a lot of fun when we were with him. And, I'd have had to been blind not to notice he liked the ladies—there were always several around him!" He took a sip of wine. "But, while he was a good bartender, he was a crappy manager. Times were hard. I remember, at one point, we had to live in a car for a time. Leonard and I stole food because we were hungry. We ate a lot of mayonnaise sandwiches that year."

"Somehow our Mom heard about this and that ended that—back we went to live with her. By then, she was already having lots of difficulty walking. The man she worked for at the car dealership introduced her to a man who lived in Capitola, Peter Townsend. He was a nice man, a good man. He took us in and without any complaints took good care of all of us. Leonard and I were little shits, and I'm sure it wasn't easy for him or my mom. We stayed with him until she died." He stopped.

"Why *did* Peter Townsend take you all in?" Rose asked.

"After we'd been with Peter awhile, I was alone with him one afternoon and I asked him that same question." Luke stared into his orange glass of wine. Rose waited.

"He told me he had been married before and that his wife had died of cancer. During her illness, now and then he needed help to take care of her. His old friend, Wayne, the guy who hired my mom after my pop split, was always there to help out. It was never a question of "if" he would help; it was only a question of "how" he could help. Peter told me he didn't know how he would have made it through his wife's death if Wayne had not stepped up to help him." Luke paused, taking a sip of wine.

"Peter went on to tell me he always wanted to be able to do something to return the favor to Wayne. When he met my mom and Wayne told him about her, my brother, and me, he knew immediately that taking us in was how he would do it. Then he sat down and looked me right in the eye and said, 'But the real reason I did it, Luke, is that it was just the right thing to do. Your mom needed help and I was in a position to give it. You remember that son, as you grow older. You'll find there are always opportunities to do the right thing.'"

Rose was misty-eyed when Luke finished the story. She let a few moments of silence pass before she asked, "How old was Aunt Mamie when she died?" Rose asked.

"She was only thirty-nine, Leonard was fifteen, and I was twelve. That's when we went to live with Aunt Angie. Of course, that didn't last too long. Poor Aunt Angie, she got the short straw on that one." He snorted and finished off his wine. His full black mustache twitched and his thick eyebrows raised as he held out his glass for a refill saying, "Tell me about you, Cousin Rose Salvador Carvalho."

Rose told him about her mother and father. He was intrigued with *The Amazing Doves* and said he would love to see the painting sometime.

"You and your wife are welcome to come to Capitola and see it anytime," she said. "I think you'd like it. I painted one wall of my bedroom hot pink—a special place for *The Amazing Doves*. In fact I decorated my room around them. It's like having the heart and soul of my parents still with me."

She told him how she felt growing up in the warm embrace of the art community of Sausalito. She shared her adventures at Berkeley and how they had affected her decision to go into law.

She was surprised to learn that at the same time she was in Berkeley protesting the War, he, a lifelong liberal Democrat, was doing the same thing in Washington state. A look passed between them confirming their unspoken bond on social issues.

"I was accepted into Stanford Law School," she continued. His eyebrows shot up with a meaningful wiggle and he raised his wine glass in a toast. She laughed.

Continuing, she said, "When I was in Law School, a friend and I went to Capitola to visit. I fell in love with the town."

"*Capitola by the Sea*," they said in unison and laughed some more, envisioning the carved wooden sign at the bottom of the hill that announced the name of the town to visitors and all who passed by. Rose said she'd spent time checking out law opportunities in Capitola because she liked the town. She met a very impressive woman lawyer who headed up a firm of women lawyers. The woman, ironically named Susan Anthony, was very interested in civil liberties and working to help the less fortunate. "The bottom line is we hit it off, and now I'm part of her firm."

Luke emptied the remainder of the wine into their glasses. They finished it and set about the task of packing up. Before leaving the cabin, they stepped out on the porch for one last look at the Bonny Doon property which had played such an important, and varied, role in the lives of the six Salvador sisters including their mothers, Mamie and Annie.

The two stood silently on the porch, lost in their separate thoughts. Rose turned to her older cousin. "Luke, do you believe in heaven?"

Luke huffed. "No. Why?"

"I was just imagining all the Salvadors up there," she said waving her arms toward the sky, "maybe sitting on a big fat old fluffy cloud having a picnic. Think of all the stories they would be telling."

Luke looked at Rose doubtfully, "That's a picnic with a lot of sad stories they..."

Rose cut him off. "Oh, maybe, but think of all the love! And," she added, "there would be so much laughter." She sighed deeply.

They each turned and looked out at the blue sky and the mixed green coverlet of trees running down the hillside of their beautiful Bonny Doon. Tears ran down Rose's cheeks. Luke's dark hair, eyebrows, and the mustache, so like his Grandfather's, added to the emotions filling his dark, brown eyes.

Suddenly Rose giggled. Luke looked at her wondering if the wine had suddenly hit her. She couldn't stop giggling and Luke found it so contagious that he started to laugh, pulling his arms tightly into his stomach. She watched his hand go up under his chin as he scrunched into himself. His normally deep laugh turned into a higher pitched giggle. They had tears in their eyes. Finally Rose squeaked out, "I haven't told you the best part." Luke looked at her with arched, questioning brows. "You know the man who is buying our property— Daniel Walker?" She was starting to shake a bit.

"He has six daughters!

About Joseph's Disease

Sadly, Joseph's Disease is a non-fictional part of this story. Joseph's Disease—also called Azorean Disease or Machado-Joseph's Disease—in the simplest of terms is an inherited, fatal disease of the central nervous system. In medical terms it is an autosomal dominant neurodegenerative disorder similar to Huntington's disease. The children of an affected parent have a 50/50 chance of inheriting the defective gene.

While rare, Joseph's Disease can affect persons as early as age 15 or not until later in life. Regardless of age of onset, it will eventually take the person's life. Its progress can be slow or fast, nevertheless living with it is devastating. The symptoms can include loss of balance, loss of limb coordination, muscle tone, bulging eyes, double vision, swollen tongue, difficulty swallowing or breathing, rigidity of muscles, inability to communicate—and yet the mind can remain intact.

A sailor named Antone Joseph left the Azores in early 1800 and moved to America. He was thought to be the earliest known person to carry the deadly gene. It would not be until 1972 that the name Joseph's Disease was applied. More information on the disorder/disease may be found online at the National Institute of Neurological Disorders and Stroke under Machado-Joseph Disease.